ALSO BY URSULA HEGI

Sacred Time

Hotel of the Saints

The Vision of Emma Blau

Tearing the Silence

Salt Dancers

Stones from the River

Floating in My Mother's Palm

Unearned Pleasures and Other Stories

Intrusions

Trudi & Pia

URSULA HEGI

THE **WORST** **THING** I'VE **DONE**

{ A NOVEL }

A TOUCHSTONE BOOK

Published by Simon & Schuster

NEW YORK LONDON TORONTO SYDNEY

TOUCHSTONE
A Division of Simon & Schuster
1230 Avenue of the Americas
New York, New York 10020

This book is a work of fiction. Names, characters, places and incidents are either products of the author's imagination or are used fictitiously. Any resemblance to actual events or locales or person, living or dead, is entirely coincidental.

First Touchstone hardcover edition October 2007

TOUCHSTONE and colophon are registered trademarks of Simon & Schuster Inc.

Designed by Joy O'Meara

Manufactured in the United States of America

10 9 8 7 6 5 4 3 2 1

Library of Congress Cataloging-in-Publication Data
Hegi, Ursula.
The worst thing I've done : a novel / Ursula Hegi.
p. cm.
"A Touchstone Book."
I. Title
PS35583E4185W67 2007
813'.54—dc22
2006101171

For information about special discounts for bulk purchases,
please contact Simon & Schuster Special Sales
at 1-800-456-6798 or business @simonandschuster.com.

ISBN-13 978-1-4165-4375-6
ISBN-10 1-4165-4375-9

for Gail Hochman and Mark Gompertz

ACKNOWLEDGMENTS

A special thank-you to Nan Orshefsky, who took me into her studio and taught me about collages, and to Gordon Gagliano, who took me inside the creative process of a visual artist. They both, along with Barbara Wright, commented on early drafts. I thank Mike Bottini because I keep learning from his books about the natural history of the East End.

As always, immeasurable thanks to Gail Hochman, my brilliant agent of twenty-eight years, and to Mark Gompertz, who has edited my books with such wisdom for the past thirteen years.

THE WORST THING I'VE DONE

ONE

Annie

{ *Talk Radio* }

TONIGHT, ANNIE is driving from North Sea to Montauk and back to North Sea as she has every night since Mason killed himself. She turns on the radio. Finds Dr. Francine. Listening to people so desperate that they confess their misery to radio psychologists distracts Annie from the rope cutting into Mason's graceful neck, his flat ears lovely even in death. Distracts her for a few minutes—but only late at night, alone in her car, when she can be as anonymous as those callers.

Annie switches between Dr. Francine and Dr. Virginia during long commercials for anti-itch powder and ointments guaranteed to cure various sores. Dr. Virginia is snappy, cuts people off, tells them the solutions to their problems before they finish describing their problems. But Dr. Francine's voice is soothing. Whenever she sighs, you can feel her compassion, even for those callers who go on and on . . . like this shaky voice now, Linda from Walla Walla, Washington—talking about shrimp.

"Everyone in Walla Walla knows. Fifty-two years ago I stole a bag of shrimp from the grocery store. I don't know why, Dr. Francine. I was looking at them on display, so . . . curved and so pink." There's something oddly sexual in Linda's description of the curved pink flesh. A pink, curved longing . . .

Dr. Francine sighs. Annie can tell she's a good listener. Imagines a gentle face, lined and intelligent.

"It's the only time I ever . . . stole anything, Doctor. The store manager, she told me to unzip my coat . . ."

Annie turns from Towd Point onto Noyack Road. Clear. The sky too. Clear, with just a fist of clouds around the moon.

". . . because that's were I was hiding the shrimp, inside my fur coat, not real mink, Dr. Francine, fun fur. The manager said she'd see me in court, but no one came for me though I kept waiting, and all along my husband's mother saying she warned him before he married me. Lately . . ."

"Yes, Linda?"

"Lately, I've had the feeling everyone is talking about me and those shrimp."

"Even after half a century?" Dr. Francine asks softly.

"I've stopped leaving my house because people are teasing me about it."

"What do they say to you, Linda?"

"Oh, nothing directly to me, really . . ."

"Space cookie heaven." Mason's voice. From inside the radio?

"No." That's why Annie is in the car—to get away from him. The steering wheel vibrates under her palms as the speedometer zooms to fifty on the winding road.

"Space cookie heaven." Mason, humming Twilight Zone *inside Annie's head—*

"FUCK OFF, Mason."

"In my heart I'll always be married to you."

"That's so . . . arrogant."

Her headlights skim across a diamond-shaped road sign with the silhouette of a deer leaping left to right. Always left to right. She's on the stretch of road with water on both sides. For an instant she wonders—would it stop her rage if she were to twist the steering wheel to the right and slide into North Sea Harbor? *Not for me.* She taps the brakes. Having a child didn't stop Mason. With him, there always was that wildness, that fiery energy Annie used to love because it electrified their marriage. But for her all wildness ceased eight years ago, when Opal was born. That's why she drives fast, but not dangerously so. Because of Opal. Who is finally asleep at Aunt Stormy's house in North Sea, where they've stayed in the seventeen days since Mason's death.

Some nights it takes hours to get Opal settled because she keeps calling Annie to her bed. Knee aches. Head aches. Ache aches. All kinds of little complaints to bring Annie back to her. Tonight, a thumb ache. And when Annie held her, she felt Opal shiver, felt her own fierce love for Opal like a shiver, a blink, throughout her body, always part of her.

"Burn in hell, you bastard, for doing this."

Mason's parents arranged his funeral. Even though, as his wife, it was Annie's choice what to do. They asked her. A burial in earth? Cremation? She was grateful when they decided, and she returned to New Hampshire to stand with them, and Jake, at her husband's grave site.

It used to be safe, hugging Jake.

"AND THAT uneasiness just started lately, Linda?" Dr. Francine asks.

"Well . . . I was ashamed for a few years after it happened, but then I didn't think about shrimp much . . . until lately."

Another sigh. "I can tell how this one incident has poisoned your entire life, but it doesn't have to be that way, dear."

Now if Dr. Virginia were taking this call, she would have interrupted Linda long ago, telling her, *"You're probably getting ready to steal again."* Annie can tell right away which station she has, because if the caller is talking, it must be Dr. Francine's show, and if the doctor is talking, it must be Dr. Virginia's.

Annie can see Linda, smuggling a bag of embryonic shrimp inside her fun-fur coat. She'd bet ten dollars Linda never had children.

"Twelve dollars," Mason says. "I bet you twelve that she has at least one kid."

"I bet you fifteen. And no children. Maybe shrimp-size miscarriages. No full-term children."

"Twenty. That she has one full-term child. Maybe more."

They used to bet on anything, she and Mason. What color the desk clerk's hair would be as they checked into a hotel. What hour of the day their phone would ring first. And all those bets about Opal. Would her eyes stay blue? Her hair red like Annie's? How many weeks before she'd sleep through the night? At what age she'd take her first step. What her favorite food would be. And they both paid up, shifting the winnings between them.

"I BET YOU eight dollars she'll turn over on her tummy before Friday." Mason was holding Opal in the cradle of his arm, nudging the bottle between her gums just so.

"Ten dollars she'll turn over Saturday or Sunday," Annie said.

His lips were puckering.

Annie laughed. "Are you doing the swallowing for her?"

"I am. Do you think she's unusual?"

"What way?"

"More aware than other babies. The way she observes us." He rubbed Opal's tummy.

"You sound like a proud parent."

"Proud like entitlement-parent-proud?"

"Valid-proud, Mason." Annie traced the side of Opal's face, from her temple down to her pointed chin, as if she were sketching her. The same pointed chin that Annie and her mother had too.

"How about me?" Mason asked.

She stroked his temple, his ear and chin and neck.

"Hey . . ." He smiled at her.

Milk trickled from Opal's mouth. She was sturdy like Annie, graceful like Mason.

"Keep that suction going now. Have I ever told you that I'm crazy about start-up humans?" His thumb kept making circles on Opal's tummy. "Right, Startup?"

And that became his first endearment for her: Startup.

Startup became Stardust.

Became Dustmop when she played in the sandbox.

Mophead when she was tousled by wind.

IF ANNIE were to call one of the radio doctors—not that she would—it would definitely not be Dr. Virginia, but Dr. Francine, who'd understand why Annie wanted away from Mason. But then, of course, he beat her to it—he'd always been competitive—got away from her in the rough and sudden way that left her with the blame and the rage and the loss of everything golden between them.

Because that was how it started, knowing each other in that golden way before they were old enough to talk—she born in August; he in December of the same year to the piano teacher and the banker next door. A history of knowing each other.

Her first memory one of touch: her fingers on Mason's toes, stroking . . . pinching . . .

Her second memory: toddling alongside Mason's father, who was pushing Mason in his stroller and saying, "Hold on tight, Annabelle."

Hold on tight.

His last name was Piano, and Annie's dad liked to say he didn't know if Mr. Piano had changed his name to Piano because he was a piano teacher, or if he had become a piano teacher because of that name. Mr. and Mrs. Piano were tall and elegant, their blue-black hair touching their shoulders.

"Expensive haircuts," Annie's dad would say, "but cheap furniture."

Mr. Piano had his hair in a ponytail. The only stay-at-home dad in the neighborhood, he wore a suit and vest around the house. It made him look like a banker, which was weird, because Mrs. Piano was a banker but looked like a piano teacher, with her long fingers and long scarves.

A black scarf at the cemetery. A black scarf over a black coat. And her fingers twisted into the end of that scarf. "Come home with us, Annie."

"Opal, I need to get . . . home to Opal."

"I understand. It's a long drive."

"But I'll come back another time."

"Bring Opal," Mrs. Piano said.

"Soon."

"And Jake," Mr. Piano said. "There's something we need to ask you."

WHEN ANNIE was three, she and Mason pulled each other around in Jake's red wagon. His house was one house from Mason's, two from Annie's, and his mother was the babysitter for several kids in the neighborhood. A science teacher, she'd started day care because she wanted to be home with Jake. She laughed easily, was forever patient, and made any lunch the children wanted: waffles or ham omelets or egg salad or peanut butter with Fluff.

Jake's father worked for Sears. "An *almost* handsome man," Annie once heard her mother say to Mason's mother, and they laughed. "With a face that's just a little off because his features are tipped sideways—"

"Sideways?"

"You know, toward the left side of his jaw?"

"Still, he is the best-looking man on our block," Mason's mother said. "Sort of . . . rakish."

If Mason asked for a lunch no one else asked for, Jake would say, "Whatever the other kids are having, Mama." After lunch he'd help her clean up, while Mason ran around her kitchen, yelling, "I want I want I want—" yelling it fast as if he couldn't figure out what he wanted—only *that* he wanted.

Jake would watch him, eyes sullen. But one day he stepped into Mason's way. "You're not the boss of her."

"Remember now—" His mother pulled Jake close, kissed the top of his white-blond hair. "Mason is a paying guest."

Paying guest. Annie's neck felt sweaty. Salty. Sometimes her parents paid late. "Not because they don't have enough money," she'd heard Jake's mother say, "but because they're careless. They can't imagine people needing the money they earned that day."

"LINDA? I want you to try and remember," Dr. Francine says, "if anything has changed in your life recently to bring up that shame. And I promise we'll talk about that right after this message from our sponsor."

"I still don't eat shrimp." In her voice, again, that pink, curved longing.

"Please—" Mason says, "Don't even think about pink, curved longing."

And then it's the woman who sells tooth whitener, money-back guarantee, favored by celebrities around the globe. Flutes and harps rise above her recital of grisly side effects, making them sound beneficial.

Since the commercials are longer than the advice sessions, Annie switches to Dr. Virginia.

"—and you must examine your own role in this, Frank," Dr. Virginia says.

"All I know is my wife got home ten minutes ago smelling of—"

"Frank, I do not need to hear any more."

"But she was smelling of another man and she did it to get even because I got together that one time only with my first ex-wife and—"

"What you are telling me, Frank, is definitely a case of—"

"—that's when I informed her I'll call you Dr. Virginia—see she listens to you all day long at the office and keeps quoting you to me—"

"*You* are not listening to me, Frank. Your wife is obviously an intelligent woman who thinks independently. Tell her thank you from me."

"—so I figured you could tell me where I can take my wife to get a test done to see if she was with another man and—"

"How long have you been married, Frank?"

"Five months and if I tell her you said to get the test she'll do it because of you and—"

"At one A.M.?" Dr. Virginia sounds impatient to get to the buy-me-now commercials. "First of all, a test is not going to resolve what is truly going on between the two of you. It is an issue of trust, of you not—"

"But she just got back from having sex Dr. Virginia and there should be a trace if we do the test right away like an X-ray or peeing into a cup or—"

"You are interrupting me again, Frank."

"Sorry. I keep telling my wife one more time and that's it and—"

"Frank—"

"—it only makes her go to bars even though she knows—"

"Frank. Frank. Are you listening to a word I am saying?"

"Sure but—"

"Do you ever listen to your wife? Your problem is communication, and this jealousy of yours is sabotaging your marriage—"

"LET ME *tell you about jealousy," Annie interrupts Dr. Virginia. "About finding a penny on Mason's side of the bed . . . just a couple of months ago, while he and Aunt Stormy were in Washington, D.C., to protest any preemptive attack on Iraq. When he came home, I asked him about the penny, and he told me he didn't know anything about it . . . but then he admitted he'd put it there . . . three feet from the foot end . . . because I sleep on the futon in the living room whenever he's gone. He said if the penny had been moved or the sheets changed, it meant I had another man there and—"*

"I want both of you to go to sleep now," Dr. Virginia prescribes.

"I was stunned," Annie says. "Then furious. Told him he was twisted inside. That my loving him was never enough for him."

"And in the morning I expect you to look for a marriage therapist."

"Too late for that," Mason says.

"Unless of course you don't care to save that marriage of yours, Frank."

"If I knew from a test that my wife didn't sleep with someone else I'd feel more trusting."

As Annie drives into darkness, taking back roads wherever she can, her headlights cast pale gray circles on the black pavement. She's been driving this same loop every night: west from North Sea to Riverhead, then east on Route 27 as far as it goes to Montauk Point, from there west to North Sea, where Aunt Stormy lives at the end of a long, bumpy driveway, a strip of weeds down the middle. Big old trees. A hammock. From the driveway you can see her cottage and Little Peconic Bay all at once . . . see the bay through the windows of her cottage and on both sides of the cottage, silver-gray barn siding, bleached. Inside, a dried rose woven into a piece of driftwood hangs from the candle chandelier, along with delicate glass balls.

Annie doesn't want Opal to know she's out driving. But Aunt Stormy knows. Aunt Stormy said, "It's what you need for the time being."

"AND WHAT will it be next, Frank?" Dr. Virginia asks. "A test once a week to see if your wife has stayed faithful?"

"Do they have those?"

"There are no tests for trust."

"Right." Annie slaps the rim of the steering wheel and thinks of a day, early in her marriage, when she bought herself a golden neck chain to celebrate the sale of two collages from her Pond Series.

Mason raised one hand to her throat, fingered the gold. "Who bought this for you?"

"I did."

"I just don't think a woman would buy that kind of necklace for herself."

"You're kidding. Right?"

"It's the kind of gift a lover would buy for a woman."

As she stared at his angular face with the wide mouth and pale skin, at his blue-black eyes and his blue-black curls, it amazed her how all the familiar added up to this stranger.

And she came right back at him. "A lover? Don't you know that every woman is her own lover?" And she was, she was inventive, giving herself pleasure, not just in bed but also at the table, in the ocean . . .

"If there were tests for trust," Dr. Virginia says, "I would suggest that your wife take *you* to be tested. Because you have a habit of fabricating flaws for others in order to avoid a confrontation with your own and very real flaws."

"Can you at least give me the name of the test so that I have it for the next time in case my wife—"

BUT ALREADY Dr. Virginia is saying hello to Gloria from Albany, who is forty-four and lives with her widowed father.

"My dad treats me like a child. He tells me I have to be home by eleven, and—"

"Do you pay rent, Gloria?"

"He won't even let me close the door to my room when my boyfriend comes visiting. Just because my dad gets lonely and—"

"You want to hear a real story?" Annie asks Dr. Virginia. "Take this. From a woman who is driving fast after her husband hanged himself."

"Once again: Do you pay rent, Gloria?"

"I can't afford to. And my dad knew that when I moved in. I got this minimum-wage job bagging groceries at—"

"Gloria, listen—"

"Hey, you listen, Chickie," Annie tells Dr. Virginia. And laughs out loud because she's never called anyone Chickie. But in a magazine at her dentist's was a picture of Dr. Virginia, resembling a chicken with her round body, beak nose, and maroon bubble hairdo.

"Listen closely now, Gloria. As long as you let your father be a parent to you—and that means provide you with food, transportation, toiletries—"

"Not toiletries. He gets the cheapest store brand. No, thank you!"

"—shelter, heat—"

"I pay for my own toiletries!" Gloria sounds agitated.

"—you give him permission to treat you as his child. Now if one of my daughters came home to live with me— Those of you who listen to me or subscribe to my newsletter at www.deardoctorvirginia.com know that my four girls are still too young to be out there on their own, the oldest seventeen, the next one twelve, then seven, and the youngest two years old, spaced a perfect five years from each other—"

"Know what I think, Dr. Virginia?"

"—and giving me such insight into every age of child rearing, while—"

"Dr. Virginia? Know what I think, Dr. Virginia?"

"—on the other hand, they're benefiting from my professional insights into parenting, which can be yours too at an introductory rate, fifteen months for the price of—"

"I think it's all about my dad being lonely and wanting me home for company."

"Listen to me now, Gloria. I'm not merely talking about the independence of paying your own—"

"You listen now, Chickie."

"You have every reason, Annie, to despise yourself," Dr. Virginia says.

"I can turn you off," Annie threatens.

"Not only because of how Mason manipulated you and Jake in the sauna but because you pulled this off together."

"You tell her, Dr. Virginia," Mason says.

"Because of what you can become when you're with him," Dr. Virginia says.

"So true," Mason says.

"For Christ's sakes, Annie," Dr. Virginia says, "you're a mother. You have to admit to yourself that, on some level, you got off on it too—"

"Christ's sakes . . . ? Getting off on it . . . ? You don't sound like yourself, Chickie."

"—and that you saw it as a way to strike out at your husband."

"Thank you, Dr. Virginia." Mason sounds grateful and considerate and so mature.

"You have such good manners," Dr. Virginia tells him. "So considerate and mature."

"Bullshit artists," Annie says. "Both of you."

"We don't need to subject ourselves to Annie's crude language," Mason tells Dr. Virginia.

"You're brownnosing, Mason," Dr. Virginia says. "Cut it out. And as for you, Annie, you outbet each other. Except he lost."

"We both lost," Annie whispers.

That seems to satisfy Dr. Virginia, because she starts preaching to Gloria about responsibility.

"ENOUGH OF *you, Chickie."* Annie switches to Dr. Francine, whose caller, Mel, is afraid of his new roommate.

"He is a bully. He shoves me, punches me. And he won't move out though we fight all the time."

Now if Mel were calling Dr. Virginia, she'd interrupt him. *"It's a problem you got yourself into, Mel, because you are spineless and excessively needy."*

But Dr. Francine is not like that. Forever patient and compassionate, she sighs as she listens to Mel and coaches him in healthy assertiveness. "Make a list of acceptable behavior with the bully roommate."

"What if he doesn't want to?"

"Find some way to get him to participate, and then agree on a date for the roommate to move out if he falls off the list."

"He'll get mad at me, Dr. Francine, and—"

"Hold on, dear."

An emotional voice is selling foot powder: testimonies of agony and of relief, of before and after. Annie drives around the traffic circle in Riverhead, heads toward Hampton Bays. The flicker of their headlights: three cars coming toward her. A sign: FIRE AND AMBULANCE VOLUNTEERS NEEDED. Darkness again. If she kept driving south, she'd drive into the ocean.

"Did you both sign the lease, Mel?" Dr. Francine asks.

"No no, it's mine. I signed it."

"Good. Very good. That'll give you a way out. Now take a blank page, draw a line down the middle, and write down the reasons why you and Humphrey—"

"Hubert, not Humphrey."

"—reasons why you and Hump——"

"Hump." Annie shakes her head.

"I'm sorry," Dr. Francine says. "Very sorry, Mel. I mean Hubert . . . why you and Hump—ubert . . ." A cover-up cough. ". . . Hubert should or should not cancel the cruise."

"What cruise?" Annie passes the sign: HAMPTON BAYS 8 MONTAUK 42. End of the island. *End of the world.*

"How do I know"—Mel starts sobbing—"that Hubert won't get . . . cross?"

Another one of Dr. Francine's deep sighs.

"I bet you she has a sigh button on her microphone," Mason whispers.

Annie has to laugh. "Right. And she pushes it at appropriate intervals."

When she crosses the Shinnecock Canal, she opens her window. Cold night air whips her face, makes her eyes tear. She stays on 27. Passes Premier Pest Control. Outside the Elvis store, life-size animals in garish colors—giraffes and cows and elephants—are arranged as if about to trot into the road. Annie doesn't know the store's real name. Mason had called it the Elvis store ever since he saw a plastic bust of Elvis for sale. He loved to go there with Aunt Stormy, searching through the staggering accumulation of chain-saw art and rococo furniture, old jukeboxes and watercolor landscapes, cowboy figurines and Adirondack chairs, stained-glass windows and plastic napkin rings.

"Mason made sure I'd be the one to find him." Annie tells Dr. Francine about the rope too thin for hanging. A heavier man might have snapped the rope, saved himself, spared her from seeing the rope slicing into his neck. Seeing before trying not to look—Mason—his face a face that's not-Mason.

Annie feels dizzy with hunger.

"When he did it, I was out, imagining myself leaving him, taking Opal with me, and letting him have the pond house and that goddamn sauna, where I figured out that I had to leave him."

But he did the leaving for her. Impulsive. Vindictive. In her studio, spoiling it forever. Not giving her a chance to reconsider. But looping a rope across the rafter and stepping off her worktable, tipping it over, spilling tools and supplies for her collages—scissors and twine and wire and glue and box cutters, baskets with eucalyptus pods and wisteria pods, her brushes and jars—as if he wanted all that as the backdrop to his body, his death her final work. Jealous here too of the time she spent on her collages.

Annie tells Dr. Francine how she climbed on the table, whimpering, hacking through the rope. *What if he's still alive?* Hacking till he fell, the man who wore Mason's green Earth Day T-shirt but whose face was not-Mason.

"The police said I shouldn't have touched anything," Annie says.

"I was looking forward to . . . the cruise." Mel is sobbing. "We both were."

"Mel, listen to me—" Dr. Francine starts.

But Mel is sobbing.

On Annie's right, the Southampton campus. And now one lane only. A liquor store. Two marinas. Sunoco.

"When I found Mason," Annie tells Mel and Dr. Francine, "all my collages were pulled out . . . propped against the walls . . . against the legs of my worktable. And all I could think was that the air smelled of smoke. The smoke had nothing to do with Mason's death but with fires in Canada."

They'd been burning ever since lightning struck the parched ground two weeks earlier. And the smoke kept drifting south—more than five hundred miles south—crossing the border, spreading through New England.

Mel. Still sobbing.

Annie pulls into the 7-Eleven, where a wild-haired man is limping across the parking lot in some bizarre pattern of three hops to the side, three forward. When he bumps into Annie's car, he stares at her through the passenger window, the kind of stare small children will give you before they've learned it's not polite.

She waves him away. *Tells Dr. Francine and Mel how, the day after Mason's death, Opal wanted to take the garden hoses to go north and fight the fires in Canada. "As if fighting the fire could still save Mason's life."*

She turns off the engine. Waits till the man has limped into the 7-Eleven. When she enters, he's trying on sunglasses by the tiny mirror on top of the display case, raising his chin, making badger teeth. Two teenagers are studying the candy rack. By the hot food section, four young Latinos are buying burritos. Good idea. Annie buys a burrito, fries, chocolate milk, two doughnuts.

Driving while eating is better than driving without eating.

And driving while eating *and* listening to talk radio is even better because there's space for little else.

Annie's mother used to sing in the car, Hildegard Knef songs that she'd translate for Annie and Annie's father, smoky-voiced songs about stealing hours of happiness by talking them away, songs about lies we tell ourselves and take for truth. She sang her Knef songs in the car the morning she drove with Annie and Mason to Boston to protest against the Gulf War. Their first protest, and they were fifteen, exhilarated to march with her because she didn't behave like someone's mother—more like a friend with a driver's license, waving her protest sign, red hair flying—and they were awed when she told them she'd been arrested. She and Aunt Stormy had been to so many protests, starting with Vietnam when they'd arrived in America, that they had seven arrests between them.

CHEWING HER fries, Annie continues east on 27, waiting for Dr. Francine. But it's the man who sells hair thickener. Then the perky people from foreign language by mail.

Dr. Virginia, then. "If you only think skin, Kevin, you are missing the cause. Don't you see what you are doing to yourself?"

Silence while Kevin deliberates. The moment he says, "No . . . ?" Dr. Virginia is on him.

"Self-esteem. Because you hold yourself in such low esteem—"

"Not really. I have a graduate degree in communications. I work out four days a week. I have my own business, and I recently got married."

"—and you're so defensive about your low self-esteem"—Dr. Virginia's voice rises—"that it's only natural how ugliness rises to the surface, erupts."

"That is such crap," Annie tells her.

"So what am I supposed to do?" Kevin asks.

"I just told you," Dr. Virginia snaps.

"No, you didn't," Annie snaps.

"No, you didn't," Kevin snaps.

"Some people never learn to listen."

"I thought you could tell me what to put on the pimples so that—"

"It has nothing to do with what kind of ointment you put on your face—"

"Wait—" Annie cuts in. "What about all the ointments and stuff you peddle during your commercials? Don't you want Kevin to buy them?"

"—although there are a few exceptional products I endorse on my show—"

"You bet, Chickie—"

"—but what you need to do, Kevin, in addition to applying those products according to directions, is think of the self-esteem as a layer beneath your skin, a layer you have control over— Hello? I'm talking with Brittany from Newark."

"Thank you so much, Dr. Virginia, for taking my call."

• • •

"THAT'S WHAT *she gets paid for," Annie tells Brittany. "That's how she hawks her pimple cream."*

The moment Brittany starts talking about her daughter's drug use, Dr. Virginia berates her. "It's because of your selfish parenting."

Annie tries to get mad at Dr. Virginia, to side with Brittany. But she can't get inside their conversation. Though she punches up the volume, she can't get it loud enough to blot out the rope— Quickly, she substitutes another picture—one she's carried within her since she was thirteen and came upon Mason and Jake on the raft at their summer camp—a picture she can evoke any time, because that afternoon the golden inside her grew warm and heavy toward both of them. Above the glitter of the water, shoving each other off the raft, hooting—laughing?—and climbing on again, their movements one continuous dance . . . Mason, the spider, the monkey dancer, all limbs and motion . . . Jake, the centaur, calves thick and feet broad, the rest of him slim, all the stability of his body below his knees.

Raft/1 was inspired by what Annie saw that summer afternoon, the boys merging in the center of the raft, a huddle of arms and legs arching toward the edge with immeasurable grace, a grace that embarrassed them when she showed them the collage.

So far, she has eleven raft collages. Train Series she completed in two years. Pond Series in four. Most of her collages are not part of a series; but the Raft Series has tugged at her for more than half her life now, and each collage has revealed more than she believed she knew. Like how that dance above water defines her connection to Mason and to Jake—*one of us always looking on.* If she already understood the image, she wouldn't need to search for it. It's like that when she works . . . the unknown sucking her in. She rather lets her materials influence what she'll do, a conversation of sorts: she'll lay out an array of papers the way a painter will lay out her palette; tear and bunch and crinkle them; layer them to change colors and textures and depth; and strive for that flicker of a moment when the real becomes unreal and the unreal real, when—in the instant of shifting and becoming—they're equally real.

• • •

"I BELIEVE in being open," Dr. Francine says.

"Right. Opal can discuss anything with me."

Slurping cool chocolate through her straw, Annie drives past East End Tick Control, Burger King, Fast Lube, Mobil, Gulf. Past the animal hospital and plumbing supplies. Past empty side streets that are jammed during the day.

"Whenever I see parents who have trouble with their children, I figure they have to be tight-assed." She expects Dr. Francine to tell her tight-assed *is not acceptable for talk radio.*

But the doctor says, "Excessive tact often masks an unwillingness to communicate."

"If those parents weren't tight-assed," Annie says, "those kids would talk to them, talk it out. I've answered all of Opal's questions. She has torn photos of Mason from albums, taped them to the refrigerator. It makes me sick, but how can I not let her? She adored Mason . . . still adores him, though she knows what he did . . . and how. I keep watching her for signs of . . . trouble. Encourage her to talk."

With Mason it used to be talk and talk, wonderful talk, excessive talk, draining talk. *"We had periods of silence, of course. Every marriage has those, right?" Annie asks Dr. Francine.*

But even after Mason's jealousy binges that made her feel exhausted and judged, they always talked—except after that night in the sauna when he pushed her and Jake beyond the line that had shifted since they were children, separating himself from them forever.

"He watched us as if counting on us to stop him as we had so many times before . . . like pulling him away from some cliff."

Dr. Francine sighs.

Annie stuffs the last three fries into her mouth. Aren't widows supposed to waste away from sorrow? In the movies they do. But not Annie. She's never been the type to waste away, and she's been absorbing weight since the suicide, courtesy of Mason. Fourteen pounds already. Going for twenty-four.

"Thank you for that too, Mason." She bears left, past the diner and Pier 1. Signs for the vineyards: Wolffer, Duck Walk. Channing Daughters.

"I bet you eighteen pounds max."

"You can't bet. You're dead."

"You're gorgeous whatever weight you are."

"If you figure fourteen pounds in seventeen days, that comes to over three quarters of a pound a day. Right? In one year, that would add two hundred seventy pounds."

"YOU'RE GORGEOUS—" Mason pressed himself high inside Annie, so slow and sweet and again.

A thud against glass. Beyond Mason's shoulders, outside the window, a streak of gray, a squirrel, falling as if shot from a tree.

"What is it?" Mason asked. "What—"

Annie touched one finger to his lips.

Scratching. Then the squirrel's head and white belly as it scaled the windowsill and hurled itself against the glass. Another thud. And the squirrel plummeting.

"We have a voyeur," Mason announced. "Must be the incarnation of some ex-lover of yours."

"In that case . . . get ready for at least two dozen squirrels."

Startled, he laughed.

She was glad she'd stopped him with that. Because if she'd told him what she really felt—*I wish you wouldn't say stuff like that . . . you know there wasn't anyone else*—he'd be asking his jealous questions. So jealous of any moment she was away from him. Except when it came to Opal. With her he was generous and playful and—

The squirrel was readying itself for another leap that would bounce it off the glass and back on the ground.

"I know what it wants." Mason. Slow and sweet and again.

She pulled in—her breath . . . him . . . and managed to say, "Must be cold out there."

"Not in here."

"No compassion for the furry."

"I bet you it'll jump again."

"Twice."

"Three jumps. I bet you three."

The squirrel repeated its ritual outside the window. Through it all, Opal did not wake up in the next room; and Annie was glad for the peace.

"Three jumps," Mason said. "I win."

"You win."

"You'll win next time." Skin so transparent.

Annie traced the fine, strong lines of his bones beneath. The bridge and length of his nose. The angles of jaw and forehead. *Sexy Trouble.*

"Sexy trouble," she'd heard Aunt Stormy tell her mother when Annie was still in elementary school. "That neighbor boy will be sexy trouble someday. Such wildness and beauty."

Tooth whitener.

Ointment for cold sores.

Dr. Virginia. "Yes, David?"

The rope, too thin, forever cutting into Mason's long neck—

All at once, Annie knows she'll use his death as insurance against other catastrophes. Nothing horrible will happen to Opal and her again. It's a fact Annie understands deep inside her bones, and it makes her invincible. In an odd way—beyond the grieving, beyond the regrets—there is solace in that.

"I am increasingly worried about my wife—" The caller's voice is anxious, so anxious. "She has been twitching and—"

"Have you taken her to a neurologist?" Dr. Virginia interrupts.

"No, but I have—"

"To a cardiologist?"

"No, but—"

"How long has this been going on, David?"

"Let me think . . ."

"I do not have all night."

". . . thirty-five years."

"Are you telling me your wife has been twitching for thirty-five years?"

"That is correct, Dr. Virginia."

"Of course it is correct. I listen—"

"What an egomaniac," Mason says.

Annie agrees. "Ego-Chickie."

"David," Dr. Virginia asks, "why have you waited until now to call me?"

"That is how long we've been married, Doctor. But I'm getting more concerned."

"Have you taken your wife to be tested for seizures?"

"Not yet."

"For epilepsy?"

"Not yet. I have my own appliance business—"

"What does that have to do with taking her to the doctor?"

"Long hours. Very—"

"How long do your wife's twitches last?"

"Oh . . . used to be twenty or thirty seconds. But the older she gets, the longer the twitching. . . . It keeps going on and on . . . long afterwards. Sometimes I think the twitching is over, but then it starts again and—"

"Are we talking hours here, David?"

"Not hours. No."

"Minutes?"

"I timed her last night because I knew you want your callers to be specific, Dr. Virginia."

"Commendable. I appreciate specific."

"Twelve minutes and forty-three seconds."

"When does this happen, David?"

"The twitching?"

"Yes! The twitching!" Dr. Virginia sounds testy.

"After we are done . . . doing it."

"After you are done doing what, David?"

"After they're done fucking," Annie explains.

But David is not nearly as blunt. "You know . . . ," he mumbles.

"David—if you want me to find a solution to your problem, you have to provide me with *all* the specifics of your problem. Is that clear? I refuse to engage in guessing games."

"Copulating."

Dr. Virginia is silent. A first.

Mason is giggling. "Multiple orgasms," he tells the caller.

Dr. Virginia is still silent. It's a whiteout, soundproof silence. More silent than a quiet person's silence. The kind of silence you'd better enjoy, fast, because it won't last. "Multiple orgasms," Dr. Virginia clarifies. "The twitching that your wife experiences is an orgasm. And extended twitching—"

"Extended twitching—" Mason imitates Dr. Virginia's voice.

"—the way you describe it, David, means that your wife is experiencing multiple orgasms. The older a woman gets, the longer her orgasms continue. Perfectly normal."

Outside it is dark except for the headlights of one other car. A siren far away. A few miles to the right, parallel to 27, lies the ocean.

Inside Annie's car Dr. Virginia: "And who is watching your child tonight, Annie?"

Mason

—ask me, Annie. Ask me what's the worst thing I've done. Ask, goddammit. Because then you'll know I'll never go beyond last night. You'll know and let me stay with you and Opal.

You've left to drive Opal to school, and I'm

searching through your collages. I want the one you'll miss most. From your Raft Series, Annie? Your Train Series?

You think you know the worst thing I've done? It's not that simple, believe me. Because it turned on itself last night in the sauna when you and Jake lay on the bench below mine, glistening in the soggy heat. I took some crushed ice from the cooler, dribbled it on Jake's chest, and as he swatted it away without glancing at me, I suddenly wondered what it would be like if your bodies came together, Annie.

Out of that came wondering what it would be like for *me,* watching you make love to Jake. And then I was sure both of you were imagining that too. Of course, then, I had to ask.

I asked, "Have you ever imagined making love to each other?"

You both laughed, the kind of nervous laugh that's meant to hide something.

"Of course not," Jake said.

"Drop it, Mason." You were sweating, Annie, sweating-beyond-sauna sweating.

"Listen," Jake said, "we've been friends forever, you and I—"

"And Annie," I reminded him.

"Who is married to you."

"As if I didn't know that."

"Just drop it," you growled at me, Annie. She-bear. Female. Haunches muscled, strong. Everything about you abundant, generous: your curls, your nose, your appetite for exertion and food.

"The Canadians are waiting for rain," Jake said.

"Nearly fifty fires," you said, "burning the forests and—"

"You are not going to distract me with Canadians," I said.

"They need rain," you said. "The ground is so dry that—"

"Rain . . ." I picked up the wooden ladle, poured water on the coals, chanted, "Rain rain rain . . ." into the sudden mist.

Did you hear Opal's breath on the monitor, Annie? Because you looked at it, there on the shelf by the door. So did Jake. And as we listened to her sleeping breath—deeper and slower than it used to be—I thought of her in the house, in her bed.

"Rain rain rain . . . Isn't it strange how skinny-dipping in the pond or being in the sauna as often as we are, it has not occurred to you to wonder? I bet you—"

"It's not something I wonder about," you interrupted. But your eyes lied, Annie.

I knew because I watched your lips: they were restless, while your eyes stayed calm. And I bet against you. Because your mother taught us both to read people by separating their mouths from their eyes, to study their lips without letting their eyes distract us. And your eyes, Annie, did not match your lips.

"I bet you a hundred dollars," I said, "that you've both wondered about making love."

"Quit it," Jake said, uneasy as hell.

"It's what you really want," I said. "Why not admit it?"

I didn't want it to happen, Annie—

TWO

Annie

{ *A Thousand Loops* }

THE DAY I married Mason, my mother's belly was enormous. Ankles swollen, she danced with my new husband—her strawberry hair wild; her purple dress not a mother-of-the-bride dress—and when she cut in on my father's dance with me, she mocked tradition, led me in a tango like a big-bellied man pressing into me, her ring flickering where her hand guided mine. As my sister kicked from within her, she filled all space between us as though the three of us were intended to fit together, like this.

On the drive home from the wedding reception, a truck jackknifed into my parents' Honda, swatting them aside, killing my father. My mother lived just long enough to have my sister cut from her in the ambulance.

Whenever I imagine my mother and sister still joined by the cord in those minutes between birth and death, my sister's mouth is sucking air, seeking my mother. My sister is pink—not yet the bluish-white of thin milk; not yet inert and scrawny; not yet attached to wires and tubes inside the incubator where I would see her that night, and give her the name my parents had chosen when the ultrasound had revealed a girl: Opal.

Mine to keep?

To raise, then?

. . .

THE MORNING Mason and I brought Opal home to our apartment at UNH, we propped the hospital's car seat on our bed and sat on either side of her, scared to speak or move, watching over her as she slept, her tiny body one pulsebeat like that of a bird, if you cup it in your palms to see if it's injured.

When she awoke, screaming, arms flailing, I swept her against me. Her legs scrambled, and her screams ripped into me till she became my sorrow, knees kicking my breasts as if she were trying to climb through my skin and into my womb.

"I feel like such an impostor," I said.

"We're both impostors." Mason stepped behind me, brought his arms around me, around her.

"You think her body remembers the accident?"

"She wasn't born yet."

"Still . . ." I molded my back against him, and he rocked me . . . us . . . while she kept screaming. I was terrified of her.

"Since we are impostors and since she is ours now . . ."

Her snot and tears hot against my neck.

"She will be ours . . . right, Annie?"

My parents' lawyer had mentioned adoption. Unthinkable. "We can't just give her to someone else," I told Mason.

"Then we may as well be the best damn impostors we can dream up."

"Like playing house?"

"Like being awesome parents." So much hope in his voice.

"I miss them so."

"I miss them too." He kissed me between my shoulder blades.

"You think she's hungry?"

"We could try feeding her."

"I'll go read the instructions on the formula." Supporting Opal's head, I laid her into Mason's arms.

He stroked her tummy with his thumb. Murmured to her, "What are we going to do with you?"

WHENEVER OPAL burst from sleep—screaming, hair matted with fear—I was sure her body remembered the accident. We would take turns walking with her through the apartment, a hundred loops or more. Jake helped. Did his loops with her when he visited. We'd rub Opal's back or tummy, whisper or sing to her, play music for her.

Aunt Stormy and Pete arrived from North Sea with fish stew and lemon meringue pies. Pete was a dentist who ran marathons, lived in the cottage next to Aunt Stormy's, and slept in her bed. Theirs was the story of a great love. "Every full moon they celebrate being together," my mother had told me. "They paddle their kayaks from their inlet into the bay . . . drink champagne and eat cake while the sun dips down and the moon rises. In winter, they drive out to Montauk and have their champagne and cake on the big rocks below the lighthouse."

Aunt Stormy and Pete walked their loops with Opal and helped us the way they must have helped my parents when I was born. When they sent Mason and me to a restaurant for dinner—our first time away from Opal—I kept thinking I'd forgotten something. Felt too light without her weight fastened somewhere to my body.

Though I got better at easing Opal into sleep, I didn't know what to do for her when she awoke because she'd be unconsolable for the first ten minutes. Joy, then—the only moment of joy since my parents' death—happened one dawn when I was able to soothe Opal as she came out of sleep, and her face, wet and sticky, lolled against my shoulder. A moment of joy that pierced my rage and confusion.

JAKE'S DORM was a few minutes from our apartment, and he'd bring us groceries, go to the library for Mason and me. Our living room table was buried: half of it, as before, under rice paper and fabrics, receipts and ticket stubs, scissors and glue, boxes of nails, and pictures I'd cut from magazines; the other half under boxes of formula and disposable diapers, tiny shirts and pajamas that needed to be folded.

I withdrew from my art history class. I couldn't imagine leaving Opal—not even with Mason or Jake, who urged me to complete summer school. Instead I sat with her on the rocking recliner Jake had bought at a farm auction, Opal's belly on my thighs, her face on my knees—a position Mason had discovered—and I'd jiggle her softly.

"Jiggling makes her let go," he'd told Jake and me. "You'll feel her get heavy . . . content."

It was a good position . . . for Opal and for me, because she couldn't see me cry.

For Mason, being her parent came naturally, but I was struggling. *What if I drop her? Starve her? Lose her somewhere?* Nothing in my life had prepared me for suddenly being someone's mother. *Maybe if you were pregnant and carried a child inside you all those months, you were used to it. You wouldn't just set it down somewhere and forget it.*

WHEN MASON and Jake registered for their fall classes—Mason in political science, Jake in environmental conservation—I applied for a semester's leave.

"You don't have to do this," Mason said.

"If the three of us take shifts with Opal," Jake said, "we can all finish school."

"I'll work on my collages at home."

Instead I knitted an afghan in four shades of pink, uneven rectangles that I sewed together . . . something I could do while Opal was awake.

"I'll help you organize," Jake offered, pale hair sticking up in jumbled tufts, one of his earlobes lower than the other.

"I'll fix up a studio for you," Mason said.

"Where?"

"I'll figure something." Mason was always more attentive when Jake was around.

"We don't have space. And even if we did, I—"

"Your art is important."

"Don't call it that."

"Once you know where all your supplies are," Jake said, "you'll want to do your collages again." He could go from cool to dorky in no time, and he definitely looked cool today in his jeans and black T-shirt, with his hair like that. But whenever he dressed up—like when we encouraged him to bring a date—he'd plaster his hair down with a side part and wear something like plaid pants and a Mister Rogers cardigan and wing-tip shoes.

But I felt tired. Without ideas. Without urgency. Everything about Opal was far more urgent than my work.

The last collage I'd finished had come from being on the train while, from the other direction, another train whooshed past. To hold that moment, that fluency—air and movement and coats and rails—I'd shaved bits of lacy driftwood into segments of daylight that flitted by. Whatever I started out with never became the total image. A piece of bleached driftwood would become not driftwood but windows on a train or, perhaps, a child's hair. And a bird's wing would become not part of a bird but something else entirely. Wind perhaps. A skirt. A cloud.

Now, I doubted that I could ever make another collage. Far too complicated. A definite sign that I'd lost *it*—whatever *it* was called. I didn't like to name *it*, though some of my teachers had. Talent? Gift? All right, coming from them. Pompous, if it were to come from me.

I doubted that my work would even recognize me. Instead I came to recognize the smell of Opal's skin—it changed so quickly—her crying smell and her eating smell and her swampy smell and her sleeping smell. I came to recognize the strength of her fingers when she dug them into my cheek. And I came to adore the ancient look that sometimes flickered deep within her pupils when she observed me with absolute stillness. *My little crone. My little wise woman.*

ONE OF US was usually carrying her around. If she cried, Mason would rush over and pick her up right away. He and Opal both thrived, glommed on to each other with the rapt focus of infants. Jake made lists of her music: what calmed her and what didn't. Opal adored Soul Asylum but not Nirvana. Melissa Etheridge but not Alice in Chains. The Lemonheads but not Bad Religion. Pearl Jam but not the Offspring.

How many loops did we carry her that first year?

A thousand loops each? Three thousand loops? Mason in a cradle-hold, her face up in his arms; Jake with his big hands around her middle, her back against his chest, so that Opal could see where he walked with her; and I, trying to keep her from devouring me as her greedy mouth sucked at my neck.

A Thousand Loops came out of that. Usually I didn't think of a title until I was almost finished—just let my hands and the material and whatever mysterious thing inside me find the direction—but for this collage I knew the title before I began. It was to be small. That I knew too, but nothing else, when I spread a double layer of butcher paper on my worktable and made a mix of Sobo Glue and water. I thinned acrylics . . . smeared them randomly on canvas board, my way of getting past my resistance to begin at all, my fear of the blank canvas that would reveal everything I couldn't do. In doing, roaming, I could trick myself into the illusion that I was working, though I knew it didn't count as work; and yet, the not-working was taking me deeper into myself, where I knew what I didn't think I knew. Where I found roundness touching roundness, merging, softening as I swirled loops from willow switches and clock parts . . . from feathers and the fringe from a sari. And even though, here too, Opal cut into the making of *Loops* with her needs, I was more at ease with her, held her till her body surrendered, molded itself against mine.

And I took that into my work.

ONE MORNING in November, while Opal was still asleep, I propped my raft collages against the walls of the living room and walked from one to the next. Why wasn't I done yet? What was it about the two boys and the raft that didn't leave me alone?

If I could capture it all at once—the boys and the raft and the continuity of their motion—would I know then what I saw? So far I'd caught them in separate images, atop the raft . . . next to the raft . . . under the raft . . . and, in my last version, Jake shoving Mason over the side and leaping off in one shining arc. I stopped—

Why haven't I seen the girl before? With each collage, a girl, all red, had come closer to the boys on the raft . . . her hand in *Raft/1*; her lower arm in */3*; her elbow and shoulder in */4*; her profile in */6*. I skimmed the red profile with my fingertips, closed my eyes because touch without sight is more sensitive to texture.

Curious to find the next image that would move the girl closer yet to the raft, I stirred white glue into a jar of water, brushed it across a piece of heavy watercolor paper. Overlaid the buckled surface with torn bits of mulberry paper and green rice paper . . . Different depths of water, yes. For the raft, I chose twine and—

Opal cried. Quickly, I washed the glue from my hands. Picked her up and changed her, fed her, and sang to her, all along thinking about how I'd weave the twine from the center outward, raising it above the water. After I took Opal for a walk, I tucked her in for her nap.

Then I spread the twine into a maze, a rectangular shape, pressed it down and brushed on lots of glue mix. To make it stick, I covered it with wax paper and ran my rubber roller across it. But I didn't like how the raft just sat there, too symmetrical . . . like some hooked rug. The background was much stronger, a multitude of fragments that suggested more than what they were . . . especially the horizon, a torn edge with something brown beneath, perhaps a mountain ridge in the distance. It introduced a different scale. Intriguing . . . I hadn't thought of mountains while I was working. Now I wanted to see some resolution to the raft, the same complexity as the background.

Opal cried. I rushed to get her, bathed her, fed her, rinsed my brushes, laid them to dry on a paper towel, read to Opal, propped her on my hip while I cooked dinner.

When Mason came home, he sniffed the air. "You're working." He sounded delighted.

"So it's not my cooking?" I teased him.

"You want to keep going?"

I nodded.

He held out his arms for Opal. "Don't we just love the smell of Annie making collages?"

I opened it more, the image, went in with my hands, mushing it up— And was snagged by a sudden panic. *No boys yet.* The surface of the lake was smooth—*both of them under*—smooth for too long. It was a panic that knew more than I did, knew already and forever, and the wisdom of that panic, *almost knowing, almost—*

Tearing at the too-smooth water, I remembered something Diane Arbus once said—a photo is a secret about a secret—and I kept tearing new strips of paper till one head broke through. *A trick of light?* One head only. Yellow, all yellow the head, rising from the too-smooth water—

It's a trick of— Suddenly, then, the other head . . . both visible now . . . yes, shoulders and arms . . . Finally, the urgency again. The flame and eagerness. It rarely happened like this—shapes flinging themselves at the background and adhering as though they'd been meant to converge—but when it did, I knew it was a gift and stayed with it. With the bliss of it.

WHENEVER OPAL napped, I worked, building up the rest of the image to balance the raft. Layers upon layers on the boys and the girl, using the colors of their hair for their bodies: Jake all yellow, Mason all brown, and red for what I saw of the girl. Bits and scraps and twine . . . crumpled strips of rice paper in different colors . . . more glue mix on top of the layers.

"Why the raft again?" Mason wanted to know.

"I don't know."

"I like the *Thousand Loops*. Why not another one of—"

"That's done." My fingertips felt like old skin. It was the dried glue, no longer sticky, and I peeled it off like shreds of skin after a sunburn.

"How do you know it's done?"

"It just is."

"That raft—such a long time ago." He touched the red along the upper edge. "That's not blood, is it?"

Blood . . . I hadn't thought about blood. "It could be seen as blood . . . fanning out in the water." *Something other than what it was. Like the raft now, finally, starting to transcend what it was.*

"But it's not blood?"

"I don't know."

"WHO GAVE you those hickeys?" Mason teased me one afternoon when he and Jake came back from taking Opal out in the stroller.

"They're baby hickeys." I held out my arms for her, and she babbled, jiggled her legs as if walking the air to me. Nothing scrawny about her anymore . . . her face round, her body growing.

"You should have seen those two guys at the park," Mason told me. "They were there with a little boy, Opal's age, and—"

Jake interrupted. "One of them asked us, 'Did you adopt?' And when we told them that Opal was not adopted, they asked, 'Is the birth mother someone you know?' "

"So I said: 'Indeed.' Now get this—" Mason laughed. "Then the other guy asked me, 'Did you use your sperm or a sperm cocktail?' And I said, 'It's my father-in-law's sperm.' "

"They had to think on that one," Jake said.

"So do I."

"They thought we were a couple, Annie."

"Two fathers," Jake added.

"Simply because they were. And had adopted."

"I figured," I said. "Good. You're so grounded in your . . . manliness that you didn't freak out."

They postured . . . biceps bulging, chins raised.

"Look at those two," I told Opal. "Competing so you'll notice them."

She made herself heavy in my arms. Squirmed.

"You know what would have freaked them out more?" Mason asked. "If I had told them my mother-in-law was the carrier."

Jake shook his head. "Carrier is for diseases. You mean egg donor."

"Opal does have two fathers now," I said.

"Cool." Jake blinked. Wide-spaced eyes. Green. "Thank you."

"You should get your own family," Mason told him.

Jake looked stricken, and we were back to being four years old . . . so careful because Mason wanted me to like him better than I liked Jake, wanted Jake to like him better than he liked me. If we didn't, he'd ignore Jake or shove him or make fun of him.

"Drop it, Mason," I said. "You know what's going to happen. You always—"

"I need to be off." Jake headed for the door.

"Don't go, Jake," I said. "Please?"

He hesitated.

I turned to Mason. "Can we skip all this? You're always bashing Jake till he stays away from us. After a week you start missing him, and then you go over to his place and drag him here to us. Can't you—"

Mason pulled Opal from my arms and kissed her. "Wouldn't you like a little brother or sister?"

"You," I said, "are insane."

"I am serious."

"Seriously insane."

"She already has a sister," Jake said.

"I'm not counting Annie as her sister."

"That's obvious."

"It's just that we're getting so good at being parents, Annie. She hardly cries anymore. Look at her." Mason touched his nose to her forehead. "My dad said I used to cry constantly."

"I don't remember you ever crying," I said.

"Because he cured me. Sometimes, when we had company, he'd tell this story about how much I used to cry. Constantly, he said." Mason laughed. "To give him and my mom some quiet time, he'd put me into my carriage, wheel me into that garage behind our house, and leave me there for a couple of hours. By the time he'd get back, I'd be all cried out and asleep."

"Jesus Christ," I said. "Why are you laughing?"

"I remember my dad laughing whenever he told that story . . . and I'd be laughing with the grown-ups."

"Your mom too?" Jake asked.

"I . . . think so."

Jake rubbed his chin. "They thought it was funny?"

"Must have. He certainly told that story often enough."

"No wonder you don't let Opal cry." Jake laid one hand on Mason's shoulder.

But I didn't. Because I felt uneasy. Was this just another one of Mason's games to hold Jake here by making him feel sorry for him?

"There's no reason to let a baby cry," Jake said.

THE MORNING of our first anniversaries—my parents' death, Opal's birthday, and our wedding—I was the one who woke screaming.

"Sshhh, Annie . . ." Mason wrapped his long, bony arms and legs around me, angular where I was soft, not enough width of him to envelop all of me, though he tried, as if he believed that could stop my shivering.

That Annabelle is too big for a girl.

"Sshhh—"

I held on. Tight. Both of us shivering.

In first grade, I'd bullied the boys who bullied Mason. He was small, then—still years away from his astonishing growth spurt—and when other boys shoved or tripped him, I'd run at them, windmill arms and yelling so the teacher would hear me, slugging them if they didn't flee.

Mason's father said it should have been reversed: "That Annabelle is too big for a girl. A girl like that makes a boy look even shorter."

Only it never bothered Mason and me. So close we were, so wondrously close—a girl-boy being, the best of both in one. And it was like that with Jake, too. From childhood on, I believed I was linked to both: one to marry; the other my friend. Not sure which. Yet. But I didn't mind not knowing because I loved them both, loved how they gravitated toward me while I kept their friendship in balance. That thought alone was seductive . . . how I could do this for them.

My first kiss: Jake when we were twelve. Snow in our hair. Snow to our ankles behind the school.

We never told Mason, because he would have been devastated. Jake knew. I knew.

And we both knew that, one day in Morocco, on the walls of Asilah, I wanted him more than Mason. That pull between Jake and me was always strong, just as it was with Mason. More so, at times. But we stayed apart, Jake and I, in that way at least, far enough apart . . . a flux of retreating and advancing.

MASON BROUGHT his lips to my ear. Whispered.

"What? That tickles."

"I have an outrageous idea."

"Oh?" Being outrageous had drawn Mason and me together from the time we were kids and had chased cars to make them stop for our lemonade sale. Outrageous meant being daring. And the shock of saying anything. Outrageous meant traveling through Morocco right after high school graduation. Mason's parents insisted Jake come with us—"He's so mature," they said—but Jake didn't want to be our chaperone . . . only came along because he loved us both, still loved us both, then, before he loved only me and came to fear Mason.

"You like outrageous," Mason reminded me.

I held him as he whispered, our bodies sweaty where they touched. "Let me get the camera, Annie."

"No way."

"It would be so outrageous." Black tousled hair, black eyebrows.

"It would be disrespectful."

"That's why your mother would be the first to laugh."

Sudden sorrow—*her hand on my waist, leading me in that dance. Her tangled hair against my cheek. That laugh of hers.*

"Hey . . . you're sad again." Mason stroked my lower lip. "We don't have to—"

"Maybe it'll be something we can laugh at . . . eventually?"

"I knew you'd say yes."

"I haven't really—"

"Yes? It'll be a great present for Aunt Stormy. I'll take the film to the one-hour place, and we'll pick it up when we leave for Long Island. Say yes?"

"Yes." I shoved him off me. "All right?"

He pulled on his sweats, headed for Opal's room, singing, "Happy birthday . . ."

From the top shelf of our closet, I pulled the box with my wedding dress.

Heard the faucet in the bathroom. Mason's voice: "Do you know it's your birthday, Stardust?"

In front of the mirror, I stuffed a pillow into my underpants.

"Better clean you up, Stardust."

As I tugged my wedding dress over the pillow bulge, I pictured my mother—wide shoulders like mine. Wide hips. And that irreverent smile.

"What a face," Mason was telling Opal as he carried her into our bedroom. "May I ask where you got such a funny, beautiful face?"

She stretched out her arms for me.

"A face like Annie's! That's where you got it. Annie is a bride. See? Here you go."

I kissed her, propped her on my hip, my naked sister, posing with her for Mason's camera, thinking of my mother, thinking: *Opal is yours . . . she'll always be yours.*

IN MASON'S photos, I'm a very pregnant bride, one child already on her hip.

"Opal has a present for you," Mason told Aunt Stormy and placed the photo envelope into Opal's hands, guided toward Aunt Stormy.

"For me? And here it's your birthday, Opal." She pulled out the photos. Laughed aloud. "Brilliant . . . a bride who may or may not reach the altar before her next child pops out. Whose idea was this?" she asked Mason, as if she already knew.

He shrugged. Grinned.

"I didn't think I'd be able to laugh today," Aunt Stormy said. "Thank you for that, Mason."

The instant she hugged me, I was crying.

So was Aunt Stormy. "At least we're . . . together . . . a ritual to be together . . . this anniversary of anniversaries . . ."

"Hey—" Mason brought his arms around us. "Aunt Stormy? Doesn't Annie look beautiful being pregnant?"

"I'm not pregnant."

"Even make-believe pregnant, you're beautiful."

"Sure . . ."

He swung Opal into his arms. "Let's you and I go and investigate the ducks." He went outside, into air so clear that the shadows were crisp.

"He's amazing with her," Aunt Stormy said.

"Amazing . . ."

She took my face between her palms. Wiped back my tears. Our tears.

AUNT STORMY taught my mother—and later me—how to keep from disturbing trees, even tiny ones, by letting the path wind among them. Taught us how to brace broken trunks and branches with the V shaped joints of fallen branches. But she was merciless with briers, clipping their bright green stems so they wouldn't smother trees and bushes. Their thorns would scratch her arms and face. And she'd keep at them till she had them all. Then she'd wind them into big circles and press them into the thicket along the north edge of her land so that birds could use them for nesting.

Aunt Stormy and my mother weren't real sisters. They weren't even from the same town, but at least from the same region by the North Sea in Germany, not far from Holland: my mother from Norddeich, Aunt Stormy from Benersiel. They became sisters-by-choice, as they called it, when they met as au pairs, doing child care for two families in Southampton, on the East End of Long Island. In old photos, my mother was sturdy and tall with stiff red hair, Aunt Stormy short with a dark braid to her waist. But somehow a resemblance emerged in their faces as they grew older. Their names were Lotte and Mechthild. For the small children, Mechthild was impossible to pronounce, and they called her Stormy because she liked to dance with them outside when it was stormy. Mechthild liked her new name so much better than the name she'd inherited from a great-aunt she'd never met, that she began to think of herself as Stormy.

Alone with preschool children day after day, Lotte and Stormy didn't recognize the America they'd been promised by the au pair agency—culture and travel and education. Instead they were cocooned within expensive houses; within the vocabulary of little children; within the routine of these children.

"What kept us from going nuts," my mother had told me, "was that their houses were side by side."

Lotte and Stormy would have felt a thousand continents away from home, had it not been for each other, for talking in words that matched their thoughts. Though they'd both studied English in school, the leap of translation took away some of their swiftness and confidence.

Their employers were kind people who believed they were generous when they included the au pairs in family outings and family dinners; but that only added to all those hours of feeding and bathing, of jam-crusted fingers, a baby's wail and loving. And since these children knew their au pairs better than their parents, they turned to them, of course, for play and solace during family times, freeing their parents to turn to each other for grown-up talk. They praised the devotion of their au pairs—though Lotte was messy and Stormy often late—because what mattered was seeing proof that their children would be loved while the parents were at work or had appointments . . . even if it made them uneasy how much their children adored their au pairs.

They were inventive, Stormy and Lotte; took turns fixing meals and snacks for the children, seven of them altogether; found games that all of them could play; danced with the children to the records they'd brought from home: Edith Piaf and Hildegard Knef and Charles Aznavour.

In winter the town emptied itself, felt isolated. But summers were glorious because they were a five-minute walk from Coopers Beach, where they spent all day with pails and umbrellas and blankets and picnics, talking while they watched over the children as they chased one another through the shallow water or took their naps.

"We often talked to them in German," Aunt Stormy had said to me. "The little ones responded the same as to English."

My mother had agreed. "It was in the sound of the voice, Annie."

"Where we walked from one house to the other, we wore down the grass."

They lent each other their favorite books. Lotte's poetry collections: Annette von Droste-Hülshoff, Heinrich Heine, Rainer Maria Rilke.

Stormy liked novelists, especially Ilse Aichinger and Hermann Hesse. They'd both brought Pearl S. Buck's *Die Mutter* across the Atlantic. The first English-language book they finished all the way—trading off between chapters—was *Peyton Place*, more risqué than anything they'd read so far.

On their day off, Sunday, Lotte and Stormy took the train into Manhattan, walked for hours through different neighborhoods. Like all of Europe—no, the world—in one exhilarating city. They went to concerts, to protests against the Vietnam war, to the bakeries on Eighty-sixth for *Kuchen*, to Greenwich Village, to museums . . .

Away from their birth country, language was a stronger bond between them than it would have been at home. And yet, when people said, "Your accent . . . where are you from?" they learned to say, "Holland." Lotte started it. Because if they answered "Germany," there might be that pause . . . that shift from curious to watchful. "I hear the streets are very clean," someone might say. Or: "The Germans make good beer." Or: "Don't the trains always run on time?"

"But what if they know Dutch?" Stormy had asked Lotte.

"Very few people here speak Dutch. And if so, only a few words. It's a small country."

"But what if—"

"We'll tell them we've made a pact to practice English by not speaking Dutch for one year."

Much later, my mother would tell me that beneath all that was the horror at Germany's savage history and their uneasiness at being forever linked to that. They were mortified by how little they knew about the Holocaust. In Germany, their history lessons had left that out entirely, but here in America, it was part of the curriculum. To many of the Americans they met, Lotte and Stormy were representatives of Germany—punctual and obedient and rigid and clean and cruel and humorless like movie villains—making them feel more German, but in a sinister way, than if they'd stayed there.

OCCASIONALLY MY mother would hide things before Aunt Stormy came to visit us. "Stormy admires things away from you," she'd say.

I grew up with my father's story of Stormy and the blue glass ball he'd bought for Lotte at a glass blower's studio when she got pregnant with me. "Because it made me think of you levitating in a sphere like that within her, Annie . . . all blue light."

The day of my birth, Stormy arrived with books and wine for my parents, a lacy white jacket she'd crocheted for me, a crate with vegetables and fruits from her favorite farm stand. For two weeks, she cooked and cleaned and shopped, bathed me, carried me to my mother, who would nurse me.

One morning Stormy noticed the glass ball. "Such an extraordinary shade of blue."

"That's what Phillip and I love about it too," Lotte said.

"I haven't seen anything like it."

Lotte nodded. Switched me to her other breast.

"Can't you picture it hanging from the candle chandelier in my kitchen, Lotte?"

Still, Lotte did not offer it, though usually, when Stormy pointed to something and said she liked it, Lotte would insist, "It's yours, Stormy." Because that was what Stormy would do for her.

"I could see doing more with that blue . . . beads perhaps, or pegs for coats . . . doorknobs. It could set the tone, that blue. You wouldn't—" Stormy shook her head. "No. I shouldn't ask."

Lotte stroked my hair. Hummed to me till she felt the hum vibrate in her teeth.

"Would you at all consider . . . trading it?"

Lotte was too stunned to answer.

"Maybe trade it for my bowl from Hong Kong? The one you've always liked?" Stormy had gone to Hong Kong with her au pair family for three months and returned with hand-painted bowls, stories of the Feast of the Hungry Ghosts, distressed souls who didn't have a proper burial. She had plans to have her own burning of a Hungry Ghost on the beach, make offerings to send him away happy.

"You don't have to give me that bowl. You don't have to give me anything in return," Lotte said, figuring that would stop her.

But Stormy took the blue glass into her hands, holding it with reverence. "Thank you, Lotte. Aren't we all custodians of belongings that pass through our hands?"

That night in bed—with me sleeping between them—Lotte asked Phillip, "Do you think being generous only means giving away something you want to keep for yourself?"

"That doesn't feel natural."

"Stormy comes from a poor family. They never had much. Maybe that's why—"

"Are you being a reverse snob?"

"I'm trying to understand why she's doing this, Phillip."

"It's only a gift if it is freely given."

"How did you get so wise?"

"From being with you."

"I think Stormy believes it's freely given."

"The way you pretend with her, I can see why."

"It's impossible to deny her anything . . . considering how generous she is."

The courage it must have taken Lotte to ask for that glass ball back! In the morning, she took Stormy's hand, sat down with her. Heart racing, she told her she wanted to keep her blue glass ball.

"But of course," Stormy said right away. "I'll get it for you." When she returned, she set the blue ball next to the toaster, where its reflection doubled into two glass balls, one for each of them.

"I'm sorry," Lotte said.

"It's all right. Really."

"You're not disappointed?"

"I'm glad you told me."

Lotte felt stingy. Selfish. Still—not to have asked for it would have meant letting herself down. "Stormy?"

"Yes?"

"Please, pick something else of mine that you like . . . please?"

"Being here with you and Phillip and Annie is all I want."

But the day after Stormy returned to North Sea, Lotte couldn't find her blue glass ball, and though she searched throughout her rooms, she knew it was no longer there; and she wasn't surprised when, on her next visit to North Sea, she found it dangling from Stormy's candle chandelier. Still, Lotte was furious, and she fantasized stealing it back. Feeling wicked and justified, she fantasized uncoupling it from the chandelier while Stormy was outside and, without saying a word, hiding it inside my diaper bag to take home with her. Later, she would tell me that she didn't know what kept her from stealing it, that perhaps it was enough to see it floating above her, attracting blue light from the candles and windows.

"LET'S GET Opal some food for the ducks." Aunt Stormy opened the lid of a metal trash can she'd secured with a bungee cord to keep the raccoons out. It was filled with cracked corn, and she scooped some into a little pail.

We walked down her path, through stands of phragmites, along the boardwalk, flat across the wetlands. Where it arched over the tidal inlet, Mason had propped Opal on the railing. His arms around her, they were looking down into the water.

"Here, *Vögelchen,*" Aunt Stormy called out.

"Duck . . . ," Opal sang.

"*Vögelchen* means birds . . . ducks and chickens too. All kinds of birds." Aunt Stormy ran her bare instep up her other calf to clear off twigs.

Wind seized us, shook us, and Opal laughed aloud. Two great white herons flew in from the bay, swerved, and landed in the crown of BigC's black cherry tree. BigC meant Big Calla. Big Calla Holland. Not because she was big but because her house was much bigger than Aunt Stormy expected. A red clay roof sat like a lid on the pink stucco mansion. Nightmare in pink, the neighbors called it.

In the late sixties, Aunt Stormy had bought her cottage in North Sea because the name evoked the German North Sea for her. It was affordable on a teacher's salary; but when the taxes got too high for her, she sold half an acre to BigC, a commercial artist who had an apartment in New York, where she painted murals for restaurants. Every other weekend BigC came to North Sea, but when she had tenants, she stayed at a bed-and-breakfast in Southampton.

"DUCK . . . ," Opal sang.

Mason joined her. "Duck."

When Aunt Stormy rattled her pail, ducks scurried down the inlet as if they'd been waiting for her. "Open your hands, Opal. I got something for you and the *Vögelchen.*" She dribbled corn into Opal's hands.

But Opal latched her fingers around the kernels and brought her fists to her mouth.

"Not girl food." Mason stopped her. "No, no . . ."

Opal shrieked. Sucked at her fist.

"No no . . . It's food for the . . ." He grinned at Aunt Stormy. "Wig-geltchen?"

"*Vögelchen,* Mason."

"That's what I said." He uncurled Opal's fingers. Flung the corn to the ducks. "See? Like this."

Aunt Stormy handed him the pail. "Are you going back to school in the fall, Annie?"

I nodded. "Mason and Jake and I are scheduling our classes so that one of us will always be with Opal."

"I'm glad."

Mason was letting Opal reach into the pail and feed the ducks. A few times her hands would instinctively go to her mouth, but he'd distract her, weave his hands between hers and detour them till she laughed and gave up the corn to the ducks.

"They're your ducks from now on, Opal," Aunt Stormy said.

"Wait a minute." I pretended to be confused. "That's what you used to tell me."

"They were yours." Aunt Stormy nodded. "Until a new child came along."

"You have to share, Annabelle." Mason tilted his face to me, light on his cheeks, his lips.

EVERY AUGUST, on the night before the full moon, Aunt Stormy celebrated her own Feast of the Hungry Ghosts. My parents and I would stay with her. Most years we'd bring Mason and Jake along. On the way we'd stop in Chinatown, buy lots of Chinese spirit money for the ghost; tinsel and crepe and streamers; yards of flimsy red and purple tissue paper.

Every year, the ghost would be different, and the one I still liked best was the ghost with two heads. We were seven when we helped Aunt Stormy and my parents build the skeleton from bamboo poles that Pete cut from behind his garage. We filled in the ghost's body with newspaper and papier-mâché. Taped the Chinese spirit money and golden streamers to the ghost's purple robe, which spread out like a tent. To the long bamboo arms, we fastened big bamboo rake hands.

My mother and Aunt Stormy were laughing and talking in German, that familiar singsong below their voices that wasn't there when they spoke English. When my mother ran up the steps to the guest room and returned with her oldest swimsuit, the two of them got giddy.

"Double D!"

"Triple D!"

They cut one big bra cup from the suit and squeezed it into a nose for the woman-head of the ghost. It had a red licorice mouth, red streamers for hair, and a long neck that positioned it a bit higher than the man-face with its paper-towel-tube nose and a forehead made from a horseshoe crab.

"More creature than human," my father said.

"Horseshoe crabs were around over a million years before dinosaurs started," Aunt Stormy told me.

The Hungry Ghost was twice as tall as my father, and when we hauled it to the beach, we walked in single file on the boardwalk: Jake and I carried the heads of the statue, my parents and Aunt Stormy the middle, Pete and Mason the ghost's feet.

By the edge of the water, Aunt Stormy's guests were already waiting for us: some of her neighbors and favorite clients; friends from Amnesty International who met every month for letter-writing campaigns; teachers from the elementary school where she used to teach until she opened her first business, taking care of summer homes. She tucked the houses in for the off-season, opened them for the holidays, scheduled contractors and various services to maintain them, and checked in while their owners were away.

All her guests had brought beach chairs and umbrellas, tables covered with Indian bedspreads, amazing food. They took photos of the ghost and of each other *with* the ghost, toasted the ghost with wine or juice. After we'd eaten, we slipped offerings beneath the ghost's robe to send along in the fire: bad dreams and consumerism and guns and sadness and corrupt politicians and entitlement and lies and summer traffic . . .

What we want the Hungry Ghost to take away.

Aunt Stormy knelt down, her trousers the color of sand, her caftan a brilliant blue, her dark braid dividing her back. Soon, the moon would rise, not full yet, not until tomorrow, when we would take out the kayaks for the second day of the ritual, witness the sun go down and the moon rise in its August fullness.

Lighter fluid in her hand, Aunt Stormy squirted beneath the figure and across the robe. My father squatted next to her, his long thighs parallel to the ground.

"Not so close," my mother called out, cautious only near fire.

When the first flames curled up around a newspaper photo, clearing a circle in the photo, brown margins, orange flames, my father came to stand behind my mother, who leaned against him as he folded her into his arms, while she folded her arms around me, the three of us facing the ghost. Ablaze, the figure was in motion—standing still, but in motion—the streamers rippling in the flames, the arms already gone. And when the figure leaned into the flame, into itself, it became the flame, a flutter of red and yellow.

"I'VE MADE a picnic," Aunt Stormy told Opal. "For your birthday dinner, sweet one. We'll take it to the ocean. We just have to stop at a client's house to make sure the furnace has been repaired."

On Noyack Road, a police cruiser was pulling up behind a beige dented car, lights flashing.

"If this were not a Latino driver," Aunt Stormy said, "the cop wouldn't bother. Makes me want to stop and remind him that all of us are immigrants in this country—except for the Native Americans, of course. It's always the most recent wave that gets it. That cop should go after tailgaters instead."

"I always notice tailgating more out here," Mason said.

"Because they're used to driving in the city. Right on your tail." Aunt Stormy glanced at Opal and lowered her voice. "Guess that's where assholes belong. I used to give them the finger, the entire arm, but then I started hearing about road rage, and now I slow down. Makes them nuts."

A block from Sagg Main Beach, she pulled in to the driveway of a yellow house with covered porches. "Two sisters live here," she said, "both in their eighties. Never been apart. Grew up in Westchester and moved out here when they retired."

"Living together their entire lives . . . ," Mason said, "sounds so peaceful."

Aunt Stormy laughed. "You wouldn't say that if you met the harpies."

"Why harpies?"

"They're always fighting, talking smut with their sharp little voices, trying to impress me with all the famous people they supposedly know. I'll show you."

In the living room, hundred of snapshots crowded the walls. In each frame two old women—lots of hair and makeup, smiling hard—hovered over one or two people at a table, different people in each snapshot, yet with the same bewildered expression.

"That's what's they do, the harpies . . . walk up to famous people in restaurants and get a waiter to snap a picture before their victims can say no."

"So that's why the deer-in-the-headlights look," Mason said.

WHEN WE got to Sagg Main, the lifeguard was blowing the final whistle, motioning swimmers in for the day. As soon as the lifeguard chair was empty, kids swarmed up the ladders like locusts. Jumped down into the mountain of sand the lifeguards had shoveled in front of the tall chair. Then up again.

"I used to do that," I said and spread out an old bedsheet, while Aunt Stormy unpacked our dinner.

A man and a woman, both heavy with masculine features, arrived with towels and shovels. He was about thirty, she twice his age. When he lay on the sand, facing the water, a towel under his head, she began to cover him with sand until he became this mountain of sand, only his head and neck visible. Walking into the water, she rinsed the sand from her hands, did a few deep knee bends, boosting herself up with her fists against her knees, and ambled to her mountain of sand.

"Help me with the umbrella." Aunt Stormy poked the sharp end of the pole into the sand.

"Let me," Mason said.

"We'll need some shadow," Aunt Stormy said.

I smiled but didn't correct her. My mother too had confused *shade* and *shadow.* In German, both words were the same: *Schatten.*

Opal half-walked, half-crawled to the edge of the sea, and I followed her, knelt down, and pulled her into the curve of my arms so that we faced the waves and felt their power . . . as I had at her age, naked and scuttling toward those white and curling waves that were so much taller than I was, and my father, strong and summer-brown and running, sliding himself on the sand between me and the water, a people-wave stopping the water-wave from getting me. Then, stepping behind me, my father pulled me up by my hands, and the instant the wave was about to knock me over, he let me fly across it—*bird . . . fish . . . bird-fish*—and I flew above the wave till he landed me on the sand, my father, shy on land but a hero in the water. He raised me up again so I could fly across the next wave too, each bigger and faster. Not one knocked me over. Because I could fly. And when he landed me for the last time, he turned me toward my mother and Aunt Stormy. I squatted and grasped fists of sand for them.

How do I remember, Dad? From stories you told to me? From what I still feel in my body: the flying . . . the lightness . . . the certainty that there is a way across. "A way we haven't thought of before," you liked to say.

"Fly . . ." I lifted Opal above the waves, and she gurgled with pleasure. "Fly . . ."

"Fly . . ." Mason brought his lips against my ear. "You and I . . . we'd make fantastic babies."

"You're not serious."

"Too soon?"

"I barely know how to take care of one. While you're playing house."

Aunt Stormy came up next to us.

Mason tilted his head. "Don't be pissed at me, Annie. It's just that—"

"What are they doing?" I pointed to the woman who had buried the man. She was laying her folded towel next to his and stretching out so that her head was next to his, but her body facing in the opposite direction from him, away from the water. Then she started digging herself in, using the smaller of the two shovels to scoop the sand from around her body and heaping it on top of herself. At first she was sitting up, reaching for the sand with her shovel, but then she had to lie down, let the sand sift across her till it was up to her chest.

"It's what they do when they go to the beach," Aunt Stormy said.

"But why?" Mason asked.

She shrugged. "It's what they always do."

The woman closed her eyes. Rested. There was something ancient about those two, the burrowing in, something foreign and intimate.

"Are they married?" Mason asked.

"I have no idea."

"I bet they're mother and son." I squatted, balanced Opal on my knee, and drew their outlines into the sand. *A man and woman burying each other.* Someone else might see it as a burial. I knew it wasn't. Imagined the delicious weight of cool sand. *What they do when they go to the beach . . .*

"I bet they're married," he said.

"She's much older than he," Aunt Stormy said.

"So?" Mason asked.

Aunt Stormy laughed. "Good for you, Mason."

"I bet you ten dollars they're mother and son."

"Ten that they're married," I said.

"And how will you find out?" Aunt Stormy asked.

Mason grinned at her. "We'll send you to ask."

"Oh no. You two . . . you'll go broke."

"Whatever money we lose to each other," he said, "never costs us anything. And even when I'm winning, I want Annie to win too. Not that moment, but soon."

"Fly?" Opal was squirming.

I stood up, raised her in my arms. "Fly . . ."

"Lotte was like you in the water," Aunt Stormy said, "a fish."

As Opal's chubby feet kneaded the air above the waves, it came to me that she was not only my sister but also my daughter—links far tighter than either one link by itself—and that, through her, my parents were continuing to live in my arms.

I raised her higher. "Fly . . ." *Daughter.* And pressed my lips against her back. No longer her make-believe mother. But her real mother. *Now.*

My daughter giggled.

Aunt Stormy was digging her toes into the sand, dislodging something.

"What did you find?" Mason asked.

"A critter bit?" I asked.

She bent. Picked up a piece of cartilage attached to a bone and a couple of feathers. "An excellent critter bit."

As a child, I'd loved searching with her along the beach for wings and bones and skulls and spines.

"Oh dear," she would say, "those critters have come apart."

We'd collect the critter bits, carry them to her cottage, and assemble them with string and wire and nails, creating an animal unlike any other; and when I'd try to breathe life into the bleached bones, I'd feel all-powerful. It was there that my fascination with collages began, with the boldness and conviction that I could resurrect these animals as I envisioned them, or—perhaps—as they were destined to be.

Mason

—but the moon and the rocks were getting hotter, your breaths faster. And though you and Jake were not touching—not yet, Annie—I saw you together.

"For Christ's sakes— Just do it."

"Will you please quit?" Jake snapped at me. "Please, Mason?"

That's when I needed proof. The kind of proof you get by offering people something they claim they don't want. "If you make love now, I'll believe it's not an issue between you, that you're telling the truth."

"That is some fucked logic." Your voice was so furious, Annie, that I knew I was in for chaos with you, even if I quit now.

But I couldn't quit. Because Jake's wanting of you was so . . . blatant. It's not like I invented it, Annie. It was all there, like it often is with him. Like when he throws back his head, or when he positions himself in Aunt Stormy's hammock just so, as if daring you to touch his jaw to make sure it really is that unbearably smooth.

"Just do it," I told him.

"I'm getting out of here," he said.

And I was so relieved . . . relieved beyond relieved, Annie . . . and already pictured myself following Jake from this drowsy and blighted heat . . . the night cold against our skin and yet already turning into glow . . . bracing us for that leap into our pond that will conceal our movements.

But Jake did not get out.

Jake said, "Quit being such a weird fuck, Mason."

But I could see the change in you, Annie. How you and Jake suddenly considered each other's bodies. Speculated. Forbidden. Like Jake and me at summer camp, Annie, and you finding us on the raft. Forbidden. Scared and turned on and sure he'd kill me if he could.

That same urgency last night in the sauna. That same urgency this morning in your studio. One collage is not enough, Annie. I used to love being in here with you, the two of us organizing your supplies, arranging your rice papers by thickness, and I'd listen to you think aloud about your next project.

Like *White on White*. The pond in winter. You said it had to do with memory and coldness, and I was awed by how you brought those two together in rich, deep whites. But you didn't like it enough, never exhibited it.

You don't honor your art the way I do, Annie, won't allow me to call it art. Whenever I say your art should be in museums, you tell me it doesn't work like that.

White on White. I hold it up to the window. Outside, the air is gray, the way it gets moments before a storm when you think it can't be evening yet though it's dark. Drive carefully, Annie.

In the sauna last night, that peculiar smell of wood—swollen and contracted a thousand times—rose from the slats.

"Doing it now," I said, wanting to cancel that urgency, to cancel all of this, "is the only way you can convince me it doesn't matter."

"You're hassling us, Mason." You, again, Annie, growling at me.

More steam, as I added water, and when I lay down again, the hot slats dug into me, measuring me, defining me. "Nothing will change," I told both of you. "Because of the trust we have among us."

"You've done some miserable things," you said, "but this is the worst. At least lock the door."

I got up. At the door, I suddenly wished I could escape. And I thought: Why not? Tried to figure out what to say to undo all this, maybe pretend it was some joke all along—not this wretched jealousy that stalked me, tackled and leveled me, again and again. You think it's easy, lugging that with me, Annie?

"Jake?" You leaned toward him. "Jake?"

When he—

THREE

Mason

{ *Pond House* }

THE MORNING AFTER all the anniversaries, rain smudged the browser bushes and phragmites outside Aunt Stormy's windows. Mason felt lazy, content, as he lay on the old velvet couch, his head on Annie's knees, his feet on the stack of books Aunt Stormy usually kept on the couch.

"Little turtles are the most intelligent ones. See?" Aunt Stormy turned a page of *National Geographic.*

Opal's hands padded the magazine as Aunt Stormy made up stories for her.

"Especially turtles with red on top like you."

Mason felt Annie's fingers in his hair. "Don't you stop."

"What is it worth to you?"

"My life," he said without thinking but meaning it, knowing it to be true.

"Is that so?" Her face above him, open, wide. Her smile mischievous. But her eyes sad. *Not matching her smile.* Not back—*yet?*—to the light from before her parents' death.

Yesterday, on their anniversary, she'd woken up crying, hard, and last night she'd cried for her parents again in his arms, quietly, because they were in Aunt Stormy's guest room with Opal sleeping nearby in the crib. He'd held Annie like he had all those other nights she cried; but all at once he'd felt furious at her parents. For dying on his wedding day. For squeezing the light from Annie. For making their anniversary a day of mourning—now and to come.

It's my day too. He'd loved her parents, especially her mom, who'd looked at him with such joy from the time he was a kid and knocked at her door. If only they'd died a week later, say, or even a month, he and Annie could have their day of celebration. And later their day of mourning. Instead of having their joy sucked up by grief. *Is it selfish, wanting joy and grief separate?*

No. It's Opal's day too. Her birthday.

"YOU'RE VERY strong, Opal," Aunt Stormy said.

"What did she do?" Mason asked.

"She untied my shoelaces by pulling at the ends. And she pulled my foot into the air."

"You are strong, Stardust," he told Opal.

By the windows, she was nestled against Aunt Stormy atop a mound of rugs and blankets from Your Personal Taste, Aunt Stormy's second business. It had nothing to do with cooking or eating but was a service for summer people whose tastes were offended by their landlords' decor. Her ads in *Dan's Papers* read:

YOUR PERSONAL TASTE
improves any rental house

Many of her clients came to her summer after summer, reserving certain bedspreads or dishes or slipcovers far ahead of the season. She always had stories about them. Like the heart surgeon from the city who sulked because his decor had already been rented by another client.

Her inventory was stored in the huge guest room that took up the entire second floor. Mason and Jake had installed more than a dozen wooden rods below the ceiling, where during the off-season, she hung curtains and tablecloths and sheets.

"Like the first floor of ABC Carpets," Pete liked to say.

But she bought most of her inventory—dishes, silverware, and crystal that she stored on high shelves; paintings of the ocean and wetlands that she stacked against the walls according to size—at auctions and yard sales. In summer, she'd rent all of that out, but in winter, the guest room shrank into a cocoon with gossamer dividers.

Some clients became her friends, like Valerie, a poet who'd inherited a house too expensive for her to maintain but was able to keep it by renting part of it for poetry retreats.

Aunt Stormy's least favorite client was a financial analyst she'd named Life-in-the-Colonies when he'd complained that his handyman was in Florida. "I guess they can do things like that nowadays . . . go on vacations."

ON THE VELVET couch, Mason reached up and traced the half-moons below Annie's eyes.

"Aunt Stormy was right," she said.

"About what?"

"Calling you sexy trouble way back."

"That's how you see me?"

"Sometimes . . ."

"Not often?"

"Somewhere between sometimes and often. How about me?"

"All the time."

"Trouble and sexy?" Annie asked.

"Sexy. No trouble."

"Way back, when we were little . . . ?"

"Yes?"

"What's your first memory of me?"

"You."

She fingered his hair. "What part of me?"

Mason smiled at her. That was what he liked between them . . . the playfulness that could lead them anywhere.

"What part of me, Mason? I remember your toes . . . touching your toes."

"All right. Your left kneecap."

"Asshole. And I mean this in an affectionate way."

"With a question like that—"

"Be serious."

"All of you. I remember all of you. Always."

"Always?"

"More than my parents."

"More than Jake?"

"In comparison to you, Jake doesn't count." He felt himself blush. It felt like a betrayal. But true. *Half true. I could have just said yes.*

"Is that the worst thing you've done today?"

"What?"

"Saying that about Jake?"

"So far."

"That's pretty awful."

"How about you? What's the worst thing you've done today?" It was always there between them, that question, as they upped each other, competed.

"I stopped loving you when you said Jake doesn't count."

"Will you love me again, Annie?"

"But not right now."

"Jake counts. All right?"

"All right."

"Yesterday, then," Mason said. "What's they worst thing yesterday?"

Opal was tugging a magazine from Aunt Stormy. *With her red hair and freckled skin, she could be Annie's daughter. But if Jake were here now—would Opal resemble him more than me?*

"How about you yesterday?" Annie nudged him. "What is—"

"I didn't let Opal eat bird food."

"Despicable."

"Does that mean I win?"

"No."

"Why not?"

"Ultimately beneficial."

"Indeed . . . that too."

"She could have caught some weird bird disease. Or choked. Or—"

"Okay, I have a better one. A better worse one. Day before yesterday—" He pointed to his new leather jacket on the blue glass pegs by the door. Butter-smooth and so light brown it was almost blond.

"Tell me." Annie stretched.

"I changed the price tag."

"You what?"

"I peeled the sticker from a sale jacket."

"You told me the jacket was half-price."

"I did not."

"You told me—"

"I told you I *got* it half-price."

She slid aside so abruptly that his head bounced on the couch.

"They would have marked it down eventually."

"Your logic . . . sucks."

"So do I win?" he tried, knowing he shouldn't have told her. Still . . . hard to know with Annie ahead of time. She'd be clowning around . . . then slap you down with schoolmarm values.

"You could send a check to the store. For the price difference."

"No way."

"Or you could pack it up and send it there with a note . . . anonymously."

"No."

"It was stealing, Mason."

"Correct. *If* I had done it."

"Stop lying to me."

"I made it up. To see if I could win."

She stared into his eyes as if believing she could find the truth there.

So he put it there. Without blinking. Held her gaze. Imagined truth in his eyes and shut out the high he'd felt when he'd switched tags and paid half-price, when he'd told the salesclerk he'd wear it home and walked from the store with the jacket so light that it didn't drag down his shoulders.

"Listen, Annie, the worst thing I've done today is make up that story."

"Swear?"

"Swear." He scooted toward her on the couch, resettled his head on her knees. "It doesn't come close to what you did on the train in Morocco."

A corner of her mouth moved upward.

"Is that still the worst thing you've done, Annie?"

• • •

WHEN SHE nodded, he saw her in Tangier, enraged as she bought a huge black scarf. Men had been staring at her wherever she went because she wasn't veiled. To Mason, it was exciting, but she didn't get it. Twisted this scarf around her head and shoulders as if she wanted to make herself disappear. Rushed ahead through cramped passages of the Medina, lined with stalls where you could buy orchids, bloody sheeps' heads, clothing, transistor radios, live roosters, jewelry, spices . . .

"Wait for us," Jake shouted.

A man with a bicycle shoved past Annie, sheeps' stomachs slung across the handlebars.

Their travel book had pictures of the Medina but no descriptions of the smells: blood and dust and sweetness and excrement. Even here, Mason could smell the dye vats they'd seen the day before, where boys with dye-stained legs were stomping in caldrons. Young boys. At the pottery wheels too, wearing face masks because the dust made it hard to breathe.

They ate a meal of lamb and chickpeas at a restaurant where belly dancers performed on a center stage. Unexpected in this country where women were veiled, where coffee shops were for men only.

On the street to the hotel, Annie held on to Mason's arm.

"I want to get out of here tonight," she said.

"Tomorrow," Jake told her. "We've already paid for tonight at the hotel." He kept track of how much they could spend to have their money last.

Hustlers pressed against them, tried to sell hashish.

"You stay away from me!" Annie raised both hands to stop the one closest to her.

"You are a hard, hard woman," the man hissed. Hollow cheeks. Eyes burning with hate. "Very sick."

At the hotel Annie insisted they leave Tangier that evening. Mason loved the city, wanted to stay. And Jake asked Annie to wait at least till morning because he'd washed out his clothes and they were still drying on the windowsills of the smaller room.

"Not anymore." She jammed it all into their backpacks, a whirling dervish who seized what was theirs, frantic to get away.

When they got on a late train to Asilah, Mason began to enjoy the adventure, especially since Jake was so unsettled. From the seat across from them, a man stared at Annie's breasts. She flushed, blinked, but Mason could tell that, secretly, she had to be loving this, and he felt a fast heat.

• • •

"YES, THAT'S a picture of a diver," Aunt Stormy was telling Opal. "He's come to learn all about diving from the turtles."

She carried Opal to the refrigerator, poured her a cup of apple juice.

"Look at all those photos." She held Opal close to the photos on her refrigerator door.

"Most are of you," Mason said. "There you are, see? With Annie. With me. With Aunt Stormy and Pete."

Opal patted her hands and cooed, her joy so physical that Mason could feel it.

"That's Pete trimming his trumpet vines," he told her.

But she was reaching for the photo of the pregnant bride.

Below that was a photo of Annie's parents against a sunset. And next to that a flyer announcing a fund-raiser for Amnesty International. Mason and Aunt Stormy often forwarded e-mails to each other, petitions to sign, senators to call. That was where he connected best with her, as he had with Annie's mother, who'd taught him and Annie—when they were in Boston marching against the Gulf War—that they had the responsibility to raise their voices against injustice.

"JAKE GOT so upset in Morocco." Mason seized Annie's hand, raked it through his hair. "He said you almost started World War Three."

"I would have changed seats. But the train was too crowded."

"Jake made too much of it," Mason said, though he too had been frightened when Annie had stared right back at the man—not at his face but at his crotch—kept staring even when the man became infuriated. Then she had motioned to Mason and Jake, held up her thumb and forefinger, about three inches apart, and grinned.

"Jake was sure the man was ready to attack him and me," Mason said.

"For not controlling your woman."

"As if we could."

"Jake has no appetite for getting even."

Mason pushed her hand away. "Jake is better than anyone at getting even."

"How can you say that?"

"Jake would kill me— If he could."

"I hate it when you come up with . . . suspicions like this."

"I always get blamed for what he does."

"Spare me. Please."

THEY KEPT postponing their drive home to New Hampshire, waiting for the rain to lessen, but when it didn't, Mason strapped Opal into her car seat, and Annie started off driving as they headed for the South Ferry. On Shelter Island, the rain got so dense that she pulled in to the entrance to Mashomack. The car smelled of baby and of teething cookies that Opal liked above any other cookies, sucking on them till they were mush and took on her smell.

Only two other cars were on the North Ferry, and the waters pitched at them. Mason was glad when they reached Greenport. But he wished he were driving because Annie kept slowing down on the road to Orient Point. She used to be such a natural driver, fast with good reflexes, but her parents' accident had made her too cautious.

"Just keep going."

"Don't push, Mason."

"I'm exceedingly patient."

"Hah. Mr. Exceedingly Patient."

"We'll miss the ferry to New London."

"So we'll take the next one." Neck stretched, she inched forward, windshield wipers flying, every one of her fingers hooked around the top of the steering wheel. Like a caricature of some old-fart lady out for her Sunday drive.

Mason laughed.

"What now?"

He sighed. "No reason."

Opal was asleep when he carried her to the passenger deck of the Cross Sound Ferry, kept sleeping through the long passage, when he took her down to the car again, and while he drove north, more aggressive than usual, to offset Annie's slowness. In New Hampshire, quite a few roads were closed due to flooding, and he followed signs for detours. The severe rainfall had saturated the ground.

"Let's turn back," Annie said when they came to a section of road that lay underwater.

"This car can float."

Behind him, Opal was stirring.

"Opal believes me. Right, Mophead?" In the rearview mirror, he waved at her.

She flapped her arms, bounced them off the padded bar of her car seat.

"Do you want to see this car float, Mophead?"

"Don't show off," Annie warned.

He gritted his teeth. Rolled toward the dip of flooded road. His hands were damp, but as he felt Annie's fear next to him, he drew courage from that. Now he had to prove that she did not need to be afraid. All at once he knew she believed him that the car would float . . . then the excitement because, incredibly, he was driving in water—*wheels like wings like propellers like wings*—churning him forward, forward and across the flood, where, set against a hill, a gray barn and a gray house leaned toward a pond between them.

Empty. They felt empty to him. A few hurricanes away from propping each other up. Suddenly he was certain that he and Annie and Opal would live here, as certain as he'd been last year about the internship he wanted with New Hampshire Peace Initiative, a nonprofit in Concord. That day too he'd been driving. Away from campus. And just as he'd passed a horse trailer, he'd known he'd get the internship. And he did.

WHEN THE car emerged from the flood, Mason took a left up the grassy driveway, expecting Annie to ask what he was doing, but she was staring at a scrawny tulip tree, about Opal's height, that grew in the yard. She got out of the car, touched one of the branches without disturbing the blossoms. Then she walked toward the barn. Mason unstrapped Opal, carried her as he followed Annie.

They didn't speak.

In one corner of the barn was a sauna, cold and musty, nine broken slats in the benches. The house unlocked, empty. Windows bare. Floors cracked linoleum. Bookshelves, gray as rain, on the wall around the fireplace. The faucets dry.

But Annie brought in a bucket of rainwater, and as she dissolved the pulp of teething cookies that had molded itself to Opal's hands and face as if part of her, Opal pointed to the kitchen window. It had stopped raining, and in the pond, the reflections of house and barn were reaching for each other.

"I could see this in a collage," Annie said.

"What if—" Mason curved one arm around her waist. "—you had a place for just your work?"

"My own studio . . ."

"Your studio. You wouldn't have to let anyone in."

But she wasn't talking, just looking the way she got when she was already sketching something inside her mind.

"It's only about ten or fifteen miles from campus, Annie."

"If we live next to a pond, she needs to learn how to swim right away."

"For sure."

"I could imagine working here."

The following morning, they made an offer with money Annie and Opal had inherited from their parents, phoned Jake, and celebrated with dinner at the nasty fortune restaurant.

THE DAY they moved into the pond house, Jake fired up the sauna. In the pond, Annie swam and Mason tugged Opal around by her life vest. It was still hot—with the moon yellow, full—and Opal paddled with her legs and feet like some small animal. So much of her was animal, Mason thought, that greed, that instinctive grasp, her quick rage. *All now.* She had something savage about her. *A baby wolf.* It embarrassed him, thinking this—*if I were her real father, I wouldn't.*

Slick with sweat, Jake came running from the sauna and jumped into the pond, shot up next to Mason, yelling, "Cold and clean and alive!"

"Can we have a bit more enthusiasm here?" Mason teased him.

"Even the scum on this pond feels clean."

"What scum?" Mason swatted at some floating green muck.

They both laughed.

Opal reached for Jake, her other hand holding on to Mason's ear.

"Ouch, you—" Mason loosened her little fist.

Jake lifted her above his head. *"The-four-of-us again"*—

His love for her was so transparent that Mason couldn't bear it. *Never as happy as when he's with us . . . with my family. Wanting what's mine. It's all here for him already.*

• • •

JAKE HELPED Mason build a studio for Annie in the barn, where the former owners had kept cows and horses, whose smell was packed into the dirt floor, into the walls and rafters. After they raised the floor of her studio with thick boards, they built her worktable from a massive church door that Mason had found for her at Sparky's Salvage.

It was Annie's idea to prop it on a cluster of eight filing cabinets so that she could approach her work from every angle. Mason bid on two flat files when a surveyor's office closed, and he helped Annie store her paper collection in the wide, shallow drawers. Yellow rice paper. Speckled mulberry paper made from the inner bark. Hemp paper, eggshell-white. Bookbinding paper. Marbleized paper. Porous rice paper. Coated paper that wouldn't fade.

He sorted out her critter bits, brushed off the remnants of sand that clung like an extra layer of skin to the shells of mud snails and slipper snails and ribbed mussels; to the claws of spider crabs and fiddler crabs; to the tails of horseshoe crabs. He took bits of a blue claw crab and fit them together like a puzzle.

"Look what I brought today," he'd announce when he came home with yet another gift for her studio—a jade-colored pottery jar for her brushes.

He surprised her with sheets of rice paper. Some had threads in them. Others looked as though they had actual rice kernels in them. He ordered a set of Chinese brushes for her: silky brushes from sable and fox and goat; hard-hair brushes from leopard and badger. Their tips were stiff with glue, and he soaked them in cold water till it softened and washed out.

For Opal he bought swim toys. He loved teaching her to swim, and she was faster underwater than on land. When he let her loose, she'd instinctively dart beneath the surface toward the edge of the pond, her arms strong as she pulled herself from the water, wiggling, slithering.

ON ONE of his trips to the hardware store with Jake, Mason noticed a baby monitor. "That may be good to have for the sauna," he said. "We'll be able to hear Opal in her room."

Jake took it off the shelf. "As a housewarming gift." He turned it. Checked the price. Frowned.

"No," Mason said. "I'll get it."

"I've been looking for something to give to you."

"It's expensive—"

"That's okay."

"—considering how cheap you are."

Jake gave him his pale, wounded look.

"It's true. You use tiny little pencil stubs. I swear you must go through your friends' trash to get them."

"Quit it."

"I've never seen you with a new pencil."

On class outings, Mason used to feel sorry for Jake because his father doubled whatever Jake didn't spend from his trip money. It kept Jake from enjoying the trip, reluctant to spend anything.

When Annie unpacked the monitor—two walkie-talkies with antennas—Jake told her, "We can take the receiver into the sauna with us."

We? Mason crossed his arms.

Jake unfolded the instructions. "The other one goes next to her crib. It says here you can hear a baby breathe from four hundred feet away."

"Do you mind testing the receiver, Mason?" Annie asked.

As Mason walked down the slope of the driveway—at least five hundred feet—he could still hear Annie and Jake in Opal's room, going on about how wonderful the baby monitor was. Women were always spoiling Jake, though he had an alarming ability for choosing awful clothes. Sort of dapper. They made him resemble an old fart, and even his features would change with the outfits, go flat like his hair, make him look heavy all over though he wasn't. Only his thighs. Jake's mother used to spoil him, saving treats for him only, hushing the day-care kids when Jake napped.

"Can you still hear us?" Annie shouted.

I could be still and hear what they're really saying. When they think I can't hear.

But this was for Opal. "Yes," Mason said. "I can hear you."

"If it works that far away," Jake's voice, "it'll definitely work in your bedroom, with just a wall from Opal's."

You stay away from our bedroom wall.

The following day, Mason bought Annie a cashmere shawl.

"It's gorgeous." She wrapped it around herself. "Thank you. What's the occasion?"

"To celebrate your new studio."

"Then that's where I'll keep it."

"You can also wear it when you're in the house. With me."

But she hung the shawl over the back of her working chair. "So extravagant . . . ," she said.

"BRING A date," Mason encouraged Jake. "We don't want to be selfish, and keep you all for us."

But when Jake did, it made everything different—*no longer the-four-of-us* but a new person. Jake would be wearing one of his dapper outfits, smiling too much, talking too much, and Mason would feel like a parent, patient with his hyper kid on a sugar high, waiting for the stimulation to go away.

Every one of Jake's dates was scholarly, sexy, and aloof. When Mason and Annie talked about them afterward, they named them Ice Queen 1 and Ice Queen 2 and so on. Even a repeat Ice Queen remained an outsider.

By then Jake had moved from the dorm into a small apartment not far from the pond house. He reduced his rent by scrubbing the steps and corridors of the apartment building, and when tenants left muddy tracks or cigarette butts in the lobby, he'd get pissy as though they'd trashed his living room.

A day before classes started in the fall, Mason and Jake completed Annie's studio. The house took much longer. The Fultons, who'd sold them the place, had painted the woodwork a solemn gray. When Mason and Jake tried to remove the paint so they could stain the wood, it took them two months to scrape and sand the shelves. They agreed with Annie on painting everything white, and the outlines of the rooms cleared, expanded.

MASON FELT at his best when they were all together. He and Annie and Opal and Jake. At his most possible best. All craving and uneasiness dormant.

Late evenings when Opal was asleep, they'd relax in the sauna, the baby monitor on the shelf by the door, her sleeping breath quick and light. Annie and Jake would stretch out on the second tier, Mason as usual on the tier above them, where it was even hotter, the air thick with steam from water that Jake would splash on the coals.

That winter, Mason volunteered one weekend a month at New Hampshire Peace Initiative. But he still took Opal to Sparky's, where he discovered a crate of wooden slats, just right for repairing the benches in the sauna. Once, when Opal climbed on a heap of heating supplies, it shifted, and Mason found an old tile stove beneath.

"Probably from Germany," Aunt Stormy said when they showed her photos. "We had stoves with blue and white tiles like that in Benersiel."

They were with her for the Feast of the Hungry Ghosts, and Opal was fascinated by the statue. Scooting around in diapers, she sang and pointed at the burning ghost—scary and lovely—but she kept glancing at Mason as if to make sure he was right behind her.

The following night, at full moon, they paddled their kayaks: Pete and Aunt Stormy in his two-seater; Annie in the little yellow kayak with the picnic stashed behind the seat; and Opal on a foam pad between Mason's knees in the purple kayak, her hands in the middle of the paddle, his outward from hers. It felt tippy to him. Unsettled. But then—for one instant—it all came together, that sensation of flying from his shoulder blades, causing all movement from that spot, and he knew how it could be if he kayaked every day.

"I'd love to do this every day," he said.

"Me too," Opal cried.

All at once the water felt heavy. Gelatinous. And their paddles were scooping up light, white-green flickers of light. They cried out in wonder.

"Did you see that?"

"What is this?"

"Sea walnuts," Aunt Stormy said. "But I call them lumis because they're luminescent." She dipped one oar into the bay, raised it. "Lumis don't sting like other jellyfish."

"I didn't know they were jellies," Annie said.

"They're waterfalls of light," Mason told Opal, guiding her hands so they wouldn't lose their paddle. "See? Now your paddle is the lumis' amusement park."

IN THE MORNING, Aunt Stormy grabbed her glass pitcher and took them to the bay to search for lumis. They found dozens on the sand, where the tide had left them. No longer the gauzy creatures that had lit up the sea at night, they felt like globs of clear Jell-O when Mason picked them up. Aunt Stormy filled her pitcher with seawater, a bit of sand, a few shells, and a green clump of seaweed, stem up, arms fanning down like an upside-down tree.

At the cottage, she set the pitcher on the table by her French doors.

"Lumis? Where?" Opal asked

"They're hard to see during the day because their bodies are almost all water."

But gradually Mason could make out their winglike extremities. Elegant. Weightless.

"Sometimes I think I'd like to get another dog," Aunt Stormy said.

"These floaty pets here don't quite do it for you?" Pete joked.

"Well . . . we have to set them free in the morning. And I do miss Agnes."

Annie pinched her nostrils.

Mason glared at her. "Agnes was a sweet old dog."

"A very smelly dog."

That night, Mason turned off the lights. In the dark, they sat around the pitcher and waited for the white-green flickers. Nothing . . . until Pete reached in and swished the cluster of seaweeds.

"There," Opal cried out.

A sudden flicker at the bottom of the pitcher.

"Photocytes," Pete said. "They have photocytes, cells that make the light."

"I want . . ." Opal waved the seaweed around till the flickers rose, illuminating her little fist in the pitcher. "I want . . ."

"Agnes was the size of a muskrat," Annie said.

"I think of her as St. Agnes now that she's dead," Aunt Stormy told her.

"Not just the size. She looked like a big muskrat."

Mason felt Annie's eyes pressing at him in the dark. "Don't listen to her, Opal."

"My mother," Annie said, "called her the Rodent."

In the dark, Aunt Stormy chuckled, softly. "St. Agnes—I want you to know—was part poodle and part terrier—"

"—and part rodent," Annie said.

Mason elbowed her. "Opal, look at those flickers you're making."

"We'll return the lumis to the bay in the morning," Pete said.

• • •

"I WANT TO be in the sauna."

"Four is not old enough," Mason said.

Opal splashed him. "Is five old enough?"

"Maybe once you're seven," Annie said.

Mason nodded. "We'll ask your pediatrician."

"No!" She swam over to Jake, held on to his neck. "I want Dr. Pagucci!"

"Dr. Pagucci only does splinters," Jake said.

A few weeks earlier, when Opal had had a splinter under her foot, he'd invented Dr. Pagucci for her. Dr. Pagucci knew how to undo splinters, tears, and bad luck. Jake had made a splinter kit like the one his mother used to have in her first aid box, using one of his mother's empty lipstick tubes with three sewing needles inside. He would take off his glasses to inspect splinters, poke at them with his needle, and tell Opal stories of graduating from splinter school. Afterward, he'd draw a smile with ears on the Band-Aid.

"I want Dr. Pagucci!" Opal dug her fingers into Jake's pale hair.

"That hurts. Stop it." Jake turned her around, gave her a gentle nudge away from him. "Dr. Pagucci's office hours are over. Besides, he only operates on solid ground."

Mason held out his arms. "Over here, Stardust. Over—"

But she flung herself toward Annie. "Tell me the story of how I began."

Mason dove, eyes open . . . dove along the bottom of the pond, through green-brown water. *I'm always last with Opal.* If she couldn't have Jake or Annie, she turned to him. But only then. She didn't mean to hurt him. But then why did it feel so awful? *They don't need me. Could assemble themselves as a family around Opal. Leave me out. Especially since Opal isn't mine. Comes as a package with Annie.*

Underwater, Opal's legs were scrambling against Annie. *If I want to, I can pull her down . . . like some big turtle hunting a duckling.* Every spring on Aunt Stormy's inlet, turtles and ospreys snapped up many of those baby fuzzball ducklings that skidded across the surface like tennis balls.

He popped up behind Jake, tickled him roughly.

Jake elbowed him away. "Start acting your age."

"You began inside the same space where I got started too," Annie was telling Opal.

Mason swam on his back, kicked his feet softly so he could hear.

"Inside our mom . . . ," Opal said. "Many many many years before me."

"Nineteen years. Because I was already nineteen when you lived inside that space—"

"All blue inside . . . blue light."

"That's how our mother imagined it . . . with the baby levitating in that light."

"You could feel me move."

"From the outside, yes . . . when I touched our mom's belly."

"Tell me about my foot." That was Opal's favorite part of the story, one she liked to hear again and again.

"Your foot . . . like a quick step—"

"Tell me about my fist."

"Your fist, suddenly pushing out, your tiny fist—"

"I punched you."

Annie laughed. "You did."

"And you already loved me."

"Oh yes . . . you were very real to me."

"Because our mom let you touch her belly . . . and we danced together."

"Yes, on my wedding day."

Mason swam closer.

"Now tell me the story of the ring."

Annie lifted her right hand from the water, showed Opal the ring that used to be their mother's. "Our dad gave our mom an opal instead of a diamond."

Opal's fingers closed around the ring. "When my hands get big, I'll wear it."

"Yes, we'll take turns."

Opal splayed her fingers against Annie's. "My hand is too little."

"It's growing every day," Mason said.

"For sure?"

"For sure," he said. "Now who wants nasty fortunes?"

"Me," Opal yelled, flinging herself in his direction.

Mason caught her.

"I have a date," Jake said.

"Bring her along." Mason laughed as he swung Opal around. "Look look—your toes are drawing a circle of splash."

AT THE NASTY fortune restaurant, Ice Queen 5 was appalled by her fortune. "Listen to this: 'You are no good and you will never amount to anything.' "

"That means you make good decisions," Jake interpreted.

"Better than mine." Annie read hers aloud: " 'You are a despicable person and bad things will come to you.' "

"Listen to mine," Mason said. " 'Your spirit is mean and your soul will be lost forever.' "

Ice Queen 5 shook her head. "They're horrible."

Jake nodded. "And unpredictable. That's what we love about them."

Opal held up her fortune. "Mine. Read mine."

"I'll read it for you." Mason pulled her onto his lap. Kissed the top of her red hair. "Hmm . . ." He covered the slip of paper.

"Read, Mason!"

Ice Queen 5 leaned over his arm and read Opal's fortune. "Let me," she said quickly. "Here, this is what it says, Opal. 'You are intelligent and generous and courageous.' "

Opal shrieked. "Not nasty."

"Maybe a nice fortune got in there by mistake. Wouldn't that be nice?"

Annie glared at her. "Wouldn't that be terrible?"

"Because we certainly don't come here for the food," Jake said.

"I want nasty—" Opal kicked and slapped at the table.

"I got her." Mason contained her arms and legs. "Sshhh . . ." He buffered her with his body from harming herself as she bounced herself against him in a frenzy. "Sshhh . . . " Outwaiting her, as he often did.

Ice Queen 5 brought her hand to her lips. "Is she having a seizure?"

"Of course not," Annie snapped.

"Tell you what," Mason whispered to Opal. "When you stop your tizzy, Annie will read your real fortune."

Annie nodded. "I'll wait till you're ready, Opal."

Opal whimpered. Sniffled. "Nasty . . ."

"Oh, this one is nasty. Ready?"

"Ready . . ."

"Let me make sure I read it correctly. 'Your brain is melting, and your nose is stuffed.' "

"Gross." Opal clapped her hands.

"Whoever writes these . . . things?" Ice Queen 5 asked.

"Someone very talented," Annie said.

"A sadist. I don't think they're healthy for children."

"Healthier than the fortunes that praise them for things they haven't done," Jake said.

"At least those are funny."

"Oh, but these are much funnier," Jake said.

"I don't see the humor in them."

"How sad." Jake raised his eyebrows. Yawned. "Opal seems tired."

Mason knew the cue. Jake wanted to get rid of his date and meet up with him and Annie. "You're right," he said. "Opal does seem tired."

"I'm exhausted too," Jake told Ice Queen 5. "Ready for me to take you home?"

WHEN MASON got Opal ready for bed, Annie said, "They're all clones of the original Ice Queen. You think we should stop numbering them?"

"You never like his dates," Mason said.

"I want someone more . . . fascinating for Jake."

"Someone like you?"

"That again?"

"Indeed, that again." He switched on the baby monitor next to Opal's bed.

"I'm not a baby," she protested.

"That's not why we use it," Annie said. "It's only for when we're in the pond or sauna."

They were already skinny-dipping when Jake arrived.

In the sauna, he scooped water with a ladle across the coals, and steam swelled around them. At first he settled on the upper bench with Mason, but he said it was too hot for him and moved to where Annie was stretched out on the lower bench.

Soon they both streaked out. To prove that he could endure the sauna longer than they, Mason stayed on the top tier, where the heat gathered, listening to them holler as they leapt into the pond. He waited a few seconds *beyond* where he could bear it no longer. Only then did he dash out into the cold, instantly alert, skin prickling. *A cold house keeps you alert.*

WHEN JAKE and Mason removed the linoleum floors in the pond house, they discovered wide oak boards, the color of maple syrup. They sanded them, sealed them with satin varnish.

At an estate auction in Dover, Annie bought an Oriental rug, still vibrant except for two holes worn into the center. But she darned the holes and wove woolen strands into her darning, almost matching the rest of the rug.

By spring, Opal was talking about the Hungry Ghost and what she wanted the ghost to take away.

"Seeds in oranges."

"Earaches."

"Naps. All naps."

Aunt Stormy encouraged her to draw pictures. "We'll make a ghost box. And inside we'll store slips of paper with messages for the Hungry Ghost."

"Is the box part of the Chinese custom?" Mason asked.

"No, I keep adapting the ritual."

On pink slips of paper, Aunt Stormy wrote what made her angry—tailgating, entitlement, all the dictators of the world, outrageous car repair bills, ads that cultivated greed—and stuffed them into the box.

Her neighbors saved their worn bamboo rakes for the ghost's hands, and when it came time for the burning that August, Opal gathered twigs for the flames.

IN WINTER, he liked to rub snow against his cheeks after coming from the sauna. A coldness that didn't sting but refreshed him, made him feel nutty. *Nutty* became their word that winter. Opal started using it too. Everything was nutty.

Especially the eco-nuts at the private school where Jake taught science. The eco-nuts were his most dedicated students, as passionate about saving the earth as other adolescents were about sex. One afternoon a week Jake took them out in the school van to study and clean up the environment.

Mason was a fund-raiser now. For New Hampshire Peace Initiative, the only organization he'd wanted to work for since his internship. The two women who'd founded NHPI were so taken by his enthusiasm that they created a job for him.

But Annie had another year in school. Four of her collages, all from the Pond Series, were in a group exhibition in Boston. She'd been working on those images from the day they'd moved here. Mason's favorite was of the barn leaning toward the pond as if about to drop into its own reflection.

Opening night, he stood with Annie in front of a collage she'd finished a week ago after driving toward their house and finding the sky in the pond, clouds and blues in the sheer pearl-white of morning.

"There's something elusive in your collages," an academic type told her. Probably some teaching assistant. Or eternal student.

"Thank you." Annie smiled.

"What do you mean by elusive?" Mason inquired.

"That you get one moment so fully," the man answered to Annie, "while already showing how it's changing."

"That's what I'm after." She tucked her hair behind one ear. More copper than red tonight. As if borrowing from the copper dress she wore.

"Well, you are doing it."

"I'm so glad that comes through to you."

"It's a characteristic of my wife's work," Mason told him. "I've seen it develop over the years." He wanted to make love to her against that collage. Wanted to be the light that made her transform what she saw. Wanted the admiration she was getting. Wanted to be her inspiration. Wanted it all to come through him and for nothing to matter to her except their love. Whatever came out of that love would enhance her work. But there must be nothing to come ahead.

OPAL ADORED BigC, who let her swim in the indoor pool that was surrounded by an endless mural of a Mediterranean landscape. Greek-looking buildings. Lots of columns and gardens. Everything was the wrong size. Buildings smaller than rocks. Jars larger than people. Black moss shimmers on rocks, makes them look mottled, weird.

"Ghastly," Annie said the first time she saw the mural. "The way Lucian Freud paints skin."

Realtors warned BigC's prospective tenants that she'd spy on them. But even tenants who were sure they wouldn't let her in didn't know how to send her away when she stopped by to bring them additional keys, or to pick up steaks she supposedly forgot in her freezer, or to show them how to close her sun umbrellas properly. On the patio were so many chairs and tables and umbrellas and flowerpots that Jake said it looked like one of those places along Route 27 that sold outdoor furniture.

Part of the rental package was Aunt Stormy, who maintained the house and was supposed to call BigC if tenants trashed it. But she said BigC was good to work for. Respectful and generous. Every spring she gave a benefit for the women's shelter.

One afternoon, when BigC was installing wind socks along the railings of her boardwalk, Aunt Stormy said, "She only gets weird when it comes to ducks. She likes watching them in the water but gets savage when they land on her boardwalk."

"The ducks may not quite understand her reasons," Mason said.

"She once told me that people who pay a shitload of rent have every right not to want to wade through duck shit."

"Weird enough," Annie said, "but how much is a shitload?"

"You don't want to know." Aunt Stormy shook her head. "Fifty thousand."

"Per year?"

"Oh no. Memorial Day to Labor Day. Pays her mortgage year round."

"That's crazy."

"It is getting crazy out here. Places selling for many times what they cost a few years ago. Grown kids of local people can't afford to live here. It creates resentment. Last year, a lot of the locals were angry when summer people suggested we do our grocery shopping during the week, so that stores wouldn't be so crowded on weekends. You should have seen the letters to the editor."

"That whole thing of how we share space . . ." Annie said. "It's so complicated."

MASON KNOCKED on the door of her studio. "Can you help me with something?"

"Depends on what it is," Annie shouted.

"Moving the Wall of China."

"What?" She opened her door. Frowned at him as though he'd yanked her away from something more important.

"You need to learn to be interrupted."

"I can't work with you here."

"You work with Opal here."

"Not fully."

"I stop what I'm doing when you—"

"When you're here, I count on you to take care of her, to give me some time alone."

"I wish I'd never built the studio for you."

To compete with Jake's Dr. Pagucci, Mason made up a story of his own, about a bratty girl, Melissandra, who happened to be always just one day younger than Opal. Melissandra had a night job in a lollipop factory, where she ate the lopsided lollipops so they wouldn't get sent to stores.

Opal adored Melissandra, and the story became a ritual at bedtime.

"What's your favorite flavor, Melissandra?" Opal asked him one evening.

"My flavor-favorite? What do you think?" Mason said in his Melissandra voice.

"Red lollipops."

"I figured you knew."

"What else do you like to eat?" Opal asked.

Mason grimaced. "Nothing else. Just lollipops. And I never ever say please or thank you, because that's just stuff grown-ups want me to say."

"You get into lots of trouble?"

He loved it when he could coax her into giggling like this. "All kinds of good trouble."

"Like what?"

He lowered his voice. "Like tying my teacher's shoelaces together."

Opal's eyelids closed. Opened again. "What else, Melissandra?"

"Sometimes I smear toothpaste on the chalk, and when my teacher picks it up, her hands get all yucky." In his normal voice, Mason added, "Go to sleep now, Stardust."

• • •

SUNDAY MORNING, and Mason slept in late. When he got up, Annie was by the window, reading in the rocking recliner.

"Where's Opal?" He poured a cup of coffee.

"In her playhouse."

"Look at her dancing, Annie."

Opal was twirling from the playhouse Mason's parents had given her for her birthday, arms snaking high in the air. When she reached the tulip tree, her fingers snatched pink-white blossoms.

"Opal," Annie called, "come inside."

"She can't hear you."

"She's wrecking the tree."

But he was siding with Opal, who was scattering petals, spinning through a shower of pink and white. "This is how I want her to remember today . . . blossoms all around her—"

"You let her get away with everything." Annie headed for the door. "Opal. Now."

"Don't—" He snagged her around the middle. "Her joy matters more than any tree."

"I'm all for her joy. But I also want that tree to survive."

"I'll take her to Sparky's." He kissed Annie on the lips and ran outside, where he danced with Opal around the tree.

Her little fists clutched his fingers, and now both of them were laughing as he danced her away from the tulip tree.

THE SPRING Opal was seven, the floods came back, and with the floods a letter from a Realtor, David Withers, offering to list their house: "I am currently contacting a few people like you to see if they're interested in talking with me about the possibility of selling . . ."

"What the fuck does 'people like you' mean?" Annie asked.

It went on like that: ". . . preapproved clients prepared to make an attractive offer . . . appreciate it greatly if you could take the time to . . . any buildings or pieces of land that you know of . . ."

"He means turning in our neighbors," Mason said.

A week later, another letter, recommending they sell before flood damages decreased the value of their property. Though the flood didn't reach them, their neighbors, Ellen and Fred, had to sandbag to keep their house from flooding. When Annie and Mason helped them, they found out that Ellen and Fred had received the same letters.

"My clients like the location of your property. It's in a lovely spot. . . . I hope that, with my letter, I'm not intruding on your privacy. It's not my intent . . ."

"That's a joke," Fred said.

"And here I thought our house was the special one." Ellen swung a sandbag toward Mason.

He caught it in both arms, settled it atop the other bags. "Next thing you know he'll be knocking at the door."

When the waters receded, the man who'd written the letters did indeed knock on their door. It was a Saturday morning, and Opal was playing near the front door, climbing up the ladder of her playhouse and leaping down.

"I have a surprise for you," the man said.

Mason instantly knew who he was. It was the pushiness, the disregard for privacy.

"A picture of your little girl on top of her playhouse." He showed Annie his digital camera.

"You can't do that," she said.

"It's for you. A present. Such a sweet little—"

Mason stepped up against him. "How dare you—"

"I stopped by to see if you ever think of selling your property. I wrote you two letters. I have preapproved—"

"How dare you take a photo of our child?"

"But it's not for me, the photo. I thought you might want me to make a print for you. I'll drop it off to you tomorrow."

Mason shoved his hand at the Realtor's chest.

"Or would you like me to e-mail the photo—"

Again, Mason shoved, hard, and as the man fell, Mason tore the camera from him.

"Let him leave." Annie held on to Mason's arm.

Mason shook himself free. "He has no right to—"

"You're nuts," the Realtor yelled.

"Watch this." Mason swung the camera against the front steps. Smashed it. "You're next."

Annie motioned the man away. "Just get out."

"I have your name from your letter," Mason shouted.

Cautiously, the man backed away.

"All right, Mason?" Annie asked. "All right?"

"You don't care that some stranger is taking photos of our child?"

The man turned, ran toward his car, ducking even before he slid himself behind the steering wheel.

"Of course I mind," Annie said, "but you don't have to beat him up."

"Next thing he'll be selling her picture online."

"That's bizarre. Stop it. Please," she said. "We'll file a complaint with his company."

Mason

—trembled, I felt sorry for him.

"Jake?" you asked. "Do you believe Mason has any idea what trust means?"

"No." Trembling . . . Jake was trembling. Sweat on his chest, on his belly.

And I was sure that anything the two of you might do could not hurt me like what I saw inside my head. It's like . . . like trying not to look at something, Annie. How that effort of not looking only makes me see it fully. Like that photo in the film book I still have from college . . . a razor slicing into a woman's eyeball.

You know the photo, Annie, from Buñuel's *Un Chien Andalou,* and how afraid I am to turn that page whenever I get close to it. But since I'm trying so hard not to look, I already see the razor half-buried in the eyeball—more explicit than in the book—and then I must turn to that page to modify the picture inside my brain.

You have offered to tear out that page, Annie. Or throw the book away. But I can't. And I can't give it away to some thrift shop, because someone might pick it up and be encumbered by that image from then on. Because that's where the book falls open.

That's how it was for me with you and Jake on the tier below me in the sauna, Annie.

"For Christ's sakes," I said, "just turn that page."

"What page?" Jake asked.

"Turn that page so we don't have to think about this anymore."

"You are the only one thinking about this," you told me.

One collage is not enough. Look at this, behind your worktable. *A Thousand Loops.* Roundness . . . your body and Opal's . . . curved and one within that roundness. I can't wreck this—it would screw up our chance together. More collages I haven't seen yet . . . two more of our pond where before there were only a few. The rest of the raft again.

Why do you hide them from me, Annie?

I bet you long after we're dead, Annie, they'll hang in museums.

You touched Jake's thigh. "Jake?"

Lighter wood next to his thigh than on the rest of the sauna bench. It's where I replaced four broken slats last spring. I like getting to them before they rot. A few months from now they'll blend in.

Your hand was darker than Jake's thigh with those tiny bleached hairs that make his skin look even paler than it is. When he moved toward you in the steam, so hesitant—Jake and Annie—it was like being once again on the ferry to Shelter Island and watching a man with a pregnant woman, guiding the small of her back with his spread hand.

Pride.

Mine.

You'd laugh, Annie, if I were to lead you like that. Jake is easier: to nudge, to please, to own. But with his hands on you, I had you both.

You swung yourself atop Jake and—

FOUR

Jake
{ *The Graduate* }

"Mason's father said I'd find you in the kitchen," Jake tells Annie. But she doesn't answer. Keeps her back to him as she fills a glass with water and drinks it slowly.

In the living room, the TV is on. ". . . Mrs. Robinson . . ." The old version. Simon and Garfunkel. Not the edgier version of the Lemonheads. ". . . Jesus loves you more than . . ."

Jake waits while Annie fills her glass again and empties that too. Avoiding him. Since Mason's funeral, Jake has called her twice, offering to go to the pond house, pack up whatever she needs, and bring it to her and Opal in North Sea. But all she said was, "I can't, Jake."

Can't what? Talk with me? See me?

"I could leave, Annie—"

She turns to him, her face puffy, clothes too tight.

"—if that makes it easier for you."

"Easier?"

"Not that it could be any less . . . horrible. But if you'd rather not have me here—"

"His parents want both of us here."

Shyness in our voices, our bodies.

"That's what they told me. Do you know why?"

"No. They just . . . summoned me. And now they're in there, watching TV. Don't leave me alone with them, Jake."

"I won't." He's afraid that, after today, he'll never see her again.

"You haven't said anything to them, have you?"

"Of course not."

"You think they know?"

"How could they?"

"If Mason called them before he—" She bites her lip.

"No," Jake says. "No."

Annie crosses her arms and rubs her palms up and down her upper arms. "It's always so cold in here. Even in summer."

"I used to believe they had ice caves underneath their house."

"Only Mason's house? Not yours or mine?"

". . . all you see are sympathetic eyes . . ." Simon and Garfunkel. Orchestral and mellow.

"Only Mason's house. Bluish-white caverns. And that air from those caverns rose and kept the rooms cold."

For an instant, she smiles. "My mother adored your imagination." But already she's blinking tears away. "She died on me too. Everyone's dying on me, Jake."

"I am so goddamn sorry."

"I've put the pond house on the market today."

"Do you need help getting—"

"Ellen and Fred did most of it. Before I got here."

"How long have you—"

"Day before yesterday."

"You're not staying at the house?"

"No. With Ellen and Fred. And they went with me to pack what Opal and I need. The rest is going to Goodwill."

"Not your work!"

"Fred and I crated it. It'll be shipped to Aunt Stormy's."

"So you're staying?"

She shrugs.

"I'm at my parents' for the weekend. They said to invite you for dinner if you like."

"I'm taking the ferry back once I leave here."

"And my sister said to say—"

"Give her a hug from me. How—"

Jake waits.

"How are *you* mourning him, Jake?"

"By being furious with him. And with myself."

"Me too."

"Not just for killing himself, but also for—" He wants to hold her, feel the warmth of her skin through her green shirt. But already his mind slams down. *Being together killed Mason.* He feels dirty being near Annie. Misses Mason—misses him terribly, that instant—*those intense eyes on you, so totally on you, spontaneous and direct, expressive eyes that have the potential of something else underneath, even coldness. But when that gaze turns away you tumble.*

And I've been tumbling ever since. He says, "I miss Opal." That calms him. And it is true.

Before Opal came to them, *the-three-of-us* felt right, and then it was *the-four-of-us,* and Opal made each of them better somehow—more compassionate, more responsible—as she took the focus away from *the-three-of-us. Because three-of-us can be dangerous.* Jake's last time at the pond house—the time before the time in the sauna—was just a few days before, when Opal turned eight. He's celebrated every one of her birthdays with her, and he can't imagine not being in her life.

He says it again, then: "I miss Opal."

"I know you miss her," Annie says.

"Opal . . . She's feisty like you. Impulsive like—"

"Like Mason?"

"Just . . . impulsive. So, at Aunt Stormy's . . . what do you and Opal do all day?"

"The usual. Looking at the water. Feeding the ducks. Swimming."

He nods.

"I'm trying to get her back to the child psychologist Aunt Stormy found for her. She was great with Opal, but after the appointment, Opal said, 'I don't want to see that woman again.' "

"Probably because she was good."

"She's hurting. And talking about it makes her hurt more. She refused to go to her next appointment, kicked and screamed, and so I went to explain to the psychologist, to not stand her up, to ask how to help Opal."

"Let me see Opal."

Annie shakes her head.

"I don't think it's good for her to be away from me too—"

"We've gone to a couple of antiwar protests in Sag Harbor."

"—to lose both Mason and me."

"Aunt Stormy and Pete go to the protest every Sunday afternoon. We—"

"Please, Annie?"

"—stand on the wharf in Sag Harbor and—"

"And I also miss you," he feels compelled to say though he wants to run from her.

"It's a silent vigil, actually."

"Miss you from before . . . how it was before all this."

"I can't, Jake."

"If you think that talking—" He stops himself. *Too dangerous.*

"No."

And he is relieved. Why did he even suggest talking? Someday soon he will have to tell her that he saw Mason moments before he killed himself. Tell her because keeping that secret from her will prevent him from being with her and Opal.

"Twenty-six days today," she says.

If only he'd run into her studio and refused to go away. But he still felt so angry and bewildered that he stayed outside the window, seeing Mason see him. *Do it, you bastard. It's the only thing you can do now.* Like a sudden madness . . . He had imagined Mason dead when they were boys, had played and replayed that death in his mind, so that—for an instant there outside the studio—Jake wasn't sure if this was happening or imagined, was afraid that if he admitted this was happening, he would be the one to make it so. He couldn't move. Not even when Mason climbed on Annie's worktable and stuck his head through a noose. *I've imagined worse: pushing you off a cliff, from the open door of an airplane*— Running. Then. Running and hiding inside his car and locking the door and cowering in the familiar shame that had been his since he was a boy. Then the jolt back to sanity and the morning dark with smoke harsh to breathe. Racing back to the window—*too late too late too*—and getting away though he knew Annie would be the one to find Mason dead.

• • •

"We miss him so," Mrs. Piano says.

"That's why we wanted to ask both of you—" Mr. Piano starts, but his voice slips.

Mrs. Piano takes his hands into hers. "Was he angry at us?"

"Oh no." Annie puts her arms around Mrs. Piano.

"We've both wondered . . ." Mr. Piano leans forward. Stares hard at the television, where an actor who seems somewhat familiar is floating in a swimming pool. ". . . if it was something we said or did that . . . triggered his—"

"If we could understand . . ." Mason's mother watches Annie as if waiting for absolution, or perhaps proof that it was something inside Mason that outpaced all her loving.

What I could tell you— Jake swallows. "Mason could be so generous. Once he gave his leather jacket to a homeless man, though he'd only bought it a week earlier.

Annie is staring at him.

"Do you have any idea why he . . . did it, Annabelle, took his life?" Mason's father asks carefully.

"No." She shakes her head. *Widow without a clue.*

"No," Jake says.

Annie digs two fingers into the pocket of her black pants, finds a rubber band, slips it over her wrist, and pulls her hair into a knot so severe that it tugs at her eyebrows and makes her forehead square, changing her instantly from lovely to stern.

Warning me off.

But that potential for ugliness only makes Jake love her more.

"That Dustin character—" Mr. Piano points to the screen.

"That's who he is!" Now Jake knows. "I've just never seen Dustin Hoffman young."

"—he always wants everything right away," Mason's father continues. "And he—"

"His hair looks so . . . like a rug, almost."

"—expects his parents to give it to him, while he despises them. See how he's ignoring them, Annie?"

"I . . . guess so."

"It was the style," Mrs. Piano says. "I don't think it's a rug."

"And the camera is not fair to the parents . . . makes them seem predatory when they circle him in the pool."

"Concerned, not predatory," Mrs. Piano corrects her husband.

In the pool, a woman and a man are indeed circling the young Dustin Hoffman. To Jake, *predatory* seems quite accurate. *If you consider sharks or crocodiles or piranhas predatory.*

"I used to think his parents and their friends were jerks." Mason's father takes a handkerchief from his suit jacket. Dabs his lips. "Now I think that Dustin character—"

"His name is Benjamin," Mrs. Piano says.

"—is a jerk, and that his parents are merely trying to be parents. You two probably like him."

"I don't know him," Annie says.

"We don't know him," Jake says.

"How young you are . . . ," Mrs. Piano says.

"When we were your age," Mr. Piano says, "*The Graduate* was *our* film."

"A cult film."

They continue as if they were alone.

"We liked Benjamin."

"I identified with him," Mrs. Piano says.

"He was romantic."

"Romantic and confused."

A glass vase filled with lemons stands on the gracefully curved piano. The rest of the furniture is all edges: folding metal chairs, a wobbly table, a painted church bench, where Mason's parents sit, both angular and tall. *All edges.* Jake's mother used to say the Pianos kept their thermostat set on frostbite. Whenever he went there, she'd make him take a cardigan. Still, his toes would be curled with cold. His hands he could tuck into his armpits—except when he had to pull them out for his weekly piano lessons.

"A cold house keeps you alert," Mr. Piano would say. He'd look persecuted when listening to his students, except to Mason, who started lessons when he was three and practiced exuberantly—but only as long as his father sat with him. *Look at me look at me look* . . . Without an audience, the switch went off.

Whenever Jake played, Mr. Piano would excuse himself. "Keep playing, Jake. I'll listen from the kitchen." His thin face would be pouchy when he'd return, because he'd be chewing, taking bites from something he hid in his palm.

• • •

Mr. Piano is chewing smoked almonds as he pours them from a restaurant-size bag and arranges them on a metal tray with Cracker Jacks and string cheese. "Pass the refreshments, Annabelle."

"I haven't been cooking much," Mrs. Piano says. "I'm so sorry."

"Don't . . . please." Mr. Piano strokes her arm. "You're doing all you can do."

Twenty-six days today.

"Nothing. I'm doing nothing. Because there is nothing to do." She's all in black: scarf, blouse, shoes, earrings. As if she hadn't changed clothes since Mason's funeral.

Jake's mother has told him that she cooks dinner for the Pianos most nights, brings it over and then leaves because they clearly don't want anyone there. "It's good that they want to talk with you and Annie," she told him. He is visiting his parents for the weekend. Their living room is still filled with play equipment, small desks, and shelves with coloring books and stuff for craft projects. His mother still runs her day-care center, though she used to say she wanted to return to teaching science once Jake was grown. Whenever Jake's father said he was falling over other people's children, she'd point out that two thirds of the family income came from those children. Jake would cringe. Because she didn't get paid for looking after him. That was why the other kids got preference. *Paying guests.*

Annie scoops up a fistful of Cracker Jacks. Passes the tray to Jake, who suddenly remembers Annie's mother thanking his mother by the door. "I'm so glad Annie gets the homey part of mothering from you. I'm not very good in the kitchen." Jake's mother winced. Smiled at Jake. And when she spoke, it was not to Annie's mother but to him. "We're lucky I have a job that lets me stay with you all day."

Jake tries to give the tray to Mrs. Piano.

"We've lost him, Jake. We've gone and lost him." She turns to Annie. "Don't you leave me too, Annie."

"I won't."

"You and Opal can always stay with us. Weeks or months or years."

"Oh . . . Thank you."

"It's okay if you like that Dustin character," Mr. Piano tells Jake.

"Except we don't like him," Jake says quickly. Still, he feels accused. But he doesn't know how to extricate himself.

HE PROCRASTINATED getting here. Stood under the shower in his parents' bathroom and couldn't bring himself to turn it off because he was terrified he and Annie would never be together the way they used to be since they were kids. Stood under the hot water until, with one swift motion, he made himself turn the handle to cold, gasping at the shock, forcing himself to stand below the icy water longer than he could bear it. He saw the three of them traveling in Morocco . . . *We shimmy up one of the high walls that surround Asilah. Mason is hugging Annie, but suddenly it all changes because he crushes himself against her, and she bites his neck—*

Gently? He flinches. Reaches behind her and catches her wrists, holds them there. She arches back, but his body arches forward, against hers. Does she feel the empty space behind her? She must. But she's not afraid at all. Her teeth against Mason's neck, she presses herself against him, wrestles him the way we used to wrestle as children. Except she's no longer stronger than Mason—they're matched. Is that what their sex is like? Because if they're this rough with each other in public, then—

"You idiots," I scream. "Get away from there."

They think I'm so safe. Safe because I adore them both. Safe because they think I know they belong together. Safe till that moment, when Annie suddenly frees herself and comes up against me, presses herself against me, not Mason, her breasts against me—Annie?—her mouth below my chin. But not biting me, not me. The ledge behind me. Pressing myself closer to Annie. Wrestling us away from the ledge. Annie—

And now Mason is the one screaming. "Stop it! Both of you!" He backs away from Annie and me, hops on the precarious ledge. "I bet you I'll jump if you don't stop it." Behind him white buildings and cliffs and the sea—

"HE LIKED TO . . . try out the idea," Jake says.

"What idea?" Mrs. Piano asks.

"That he could . . . jump off somewhere . . . or do it some other way."

"But he didn't mean it," Mr. Piano says.

"When we played hide-and-seek," Annie says, "and Mason couldn't find us, he sometimes yelled, 'If you don't come out, I'll kill myself.' "

"He says that to get what he wants," Mrs. Piano says.

"With you too?" Annie asks.

Mrs. Piano nods. "He starts off all nice. Then he ups it, sulks and tries to get me to feel sorry for him. And if that doesn't work, he says he'll die. The first time he said it was when he was five. Because I wouldn't buy him ice cream."

"Did you?" Jake asks.

"Buy him the ice cream? Yes."

"He said it at camp," Jake says.

"That place on Winnipesaukee . . . Mason hated it there," Mr. Piano says. "You know, a couple of times Mason tried that with me when I said it was time for bed. But he stopped that when I told him he'd go to bed half an hour earlier for every time he said that. I knew he didn't mean it." He squints. Suddenly looks sick.

"I thought it had to do with betting against himself," Mrs. Piano says. "The way he said it was . . . sort of playful, betting . . . testing if I'd believe him. That's why I thought it was important to make Mason believe that I *did not* believe him. So that he wouldn't . . . do harm to himself. And when he'd say it again, I'd remind myself that he hadn't harmed himself the time before . . . that it was just another one of his moods."

"I used to know everything about Mason," Mr. Piano says, "and then I didn't know him at all. I used to know the music he liked. He and I had the same favorites. A four-year-old who likes Mahler. Can you fathom that? And Schumann. Now I don't even know the music he liked before he—"

"Sarah McLachlan," Jake says. "He liked her a lot."

"Also the Cardigans," Annie adds.

"The Mrs. Robinson song." Jake points toward the TV. "But performed by the Lemonheads. Except hearing it now, with the movie, it's clearer what the words are about. It feels more true than from the Lemonheads."

"Lemondheads . . . that reminds me of the Lennon song," Mr. Piano says. "No connection really. Just Lemon and Lennon?"

Annie nods. "Sure."

"Did you ever listen to that song John Lennon wrote for his son?" Mr. Piano hums. Coughs. Then sings, "the monster's gone . . .your daddy's here . . ."

Annie's face is bright red.

Tears run into Mr. Piano's collar. ". . . beautiful little boy . . ."

Jake has goose bumps. *Don't do this to yourself.*

"He was the most beautiful baby in the neighborhood," Mrs. Piano says.

How can this be good for the Pianos? For any of us?

"I can burn a CD of Mason's favorites for you," Annie offers.

"Everyone said he was the most beautiful baby. Even the other parents. Not that you two weren't good-looking babies too—"

"Strangers stopped us to ask if they could look at Mason. All that black hair." Mr. Piano scrutinizes Jake's hair, which has been thinning since Jake was in his early twenties.

Jake makes an effort to keep himself from checking that it hasn't spread. *My third eye.* That circle of shiny skin behind his fontanelle.

"Mason got so excited when people smiled at him," Mr. Piano says.

Mrs. Piano touches her neck. "He never went through the no-neck phase. You know. That pudgy baby phase. Right from the beginning, he was beautifully proportioned."

"Aunt Stormy always said he was beautiful," Annie says.

"See?" Mr. Piano looks at his wife.

"Like a miniature grown-up," she says.

"Not miniature," he objects. "At least not for long."

"You used to fret that he wasn't growing fast enough," she reminds him.

"Not really."

"He had the most gorgeous skin, Annie."

"I understand," Annie says softly.

"Do you?" Mr. Piano turns on her. "You and Mason—you rushed everything."

Annie blinks. "What do you mean by that?"

BUT JAKE knows what Mr. Piano means. Jake was Mason's best man, and at the altar Mason got so moved that he started crying. When Jake handed him a handkerchief—discreetly, behind their backs, not realizing that the guests saw it—Mr. Piano was mortified.

At the wedding dinner, he told people, "Mason never cries."

"Well, he cried today," Mason's uncle said.

"Only because Annabelle is rushing him into marriage."

But Mrs. Piano took her husband's wrist, held it down next to his wedding plate and the wedding cutlery. "You of all people know that our Mason only cries when he's overly happy."

"What I mean by that," Mr. Piano answers Annie now, "is getting married when you two were just kids."

"That was Mason's plan," Mrs. Piano tells him. "Getting married was all he talked about after Morocco. I think—" She hesitates, glances at Jake, who wants her to stop, but she continues as if nothing should be left unsaid. "I think it was to keep Annie away from Jake . . . so he wouldn't ask her first."

"Show-off." Mr. Piano motions to the screen. "Hopping into his little red convertible without opening the door. A user, that Dustin character. Drives that jazzy car his parents paid for but despises them."

"At our age now," Mason's mother says, "Benjamin seems indifferent . . . lazy."

"That's true for sure," Mr. Piano says.

"And he blames Mrs. Robinson—she's his parents' friend, Annie," Mrs. Piano says, "—for seducing him though he certainly takes part in the seduction. Just because she's older."

Mason's father stares at Annie.

"Stop it," Mason's mother says. "With barely four months ahead of Mason, Annie hardly qualifies for the role of Mrs. Robinson."

Annie's lips crinkle.

More like the Annie I know.

Jake wants to touch her forehead, high where her skin and hair meet, loosen her knot of hair—a bit—to let her face rest. He stuffs his hands into his pockets. But already they're out again. He doesn't trust them. To keep them away from Annie, he picks up a piece of string cheese he doesn't want, peels off the strands just to be doing something. The taste of milk-soaked rubber bands.

"Sitting there with that fish tank, that Dustin character!" Mr. Piano sounds agitated.

"What fish tank?" Jake asks.

"You missed that part, you and Annie. You were still in the kitchen when that Dustin character was sitting in his room with that aquarium thing, letting his father make all the effort. He didn't even smile at his father."

"Our Mason used to do that," Mrs. Piano says, "not smile at me. Deliberately not smile at me and—"

"When he got into that mood of his," Mr. Piano says. "Gloomy. Not talking to us."

"It made me want to shake Mason." Mrs. Piano closes her eyes. "Once I did—"

"That way he stared past his father . . ." Mr. Piano pops some almonds into his mouth. Opens the lowest button on his vest. "Like he's bored with him. I don't think he notices his father."

In the vase on the piano, the lemons used to shimmer, but today the water is cloudy.

"WHY DON'T you have flowers in that vase?" Jake once asked Mason's father after his piano lesson.

"Because lemons don't wilt."

"Oh—"

"Lemons last longer than flowers, and once they fade or get spots, we use them for lemonade."

"Can we have a lemonade stand?" Mason asked.

"Sure. You can have these."

When Jake, Annie, and Mason got ready for their sale, they were so excited that they kept zipping back and forth on their street. From Annie's basement they lugged a card table and set it up on the sidewalk. Jake's mother gave them sugar and her insulated pitcher with the red lid. In Mason's kitchen they squeezed lemons, added water and sugar. Annie printed huge letters, STOP, on both sides of a paper plate, colored the white space yellow, and trimmed it in the shape of a lemon.

"I bet the first car is silver." Mason fastened his roller skates.

"Green," Annie said.

"Bet you a nickel—"

Just then they spotted the car—silver, indeed—

"I win!" Mason yelled and rolled sideways along the sidewalk, full face to street, like a dancing girl, Mason, waving his palms, windshield-wiper style, pointing toward the lemonade bucket.

When the car slowed, Annie wielded her STOP plate and ran a few feet into the street.

"Be careful—" Jake shouted. *Already such a good audience for their daring.*

"Go in the middle of the street, Annie," Mason yelled, "you're such a girl."

"That's what I am. A girl." She flapped her sign at the car.

It swerved. Didn't hit her. *Annie—*

"You idiot!" Jake screamed. "Get out of the street!" Hopping up and down on the sidewalk. Screaming. "You idiot!"

"Don't be so dramatic," Annie said in her grown-up voice.

"Lemonade!" Mason chased the car on his roller skates. Greedy. Fierce. "Stop! Hey! Look at me, Jake—"

And Jake was grateful because Mason singled him out for being friends. Even though grateful felt sticky. Still—he felt the excitement of risk, *the badness*, that became his when he was with Mason.

When the car got away, Mason plopped himself on the curb. Dropped his forehead to his knees. "I can't do this day." *All the light out of him. Sudden. The way he'd get sometimes.*

Annie plopped down close to him. Jake on his other side. Across Mason's curved back, they looked at each other.

"There's a car," Jake said.

Mason didn't move.

"Another car—" Annie poked him.

Four cars passed.

"We got a lot of lemonade to sell," Jake said.

"That's it." Annie knelt in front of Mason, started to undo his roller skates.

Mason tried to kick her away.

But she got them off. Still stronger than Mason. Bigger.

During the next hour, only two drivers bought lemonade, though Annie and Jake took turns swinging the STOP lemon plate at every car. They kept watching Mason. *So still. Just a lump on the sidewalk, really.* And when he stirred, *finally*, they laughed with relief.

Laughed when he demanded his skates. And when they helped him fasten them. And when all at once he was up again, doing his skate routine, adding a movie star smile. *Mason.*

By late afternoon, every drop of lemonade got sold.

"Let's make plans for the money," Jake said.

"We'll buy something together," Mason said. "Something we *all* want."

"We need poster board and markers," Annie said, "so we don't have to use paper plates for our next sale."

"First we have to buy a flashlight," Mason said. "With different color lenses."

"You want it for yourself," Jake said.

"I want it for us. The yellow light keeps bugs away, and the red light means stop. I saw them at the hardware store, and two boys at school have them."

"Poster board—" Jake started.

"I'll guard the money," Mason promised.

But Jake knew Mason would promise him whatever he wanted . . . and all it meant was that Jake would get nothing.

"My house is like a bank," Mason said.

"Your mom only works at a bank," Annie said.

"Not so. It belongs to her."

"Really?"

"Really."

"But the bank is not in your house." Jake knew. Because his parents had their checking account in the bank where Mason's mother worked.

Mason started counting the money.

"Why can't I keep it in my room?" Jake asked, wishing he'd said it differently, because asking was handing it over to Mason. He tried again. "I want to keep the money in my room."

"With all those kids running around, it'll only get lost . . . or stolen."

"You're the one who runs around."

"That's for sure," Annie said.

And it was. Jake didn't want Mason and all those others—except Annie—at his house every day. Wanted to go to their rooms instead and mess them up. Mostly Mason's, throwing his toys and clothes around, crushing Cheerios on Mason's floor so they'd get stuck to the bottoms of his feet and get into his bed and make him feel itchy. Bouncing on Mason's mattress—except in the Pianos' house, you didn't get a good bounce because the mattresses lay on the floors.

But at least Mason got punished for breaking the blue robot Jake got for his fifth birthday. Even though Jake took it into his bed that night to guard it from Mason. Once it was morning, he knew, Mason would play with it. *And break it.* Jake knew how: *First Mason twists the arms, then snaps off the head.* Jake's stomach was hot like just before throw-up. Scared-hot. Though he was bigger than Mason and could snap off his head. But Mason was family income. And Jake had to keep his robot safe. Had to— *Don't— But I have to. Stop Mason from twisting off the blue robot's arms.* Jake did it, then. Twisted off the arms. *Like this. Stop Mason from snapping off the blue robot's head.* Jake did it, then. Snapped off the blue robot's head. *Like this. Before Mason can. Mason, who's making me do this.* And when he blamed Mason, it was true because it would have happened. *Like this—*

"WHY ARE the Pianos' mattresses all flat with no space underneath?" Jake asked his mother one morning when he helped her clean up yesterday's day-care mess.

"Because they don't like to spend money," his mother said. "They let it grow in the bank."

Jake wished his parents could grow money too. Because they had less than the other parents on the street. That was why he helped his mother clean up. Pride in that, being useful. But rage too. Because what the day-care kids needed came first. While his mother was stuck with him—he knew that even when she kissed him—and once his sister was born, his mother had two children who were not paying guests like Mason, who chased Jake's mother around, making his whinnying sound, high-pitched through his nose like an ambulance and a horse, till she yelled at him, "Please? We don't run and yell inside this house!"

We?

The unfairness of it.

We.

Meaning me too.

Searching for something nasty to hide in Mason's lunch. A half-dead fly in the spiderweb by the woodpile next to the stove. *Half-dead means half-alive.* Freeing it from the web, carefully, and pressing it into Mason's cheeseburger when no one saw. *You always want something special.* When Mason took a bite, Jake's heart lifted, exhilarated.

ANNIE AND Jake outvoted Mason. "Poster board and markers."

"But I worked harder than you at the sale."

"No way you didn't," Annie told him.

"Plus I slammed my finger in the ice chest."

"So what?" Jake said, brave with Annie watching.

"I'll never do another sale with you if we don't get the flashlight."

Jake almost gave in. Without Annie, he probably would have. But with Annie, he could tell Mason no. Tell him, "We're buying poster board. And markers." Though he didn't care what they bought. Only cared about having Annie on his side. High from persistence, he repeated, "Poster board and markers."

Mason pouted. "Those lemons are from my house."

"But the sugar comes from my mama's kitchen," Jake told him. "It's her baking sugar."

Annie rolled her eyes. "And the bird turds are from my front yard. So we're even."

"Gross." Jake wished he had her guts.

Mason was giggling. "Yeah, gross."

And for an instant they were no longer at odds. Annie had pulled them once again into one. And Jake felt that warm flicker between his ribs that he got when he was with both of them. Safe. It made him feel generous.

And so he consoled Mason: "We'll buy the flashlight with money from our next sale."

Mason was kicking his left heel into the ground, watching the dust swirl around his sneakers. "Okay . . ."

And because he had a pocket with a zipper on his shorts, and because Jake and Annie had ganged up on him, they did not say no when Mason said he'd hold the money for them.

But the next day Mason went ahead and bought what *he* had wanted all along. That flashlight with three lenses. "It was on sale. So we're really saving money."

"Not fair." Annie shoved at him.

Then Jake shoved, hard. Felt Mason's bones against his fist. He pulled back, startled.

But Mason was already dancing away from him. "Now that we have the flashlight, we'll earn more when we sell lemonade."

Again, Annie shoved him. "Asshole."

Bad word. Jake was awed.

"We'll earn ten times as much—"

"Triple-dipple asshole."

"—because people will see our flashlight from far away. And then we can buy a bigger wagon to haul the lemonade."

"Jake already got a wagon."

"A bigger wagon than Jake's," Mason said.

"It's plenty big enough," Jake said.

"The more we haul, the more we'll earn. Enough for new bicycles."

"I bet you want the first bicycle," Annie said.

"Three new bicycles. We'll buy them all at the same time."

"Just don't do this again," Jake warned, wishing he had the guts to say *asshole* to Mason.

But late that afternoon, he said the word when he and Annie whispered about Mason in Annie's room. Whispered as if Mason were close enough to hear and get mad because it was always the three of them together. Whispered excitedly about what Mason had done and what Mason had said.

Annie's left ear against his lips, Jake whispered her a secret though he was not allowed to repeat anything his mama told his dad about the daycare kids. "Mason is a wild card. I heard his mom say it to my mama."

Annie smelled of sweat and dust. Her red hair stuck to her temples, darker where it was sweaty. "His own mom said that?"

"A wild card. That's what she called him."

"What's a wild card, Jake?"

"WHEN THAT movie came out," Mason's father says, the smell of smoked almonds on his breath, "I had a friend who lived in the same apartment building, Joey Robinson, and when we saw his mother . . . me and other boys . . . we'd snicker and yell, 'Hello, Mrs. Robinson.' "

"He was fifteen, our Mason," Mrs. Piano whispers, "and I grabbed him by the shoulders and—" She draws her scarf around herself. "—shook him, not hard, until he said, 'Okay, Mom, you win.' "

Annie nods. "The winning thing . . . that's Mason."

"And then he smiled at me." Mrs. Piano folds her hands on her black skirt. "Still, afterwards I felt queasy."

Jake feels queasy too. From the weirdness of the conversation. From the normalcy of watching the television screen. When Mason was a kid, the Pianos disapproved of television and didn't own one though everyone else in the neighborhood did. And now they're stuck to it.

What do you want from me and Annie?

"It's not like Mason was a baby," Annie consoles Mrs. Piano. "A baby you'd hurt, shaking like that. But a fifteen-year-old . . . no."

"It's the only time I shook our Mason."

"He was taller than you."

"No, he was still little. He didn't have that growth spurt till afterwards. Do you think— What if shaking him had something to do with . . ."

"Absolutely not," Jake says.

"You hear him?" Mr. Piano says to his wife.

"I think," Annie says, "that you shook that growth spurt loose in him."

Mrs. Piano starts laughing.

All along, Jake was taller than Mason, and he didn't like it when Mason, all at once, started growing. Coming to the height that had been Jake's alone till then.

"I should have shaken him sooner." Crying, now, Mrs. Piano. "A good shake once a week." Laughing and crying again.

"Once a week," her husband says, "we'd make up some occasion to knock on Joey's door and say, 'Hello, Mrs. Robinson. Hello—' "

"Benjamin's first date with Mrs. Robinson's daughter is brutal," Mrs. Piano interrupts.

"I think it's romantic," Mr. Piano says

"Romantic? Dragging her to a strip joint until she cries?"

"That Dustin character is just insecure. Besides, Mrs. Robinson's daughter falls in love with him—"

"Love? They don't even know each other."

"We didn't know each other when we fell in love."

"All that connects those two is that they are rebelling against Mrs. Robinson."

"Plus they're in love."

"That girl even believes Benjamin over her mother. And then he abducts her from her wedding."

Jake wonders if they've forgotten about Annie and him.

In the meantime Dustin Hoffman is swinging a cross to fight off Mrs. Robinson and Mr. Robinson and the wedding guests.

"Cutting her off from her parents like that."

"Forever. Because—can you imagine family reunions at the Robinsons'?"

Jake laughs aloud, but no one else seems to think it's funny. "Family . . . reunions . . . at . . . the . . . Robinsons'?" *Hissed conversations. Then silences. Red faces. Closed doors at night. The only one moving through the house is Dustin Hoffman, traipsing from his wife's bed to his mother-in-law's bed.*

"All that angst . . . what will I do . . . what will I be . . ." Mrs. Piano shakes her head. "And to think how I loved that movie."

Dustin Hoffman is barricading the church door with the cross . . . climbing into a bus with Mrs. Robinson's daughter, who is someone else's bride.

"That revolution against parents is no longer that interesting to watch," Mr. Piano says. "Our conflicts are more . . . civilized."

Mrs. Piano nods. "But for the young, like Annie and Jake, our conflicts are dull."

"Oh no," Annie says.

But Jake doesn't even try to clarify.

"It makes a case for living with people of your own generation," Mr. Piano says.

"An understanding of each other's conflicts . . ."

"How can that girl ever return to her parents?"

"Especially to her mother."

Mr. Piano curves his hand across his wife's. "How about those Simon and Garfunkel songs?"

"Those I still like."

"I'll get you the CD."

"Get one for Annie too."

Mason

—he cried out. Cried out like a boy.

Did you imagine me when you took him inside you, Annie? When his big thighs braced your big butt? Your shoulder wings soared toward me while I was sucking in that scalding air, not fitting enough inside me. Like not enough yeasty bread at camp and chewing fast so I won't get caught. Swallowing the it's-wrong. Furious because you're with Aunt Stormy all summer, Annie, and Jake is not enough. Not enough. Kissing you in front of Jake when we swim in from the raft though I don't feel like kissing you but claiming you— Not enough. Chewing and swallowing—

Jake could have said no at camp.

Jake could have said no in the sauna.

And you could have pulled me from the edge of dare, Annie, where you used to be with me till Opal was born and you became mother-bear protective—

I'm not done yet searching for the collage I'll destroy. It's obvious you're working on some in secrecy. Like this stack of raft collages, facing the wall. I turn them so I can see them. Leave them there and pull out two more collages, their background old letters that are written in German, ticket stubs, seeds, and flat stones, photos of Aunt Stormy and your mother as au pairs.

I open the drawers beneath your worktable, Annie. Search through the baskets on your shelves. What I still love about fixing up your studio is how we did it all together, building these shelves, painting the floor. Until you closed the door on me.

Why, Annie? When I'm the one who understands more about your work than anyone else? I can always tell when something snags you into imagining, when you get dreamy and intense all at once. I know. Because I have been there when you felt inspired.

That edge of dare. Last night, Annie, I dared you to pull me back from there, but you made me watch as you clamped your legs around Jake, rising—and that fast heat mine, mine—his eyes squeezed shut, yours locked with mine as if you could only fuck Jake by imagining it was me inside you.

It was like watching that play the three of us saw in Morocco, Annie, not understanding a word and making up our own stories for what was happening onstage and comparing our stories afterwards. But I believed what *I* saw.

Just as I believed as a boy that the bank where my mother worked belonged to her. The guardian of everything people locked up in the safe-deposit vault, she witnessed the impact of death, marriage, birth. Whenever one of her regulars closed a deposit box, she'd tell me and look at me the way she must have looked at that customer—with great sorrow and affection. It troubled her that—unless her customers told her voluntarily—she might never find out where they were moving, and what the rest of their lives might be like.

I bet you imagined it was me inside you, Annie. I bet you did.

Afterwards—

Afterwards, you and Jake wouldn't look at me.

Almost dawn, then. And you, throwing on your robe and—even in that moment of swinging it around you—shielding your body with the fabric so I couldn't see you naked. Your back to me, you stomped toward the house.

"Annie!" I ran after you. "Have you noticed how you cover yourself whenever you're pissed at me?"

"I want you out, Mason."

"How come you're naked with Jake but not with me?"

You went into Opal's room, held up one hand to keep me from following you.

Outside, the engine of Jake's car. Idling. No headlights.

And then you. Leaving Opal's room. Wrapping yourself deeper—

FIVE

Opal

{ *A House Hatching a House* }

Aunt Stormy says we're going to live with her.

She came to our house on the evening of the day Mason offed himself. Said to Annie and me: "This is what we're going to do. You're coming to live with me. For the time being."

I like *off* better than *kill*.

Because *off* doesn't sound forever.

Like *switch off*. Or *buzz off*. Which I'm allowed to say. And *fuck off*. Which I'm not allowed to say.

Aunt Stormy is not my real aunt. That's because she's not my mother's real sister. But she's still my aunt. In my school lots of kids have—

But my school is no longer my school.

In second grade of the school that used to be my school, seven kids had parents who didn't start out as their real families. Sisters and brothers too. But who became their families. Stepfamilies. Half families.

Still, different from me.

Because Annie is two people. My sister and my mother.

Annie says she'll be more like a mother till I'm grown up. Afterwards more like a sister. Or both forever. If I want her to be.

My real parents died. A big truck did it. Crashed into them. But my real mother waited with dying till I was outside of her. Safe. Because she loved me. That's what Mason told me.

But then Mason offed himself.

So what does that say about him loving me?

WE FOLLOW Aunt Stormy's little truck in our car. When I wake up, my face is sticky on my pillow.

"We're here," Annie says. "Let's go inside."

I can't make my eyelids stay up.

She takes hold of my legs.

I kick her. "No, Annie!"

But she slides me into air of salt. Air of ink. Air of salt and ink. Wind in the tall grasses. Wind along Aunt Stormy's boardwalk.

Annie carries me. Me and my pillow.

"I'm not three, Annie. I'm eight."

Carries me into Aunt Stormy's kitchen. "I know you're eight."

"Eight is four times two. Or two times three plus two."

"Even half asleep you're a genius," Aunt Stormy says.

Above me her candle lamp. White candles and a rose and driftwood.

When Aunt Stormy kisses me, she smells bad, of too-many-flowers. Smells of what sticks the smell of too-many-flowers together.

But I like her eyes. Clear and blue. Reading inside me. Reading that I want Annie to let me down.

"Our little girl wants to get down."

I kiss her back.

Annie stands me up on the floor. By myself. Unties my sneakers.

Aunt Stormy's kitchen is the only kitchen I know that has a bookcase. All the way to the ceiling. I know which books are in German because I can't read the titles.

Aunt Stormy slips down the hood of my purple windbreaker. "Would you like to sleep in your clothes, Opal?" She talks funny. It's called accent.

"Okay."

Up the stairs with Annie then. Toward the little bed where I sleep when we visit. Where a hundred veils hang between the little bed and the big bed. A flowing maze that changes when I dance. The big bed is where Mason and Annie always sleep—

Mason offed himself, stupid.

No maze. No hundred veils. Empty. Here. Empty on the high shelves where Aunt Stormy keeps glasses and bowls and plates.

My toes start hurting.

Annie tucks me into the little bed. "I'll be up soon, sweetie."

"Where will you be?"

"Not far."

She turns off the lamp.

Downstairs, her voice floats into Aunt Stormy's. Floats. Then she's crying. Aunt Stormy too.

"Melissandra?" I whisper.

Melissandra doesn't answer.

My toes are hurting worse.

"What did you do today, Melissandra?"

No Melissandra.

No Mason joking around.

"Mason!"

I bet Melissandra offed herself too.

"WHY ARE you crying, Opal?" Annie, flying at me.

Crying?

"*You're* crying, Annie."

And she is.

But it's my face. Wet.

She sits on the edge of my bed. "What is it, sweetie?"

"My toes. They hurt."

"Which ones?"

"I can't do this day." Saying it the way Mason does. The way he always says it. Knowing it. Watching Annie know it. Watching Annie's fingers fly to her throat.

The green 7 on Aunt Stormy's clock changes to 8, making it 3:28.

Late.

Saying it again: "I can't do this day." Because I won't let Annie forget. Forget Mason.

Annie finds my feet under the quilt. "Which toes?"

I have to think. Because nothing hurts now. Now that Annie is wiggling my toes. But I want her to stay. With me. With me in my bed. I tell her, "The middle toes. Of the foot closest to the wall."

"Middle toes . . . foot closest to the wall . . ." She takes them. Takes them between her fingers. "Here?"

It tickles. "Yes."

"Want me to kiss them?"

"Okay."

Annie kisses the middle toes of my foot closest to the wall. "I am not going away."

"Mason went away." Now I'm crying. Crying for sure.

"Yes, he did."

"Mason offed himself."

"Offed? Oh, sweetie . . . where did you get this?"

"With a rope. That's how he offed himself. And Jake offed himself too."

"Jake didn't . . . Jake is . . ." Annie fusses with my quilt. ". . . busy . . . very busy."

"Jake isn't here. And Melissandra isn't here."

"I'm here."

"But Jake—"

"And I'm not going away. Neither are you."

My face wet against Annie. Annie, who smells of driving. Who smells of sweating. And of M&M's she bought when we stopped for gas. A big bag of M&M's.

She doesn't let me have many sweets. Because sweets rot your teeth. That's the truth. But Annie eats sweets.

And Annie says fuck off. Said it to Mason.

Did that off him?

"Scoot over, you." She squeezes in. Next to me in the little bed. Snuggles up so her toes won't hang over the edge. Her face white in the dark. Lopsided where it dents my pillow.

Annie, smelling of driving.

And of sweating.

And of M&M's.

Smelling of carrying me.

And of toes no longer hurting.

Smelling of sleep.

SUN ON THE lids of the clouds. I climb across Annie. She's curled and little. By the bathroom sink, the floor is like a sponge. I brush my teeth. Hop up and down. Make the tiles jiggle.

The tub has dragon's feet. Dragon's claws.

Treetops swish against the windows. Like being in a tree house.

"Aunt Stormy?" I yell down.

She's working in her garden. No shoes. In winter she'll wear shoes. But never socks. Beyond her, the boardwalk and wetlands. Mason says wetlands is a fancy name for swamp. Beyond the wetlands tall beach grasses. Then sand. Then Little Peconic Bay. Which is not little but big with lots of water.

My pond house has water too.

But that water is round and little and stays in one place.

Aunt Stormy's bay has snaky water. Water that doesn't stay in one place. Snakes away with the tide.

"Aunt Stormy?"

"Opal! Good morning."

"What happens if I fall through the bathroom floor?"

"You'll land on my bed."

"And squash you."

She's moving a huge rock. A pink and white rock. Lifting it. Walking with it. Heavy. Setting it down nearby. "If you fall, you'll land on the other side of my bed, Opal, the empty side."

"Oh."

"It'll be like one big trampoline."

I RUN downstairs. "Are you growing rocks, Aunt Stormy?"

She kneels down. Now she's smaller than the rock. "How did you know?"

"Because I don't remember this rock." I touch the rock. Its edges are soft. "And I don't remember the gray rock over there. Do you look like my real mother, Aunt Stormy?"

"Sometimes. In a certain light."

An old mother. Much older than Annie. An old mother I have not seen in my real father's photo books. Six books with photos and his notes. Photos of my real parents. And Aunt Stormy. And my real parents' friends. Pictures of traveling. And of Annie. Annie being a baby. Annie in first grade. Annie every year. Every year with my real parents. But I'm not in the photo books. They stop, the photos. Stop before I'm born. And I didn't get to go anywhere. The last photo is of my mother. Pregnant. "With you, Opal," Annie says. But how do I know it's not a pillow?

"I talk the way your mother did," Aunt Stormy says. "But she looked like you and like Annie. The shape of your faces. Strong shoulders and long necks. That same quick smile. Lots of thick red curls. Her hands were so smooth, Opal. Not like mine." Aunt Stormy spreads her palms for me. "Rough skin. From gardening."

"What was her favorite color?"

"She loved purple. And tie-dyed. That day I met her—we were just eighteen—she was wearing a tie-dyed shirt, purple and yellow and orange and red. And then her red hair, of course, with a ton of hair spray. And I still remember thinking: This girl looks like one big sunset."

"One big sunset." I like that.

"Your mother, she had the stiffest hair of anyone I knew."

"Do you think she loved me?"

"I know she loved you."

"Even if she didn't know what I was going to be like?"

"She loved you from the moment she knew she was pregnant. She felt so lucky."

"How about my real father?"

"He was so excited about you. Looking forward to you."

"How about his favorite color?"

"Phillip liked to wear blue." Aunt Stormy plucks some weeds. "A deep blue, like his eyes. He was a fast walker. Most days, he walked six miles before breakfast."

"You knew my real parents before Annie knew them."

"Yes. And I knew your mother before your father met her. This sun is too strong for you."

"No, it isn't."

"I know how quickly you sunburn. You can either stand in the shadow or we'll put on some lotion."

I step away from her till leaves keep the sun from my face. "How long is for the time being?"

Her eyes. Reading me.

"You said we're going to live with you for the time being."

"That means for as long as you want, Opal."

"Your bathroom floor squeaks."

"It's how this cottage talks. A groan here, a squeak there. It's over a hundred years old."

I tilt my head toward her house. The blue door stands open. Far away, a dog is barking, then two. I wish I had a dog. "What happened to your dog, Aunt Stormy?"

"Agnes? She . . . she got spooked by fireworks one Fourth of July."

I wait for her to tell me more, but she doesn't. That's how I figure Agnes is dead. Because people get squirmy saying *dead* around me. *Dead* or *kill* or *hang*.

After a while, Aunt Stormy adds, "Agnes ran under the wheels of a car."

"Where did you bury her?"

"Where I grow squash."

"Gross. I'm not eating Agnes squash."

Aunt Stormy smiles. "St. Agnes squash, please."

"Annie won't let Mason get a dog."

"Oh."

"Annie won't let Mason get a baby."

AFTER LUNCH, Aunt Stormy takes Annie and me hunting. Hunting for catbriers.

"Touch these pine needles." She stops by a small pine. All tangled in prickly vines. "Feel how fine and long they are. That's how you can tell a white pine." She crouches. Reaches with her clippers.

"They'll scratch you, Aunt Stormy," I warn her.

She chops off vines close to the ground. But their green stems are still around the tree.

"Like a cat. They'll scratch you."

"That's why they're called catbriers." Annie's eyes are red.

I ask her, "Do you want to take a nap, Annie?"

"If I do, I won't sleep tonight."

"You can sleep in my bed again."

"Thank you. I may do that." She sits on her heels, her back against a tupelo. Pulls me close.

I lean into her. Peer into the thicket behind the white pine. Catbriers.

Aunt Stormy is yanking at the catbriers. Scratches on her wrists.

"Be careful." Annie's voice is too loud.

"Sshhh . . ." I press my index finger on her lips.

"What is it, Opal?"

"How about the bones?" I whisper.

Annie flinches. It goes through her body, like lightning.

"Bones?" Aunt Stormy's clippers are still opened.

"The bones in the catbriers. Duh."

Annie bites on her lip, hard.

Aunt Stormy says, "I've never found any bones here, Opal."

"There is such a thing like bones stuck in catbriers."

Aunt Stormy waits. "From birds and squirrels?"

"No!"

Annie takes my hands into hers. "Don't be scared."

I yank my hands free. "Bones of princes."

Annie's teeth. Deeper into her lip. Red and white.

"Because of Sleeping Beauty. In my fairy-tale book. The picture of her. Remember? With those catbriers all around her?"

Annie laughs. Laughs a quick, high laugh. Pretends it's a hiccup.

"You're being nutty, Annie."

"But the prince rescued Sleeping Beauty. So why would his bones be stuck in the catbriers?"

"Duh. Not *his* bones. The bones of other princes. Who tried to wake her up. But got stuck."

"Ah . . . ," Aunt Stormy says. "Then we'll have to clear this carefully, Opal, so we don't cover up those bones."

"If we find some prince bits," Annie says, "we can put them back together."

I can see us collecting those prince bits. Maybe not enough to put all the princes back together. But enough for one really excellent prince.

"I'll be very careful." Aunt Stormy keeps chopping off briers where they start at the ground. Still, they hold on to trees and bushes. Until she chops them into little pieces. *So there.*

I follow her, looking for bones.

• • •

Aunt Stormy takes us into BigC's pool room, where she tests the chlorine. On the walls a painting wraps itself around the corners. Cliffs and sea and meadows. The painting has no beginning or end.

"Gross." I point to a cut-off head that wasn't there before. It lies on the ground. On the ground in the painting next to a pillar.

"BigC just added that head," Aunt Stormy says. "A strong resemblance to her husband."

A tiny, tiny woman peeks from behind a jar. A tiny BigC. Her body is smaller than the man's cut-off head.

"A self-portrait," Aunt Stormy says. "Over there, those nymphs . . . they're new too. BigC and her three daughters."

"All the same age," Annie says.

"No more than seventeen years old . . . frolicking in the flowers."

"I didn't know anyone said *frolicking* anymore." Annie takes towels from the dryer.

"It's the only word that fits." Aunt Stormy helps folding the towels. Hangs them over a golden rack.

I walk along the mural, touching. "What does *frolicking* mean?"

"Dancing and hopping and skipping and twirling," Annie says.

"Frolicking . . . ," I sing, touching moss and flowers and jars. Touching the tiny, tiny BigC.

Yesterday Aunt Stormy pulled me out into the rain, frolicked with me.

"There are other people hidden in BigC's mural," Aunt Stormy tells me. "See, over there? Her parents as marble statues."

Annie turns on the hose, sprays the floor tiles.

"Don't you get me wet, Annie," I yell, wanting her to squirt me.

She squirts close to my feet. Almost smiles when I jump. Mason would squirt right at me. *He squirts right at me. Wraps me into a towel. Throws me over his shoulder. All wet. Wetlands.* Mason says BigC did away with the wetlands. Doing away with wetlands means doing away with little owls. Mason says lots of little owls used to live on Aunt Stormy's land before she sold it to BigC.

Annie and I follow Aunt Stormy through the house, and we check each room, read the Post-it notes BigC has on every mirror. Each has the same message: "PLEASE, DO NOT BRING SAND INTO THIS HOUSE."

Annie laughs. "That's asking the impossible."

Aunt Stormy nods. "Still, she gets pissed when renters drag sand in on their shoes."

"Then why did she build her McMansion by the beach?"

I think BigC has the most beautiful furniture in the world. All gold and white. The floors too. Gold and white. When I'm grown up—

"My bad-taste neighbor," Aunt Stormy says.

"It's the most beautiful furniture in the world," I tell her.

"Tomorrow we'll have dinner with my good-taste neighbor."

"Pete," I say.

"Right. He'll come to the Sunday vigil with us, and afterwards we'll have dinner. I shouldn't have said that about BigC. She's been good to Pete. Helps with driving him to his counselor, to physical therapy and speech therapy and—"

"I can help too," Annie says.

"Good."

"Pete is a bit slower than you remember him," Annie tells me.

"Pete can run faster than Mason. Marathons, Pete runs."

"Not anymore. He had something called a stroke."

"What's a stroke?"

"For a little while, Pete's blood couldn't get to his brain," Aunt Stormy explains. "It does now. But the right half of his body has to learn how to move again."

"Can he still bake?"

"Not quite yet."

"Lemon meringue pie . . . I can help him bake. And walk."

"He'll appreciate that. He gets tired so quickly. Sometimes he cries."

EVERY NIGHT while we sleep, rooms that were there yesterday become other rooms. Shrink or stretch. Three steps up become three steps down. Leading to rooms beyond where the house used to end. *A house hatching a house.*

Sunday I don't recognize Pete. I'm upstairs, busy watching an old man on our boardwalk, walking with stiff little steps, both hands on the railings.

I frolic down the steps into the kitchen, where Aunt Stormy is frying fish. "There's this old man outside. He's limping, and he's wearing a girl-color T-shirt."

"Must be Pete."

"No. Pete is tall. Pete has black hair. Pete runs marathons and—"

"My God—" Annie has opened the door. "His hair is all white."

"It turned white after the stroke," Aunt Stormy says.

"It's not Pete," I explain in my most patient voice. "It's someone else."

"He usually takes his boardwalk down to the bay and then comes up on mine." Aunt Stormy turns down the burner. Jiggles the pan. "He's getting better every day."

How can she think this old man is Pete?

The old man kicks one of Aunt Stormy's new rocks.

I run outside.

Again, he kicks the rock. It makes a hollow noise.

"Now you . . . kick it . . . Opal." His voice a tape at the wrong speed. But it belongs to Pete. Who is inside this old man with the girl-color shirt and droopy face.

I kick the rock. It budges.

"Now pick . . . it up." Stubbles in his ears. But not in his nose.

"I'm not that strong."

"Same . . . here." But he lifts the rock like a laundry basket. Shuffles his feet in a slow, funny dance.

I lift it, then, above my head, the rock. It is hollow—that's why it sounds hollow. Gray inside and out, with white lines. Like veins.

Pete claps his hands. Even his clapping is slow-speed.

"Why do you have bruises on your arms, Pete?"

"Because . . . my skin is . . . getting thin."

I squat and pull the rock over myself. All dark inside. It smells of raincoat and of earth.

Pete laughs. His laugh is regular speed. Now I know for sure it's Pete. Maybe he plucked his nose hairs but forgot the ears.

Aunt Stormy's voice. "They weigh just a few pounds, Annie."

The rock crawls away from her voice.

Aunt Stormy. Closer yet. "You can hose them off."

Not me. The rock crawls faster.

"Fake rocks are so . . . not you." Annie's voice. Above me.

Bet you don't know where I am . . .

"They're a gift from Pete." Aunt Stormy's voice. "He makes them from stuff they use on space capsules."

Now you're in trouble, Annie.

"I'm sorry." Annie's voice.

"Don't . . . be. They . . . are . . . fake."

"Where's Opal?"

"Opal . . . who?"

Aunt Stormy's voice. "You can turn those rocks upside down for weeds. Pete started me off with the rock that's moving—see, Annie?—to cover a pipe coming from the ground. Then he made me another to hide the compost."

"And . . . to hide . . . weeds."

Annie's voice. "Like a lunar landscape."

Aunt Stormy's voice. "Yes, of those first images we had of the moon. You and Opal weren't alive yet."

"Opal who?" the rock asks.

Pete's slow-speed voice. "Opal . . . the . . . rock."

The rock giggles.

"There she is," Annie says.

I cast off my rock and spread my arms and do Pete's shuffle dance.

He is trying to sit down on the porch steps, bending his knees and lowering his butt inch by inch by inch.

"Don't fall, Pete." I run over to him, slip his arm around my shoulders. Glare at Aunt Stormy and Annie, who don't help him.

"Are you sure that's comfortable, Pete?" Annie asks when he's finally sitting.

"Considering . . . that I . . . usually sleep . . . on a . . ."

My lips are moving. I want him to be done with what he's saying.

". . . bed of . . . nails."

"Really?" I ask.

"I wonder if . . . it is . . . possible to . . . sleep—"

"—on a bed of nails," I finish for him. "Sure."

He leans forward till his elbows touch his knees. "But . . . how . . . Opal?"

"I saw it on TV."

"I guess . . . you'd have to . . . tighten . . . all your—"

"Muscles."

Aunt Stormy winks at me. Shakes her head.

"—muscles . . . so that . . ."

I press my lips shut.

". . . each . . . nail gets the same . . . pressure."

"That'll work," I tell him.

ON THE DRIVE to the vigil, Pete gets to sit in front. I sit in back with Annie. The vigil is in Sag Harbor. It's called Women in Black. But there are men and kids too. And not everyone is wearing black.

We stand on the wharf by the windmill. Some of the Women in Black people have signs. Even the ones who are not women. And who don't wear black.

Peace. Now.

No Blood for Oil.

BigC is there too, holding up a sign: PATRIOTISM = DISSENT. She puts it down to give me a hug. Her coat has golden buttons.

"Maybe if enough of us speak out," she says, "we can still prevent a war in Iraq."

"It's a silent vigil," says a man behind her.

I stand between Pete and Annie. Cars and trucks drive past us. Some drivers stick up their thumbs. But one truck with huge tires and loud music races toward us. People cry out.

BigC swings her sign at the truck.

Annie yanks me behind her. "Fuck off," she yells after the truck.

I bet he'll off himself now.

"Sshhh . . ." From behind us.

I shiver. Lean into Annie. From the bay comes a breeze. Prickly and salty.

Annie rubs my face. My shoulders.

Pete says, "Shrub has . . . bad . . ."

"That's what he calls Bush," Aunt Stormy says. "Shrub."

"Shrub," I say.

"Sshhh . . ."

". . . bad manners . . . always in . . . front . . . walking or . . . standing . . . in front of . . . anyone else . . . even . . . rulers of . . . other . . . countries . . ."

"You're so right," BigC says. "I've seen it. I've just never thought about it that way."

". . . a terrible . . . host. . . ." Pete turns his neck slow-speed to look at Aunt Stormy. "What's that . . . German word . . . you have for . . . the shrub?"

"*Fahradfahrer.* Is that the one?"

He nods.

"Fah——what?" I ask.

"Fah . . . rad . . . fahrer."

"Bush is a *Fahradfahrer.* It means bicyclist," Aunt Stormy says. "Feet down, head up, kicking people below, smiling at people above."

"God, that fits him," BigC says.

Pete is still nodding. Up one down one up one down . . . slow-speed.

HE DOES that at dinner too. Nodding. Up one down one up one down . . . His lips are red from tomato juice.

No one tells him to wipe them.

Halfway through dinner, he's napping.

We have hollow noodles. I slide two over the tips of my fork. Then suck them up into my mouth. From the refrigerator, the naked bride is watching. Not the bride naked. Me naked. Sitting on the hip of the bride who is not naked but wearing a bride dress. Annie. Who says it's not a baby under her dress but a pillow. *Fake.* Annie doesn't want babies. Mason said so.

When Aunt Stormy is done eating, she stands up. Stands behind Pete. Rubs the back of Pete's neck. The side of Pete's neck.

Can he feel it? I think he does because he wakes up. He looks a hundred years older than Aunt Stormy.

That's what I tell her. "Pete looks a hundred years older than you."

She smiles. "But he's two years younger."

"Mason says—"

Now they all look at me.

Annie's mouth gets little.

"Nothing." I don't tell them what Mason says. That Aunt Stormy and Pete are like wife and husband. But without marriage. And with separate houses.

Slow so slow Pete gets up. One hand against the wall, he lifts his left foot. Takes a baby step. Brings the right foot along. Again with the left. The right. When he gets to the remote, he picks it up, raises it to his eyes, and turns on the news. A woman's head. Bigger than the screen. Because only part of her hair shows. I know who she is. Laura Bush. Talking about women in Afghanistan. And about voting in Afghanistan. I know where Afghanistan is on the map.

Aunt Stormy goes wild. "The right to vote is not enough, you insipid woman. They have to make sure their votes count. Not like in this country."

"Insipid . . . smile . . ."

"That woman always says 'chail-tren,' " Annie says.

I try it out. "Chail-tren."

And that's just how it sounds when Laura Bush says it a moment later: "Chail-tren."

"She . . . looks . . . tired."

Aunt Stormy nods. "From always carrying that dog. Probably holds him so she doesn't have to touch that George."

"A school-yard bully," Annie says. "You're either with us or against us. If you play with my enemy, I'll hate you and get even."

"Not . . . looking for . . . consensus . . ."

"Grabs what isn't his." Aunt Stormy says. "I win I win. A presidency that isn't his. And the sheep, lining up behind the thief."

PETE SLEEPS in Aunt Stormy's bedroom. By morning he's a bit stronger and not so old.

Odd things happen in Aunt Stormy's house.

A house hatching a house.

Why doesn't anyone else see that?

Last night the roof unfolded so I could count the stars.

At breakfast Pete sticks a piece of tape to his wrist.

"What's that for?" I ask him.

"Grocery . . . shopping."

At the store, he unfolds his shopping list. Peels the tape from his wrist. Fastens his shopping list to the cart. He pushes, and I put stuff inside. Only what he tells me. Not sneaking stuff inside like I do with Annie.

At the checkout, it takes Pete ten hours to open his wallet.

Well, ten minutes, maybe.

Or just five.

Long enough so I want to do it for him. Like wanting to help a stutterer finish a word. But I don't.

AUNT STORMY pulls next to me in her purple kayak. Opens a bottle of lotion.

I know that smell. Tutti-frutti. "No!"

"Put some on, Opal."

"It's stinky."

I have the yellow kayak all to myself. Better than sitting squeezed between Annie's legs.

Mason's legs are skinnier than Annie's.

Annie is at the pond house.

Getting some of our things.

Aunt Stormy reaches for me. "I should have put lotion on you before we got in the boats."

I paddle away from her. But it's too late. Smell has become touch. Clings to me. Smothers the smell that is me.

Sticky. Stinky. And I'm little again. Fighting Mason—

"Hey—" Mason. On the beach. Sand on his feet. Pulling me close to him. "Let me put some of Aunt Stormy's lotion on you."

I squirm. "No lotion."

"The sun is hot. I don't want you getting a sunburn."

"Stinky!" I scream.

"Oh . . . hold still, Mophead. Please?" Mason. Smearing lotion on me.

Stomping and wailing and tearing off my skin. "No, Mason—" Running from the smell. And from Mason. Who put the smell on me.

"Put your fingers down, Opal. I'm almost done."

Tearing it off to the me underneath the smell. Running away down the beach. Never coming back. But when I look, Mason is running behind me. Little steps. Not Mason steps. Staying always a bit behind me. The same little bit. Staying behind me and behind the stinky smell. I run. Run fast. Away. Running fast needs my crying breath. So I stop crying. Run fast with the sun hot. Fast with Mason a bit behind me. But not too close and singing: "My Stardust . . . my Mophead . . ." Till I have to laugh. Mason swoops me into his arms. Up up— Swings me. Round and round till we both giggle. Props me on his shoulders. All in one mo-

tion. I'm riding. Riding high up on Mason's shoulders. Fingers slipping across his forehead. Slipping. Clutching his hair. Bouncing—horsey—my feet digging into Mason. Giddy-up, horsey, giddy—

Aunt Stormy. Her kayak right behind mine. "At least wear a hat, Opal."

Mason—

Oh—

Paddling away from Aunt Stormy. Paddling.

Through the long grasses at Sammy's Beach.

Seaweeds under my kayak. Waving.

Egrets. An osprey nest.

Paddling away.

Away and suddenly— *Mason in the purple kayak right behind me again. Behind me as long as I don't look. His paddle slicing the water. Scooping water. Right behind me. Mason. Always. As long as I don't outpaddle him. Always right behind me. As long as I don't slow down. As long as I don't check if he's really there. That always makes Mason disappear.*

"Sshhh . . . ," Aunt Stormy hisses.

Paddling. Away.

"Opal." Hissing: "Sshhh . . ."

The purple kayak next to mine. But now Aunt Stormy in it. Hissing: "Don't move don't talk. Horseshoe crabs."

In the shallow water below us. A hundred horseshoe crabs. Or fifty. At least fifty. In clumps.

Our kayaks hang above them.

Each clump has one big horseshoe crab, digging itself into the sand. With a few smaller horseshoe crabs on top of the big one. Some of the shells stick from the water. But their legs and gills are underwater. They don't scuttle away.

"The urge to mate—" Aunt Stormy sticks one arm into the water. "—is stronger than the urge to flee and be safe."

Our kayaks wobble. Wobble in the shallow water.

She turns her kayak so she's next to me. Taking my paddle, she lays it across our kayaks. Her paddle too. Then she fastens orange rope from the front of my kayak to her kayak. "Now we're stable. Like a catamaran."

Reaching into the water, she lifts a small horseshoe crab from the back of a big one. Checks underneath. "A male."

"How can you tell?"

"Front claws like boxing gloves." She holds the horseshoe crab out to me.

I inspect the underneath of the male. Boxing gloves.

"That's how the male holds on to the female. The rest of the claws end in pincers." She touches the mouth of the horseshoe crab. "The mouth feels all bristly. Want to feel it?"

"The crab won't like it." I shrink from the bristly mouth. From those pincers and boxer hands. From the sharp, long tail.

Aunt Stormy smiles and sets the crab back into water. "The females are all pincers. They're the ones on the bottom. Much larger than the males. Fertilization happens outside the body."

"How?"

"The female digs a little crater into the sand. Near the edge of the water. Lays her eggs in there. She has thousands and thousands of eggs, Opal. And she pulls the male across the eggs till they're fertilized."

"Cool."

"Look at their shells."

I lean over the side of my yellow kayak. "Like armor."

"Right. And each one is different in what it has attached. What do you see?"

"Those little stacking shells . . ."

"Slipper shells."

". . . and crusty stuff."

"Barnacles, right. Algae . . . carrying all that like we carry our history. What have you lost? What have you taken with you?"

"What have *I* lost?"

"I mean all of us, Opal."

"Oh— My real mother. My real father."

"I'm sorry. I shouldn't—"

"Mason. Jake. My second-grade teacher, Mrs. Mills. Who won't be my teacher anyhow in third grade. Sally, who used to play Ice Capades with me on the kitchen floor—"

"You've lost so much, Opal." Her voice, gentle.

Sand in my eyes? They sting. "I want to see Jake."

"I'll talk to Annie."

"She'll say he's busy."

"I'll talk to her." She puts a kiss in her hand. Plants it on my lips. "Here. Grab your paddle. Good." She unties the orange rope. Shifts her kayak away from mine. "You go first."

I stay ahead of her. Paddle. Turn this way or that way when she tells me to. Paddle toward a fuzzy moon.

"Weird."

"What's weird, Opal?"

"The moon. Because it's afternoon with blue sky."

"Oh, that's the children's moon. That's what your father used to call a daytime moon. Because the children are still awake to see it."

STILL DAWN. And Annie is home again, asleep in the big bed.

The roof is closed. Everything is muggy. The air. The blankets. I kick them off. Get out of bed.

Hair across Annie's face. Chocolate smell in her hair.

"Your teeth will rot, Annie."

But she keeps sleeping.

In the kitchen, boxes and boxes. On the table. Around the table. In front of the bookcase.

Smell of the pond house.

My belly gets stiff.

Clothes from the pond house.

Toys from the pond house.

Aunt Stormy's door is closed. But I hear Pete sleeping. He is a loud sleeper. A breather of scratchy breaths.

Someone has set the fruit bowl on top of two boxes. I take an apple. Head for the boardwalk. Air so heavy it shimmers. Like walking through dough rising around me. Sweating though my pajamas. But knowing I can—*if-I-want*—jump in for a dunk in something wet, not half-wet like the air.

Dawn smudges Aunt Stormy's house. Makes it all wavy lines. No edges.

How can a house do that, hatch itself?

I bet Mason knows how.

Some days, the front opens like a barn and pulls me inside.

Inside is much larger than outside. Rooms run into rooms into rooms. Long after I think there can't be any more rooms.

Tall grasses tickle my ankles. On the wooden cradle by the inlet, the kayaks are upside down, their bottoms scratched.

"Designed by a woman. Light enough to be carried by a woman," Aunt Stormy would say.

Pete would laugh. "So why do you need my help then?" But he'd swing a kayak onto his shoulder and carry it for me to—

But Pete is slow now.

Anything can change in one moment.

From fast to slow.

From alive to dead.

From hairy to bald— But Jake still has hair. Around his third eye.

Not light enough for me to carry, the yellow kayak. But light enough to drag from the cradle by the orange rope tied to its front. The rope is damp. So is the kayak. When I sit inside, the bottom is cold.

I push my hair from my eyes. Stretch my arms like a paddle. My fingers are the ends of my paddle. Like flying.

Mason can fly. Fly through water that splashes up high against the car. Up from the wheels in silver circles. Where it hits the fenders, it sounds like a hose turned up high into the wheelbarrow. Mason let me hose off the wheelbarrow when I helped him build Annie's studio.

I do some butt-surfing. Jiggle the kayak forward without water.

Sun burns through dawn.

Burns a hole into dawn.

A hole that gets bigger.

Lets the world in.

A waterfall of light.

When are the lumis coming back, Mason?

Behind the seat is the life jacket. I know how to fasten it around me.

I climb from the kayak. Get myself a real paddle. Drag the kayak—*light enough to be dragged by a girl*—to the water. I remind myself to tell Aunt Stormy.

Then I'm in.

No longer butt-surfing but slicing through the water.

Flying, Mason.

Looking for lumis.

Across the inlet, a white sheet flutters high up in a tree. Higher than anyone can toss a sheet. Like a candle ghost, melted into the tree. Like the day after Halloween. *Candle ghost.* Still and draped. Then suddenly something rises. A beak. A neck. Long and white. *Not a sheet.*

I paddle to the left. Where the inlet flows into the bay.

Behind me, pecking. A woodpecker—black and white and some red—on a tree behind me.

How can one little beak make that much noise, Mason?

My hair tickles. I pull it up high, twist until it doubles over into a unicorn horn. My kayak is wobbling. *Whoosh* . . .

Under BigC's boardwalk, ducks are splashing toward the shallow water, away from the swans. One of them is all puffed up and chasing after the ducks.

I tell the ducks, "It's just showing off."

They turn their beaks toward my voice.

"It doesn't want to catch you."

When I paddle beyond the next neighbor's boardwalk, the stick heads of turtles bob on the water.

Look look, Mason. Look—

But the stick heads pull back beneath the surface.

I see a cormorant.

And there's a muskrat. Musk-rat.

Water splashes around me. *Whoosh* . . . But I'm only a little wet.

Look, Mason—a musk-rat.

Lots of people are afraid of rats.

But not Mason.

Musk-rat. I bet musk-rats are carnivores. *Carne* is meat in Spanish, Mrs. Mills says. Car-ni-vores. I bet if plants can be carnivores, rats and musk-rats can be carnivores too. When Aunt Stormy took Annie and me to the Walking Dunes, we saw car-ni-vore plants. I think they were called dew drops. They were *not* Venus flytraps because Mrs. Mills had those on her desk.

The car-ni-vore plants in the Walking Dunes had little hairs. Hairs like the hairs animals and people have on their bodies. Hairs that stuck to my fingers when I touched them. *Nutty.* They were long and thin, those plants. And they didn't eat my fingers. Because I didn't touch them for long. Not even for almost-long. Just a millisecond. Aunt Stormy said the car-ni-vore plants curl up. Like ferns when they attract a bug. Because that's evolution.

"They can't get what they need from the soil," Aunt Stormy told Annie and me, "and so they attract nourishment from the air."

I wish Mason could see the car-ni-vore plants at the Walking Dunes.

I bet Mason knows about car-ni-vores.

Because he knows how the house hatches itself. It's definitely a magical house.

Whoosh . . . Look look, Mason—another turtle. I bet you're just hiding from Annie's hissies. Hiding or disguising yourself away.

Under the boardwalk—four boardwalks from Aunt Stormy's—a crab is hiding. It has stuck itself to one of the wooden posts underwater. A big crab. Big and blue.

Maybe we can eat the crab, Mason.

Mason? Look—

Whoosh . . . I try to scoop up the crab with one end of my paddle.

But it won't budge.

The kayak wobbles.

Mason

—into your robe.

"Is Opal sleeping?" I asked you.

"Yes." You closed her door, softly.

"I didn't think you'd do it, Annie, that you'd really do it."

"You did everything you could to make us do it."

"I had to know. What it would be like for you both—"

"Why?"

"To understand . . . and if both of us understand, then we'll be able to—to get beyond this. Together."

"You're sick."

"We don't ever have to talk about it again."

"You mean you . . . forgive me?"

"And Jake." The moment I said it, I knew you'd set me up.

And you clobbered me. "You are so arrogant."

The beams of Jake's headlights bobbing on the ceiling as he backed out.

"Finally," I said.

"I want you out."

"You don't mean it."

"Out as in for good."

I told you, no—begged you, Annie: "Don't destroy the family Opal has."

"I no longer know how to be a family with you."

"Maybe not with me, this minute. But for Opal we're the family she has."

You did that impatient little breath, Annie.

"Don't listen to what Jake makes out of this," I said.

"I was there too."

"But he'll make it seem like something else. He is such a liar. Always was. Liar liar pants on fire. Breaking his toys and saying I did it. But no one believed me."

"Oh, sure . . ."

"Lying that his parents were buying a big big house. Every Monday bragging about a different house. 'Far away from you, Mason,' he'd say. 'A house with maids. Not with day-care kids like you. And when you come over, it will be to visit only. Not to stay all day. Not to mess up my room.' Remember, Annie?"

You shrugged.

"I told him, 'Your maids can pick up the toys!' Hah. My mother used to say, 'They're lookers, not buyers. That's what they do on their Sunday drives. Look and dream.' Listen—" Suddenly, then, I had this idea.

I knew it was the worst possible moment. Yet, not to tell you would have gotten the words stuck inside me, would have made me wonder—days or years from now, apart from you and inconsolable—if, of all the words in the world, these were the words that would have made you keep me.

So of course I had to say them aloud, the words: "We would be even more of a family if we had a child together."

And it was true, Annie.

So true that I could feel the presence of that child who would make our family permanent.

"Your timing is so . . . off, Mason."

"I know. But I love being a parent. When I think of myself, I see myself as Opal's parent first."

"I can't believe you'd—"

"Whenever I've talked about it before, you couldn't believe it either. And my timing was supposedly off. This may be my last chance to tell you."

"Now that I want you out . . ."

"You may think you want me out, right now, and I understand—"

"You can't get in here, Mason." You jabbed your forehead. "You can't tell me what to think."

"Except when we both know we're thinking the same—"

"We're not."

"How about that time we hiked Mt. Washington? And there was no one but us in the fog . . . trusting each other so totally as we walked from cairn to cairn together."

"That doesn't undo what happened."

"It doesn't. But up there, on that mountain—"

SIX

Annie

{ *The Raft* }

"You could have drowned!" Annie is screaming. Screaming and leaning over the railing of the neighbor's boardwalk and ready to leap in if Opal's kayak were to tip.

"Hi, Annie."

"I woke up and I couldn't find you!"

"I'm wearing a life jacket. See?"

"You're not allowed in the water without an adult!"

"I'm not *in* the water!"

"I searched everywhere!" Screaming. Not letting Opal see how relieved she is to find her. Because then Opal will go off by herself again next time she feels gloomy.

"You're having a hissy, Annie!"

The air drips, holds so much moisture that Annie feels soaked through. "Where were you?"

"And a red nose from the hissy."

"I ran along the inlet—"

"I was right here."

"—and across the boardwalk to the bay and drove all through the neighborhood up to Towd Point and then I called the police and—"

"That's stupid!"

"Don't you let her talk to you like that," Dr. Virginia snaps.

"I thought you were lost."

"I wasn't lost."

"Don't you dare talk to—"

"Stupid!"

"Not as stupid as you for almost drowning!"

"I didn't drown!"

"Stop sniping at me!" Definitely the sister part of their relationship. As Opal's mother, Annie strives to be patient and constant, but as Opal's sister, she wants what's fair and snipes right back at her.

"You stop sniping, Annie!"

"Listen to her feelings beneath the angry words," Dr. Francine advises.

The radio people have been tugging at Annie. It's like salivating. They're at her as soon as she unlocks the car, before she turns on the radio, even when she's not in the car and far from any radio, harassing her, or comforting her with—

"Whoosh . . ." The kayak sways. Opal is making it sway by leaning from side to side.

"Sit still, you!"

"Now the police will be mad at you, Annie."

"Aunt Stormy is waiting for them. I went driving, searching for you—"

"You're always out driving, Annie."

"—and I saw something floating in the inlet." *Yellow.* "The kayak and you in the kayak."

"I wasn't lost. I knew where I was."

"Well, I didn't."

"I was investigating."

"Investigating what?"

"Just investigating."

Investigating. Annie wants to punch Mason. *Attack him. Kill him. Kill him good.* Because of him, Opal isn't as safe in the world as before, when she had two parents. It startles Annie, that lust for violence. *Delights her.* She wishes someone would hassle her right now—maybe the people on whose property she trespassed, tires squealing—because then she could strike out. Within this rage, she feels stronger than any possible attacker. Within this rage she feels safe, dangerous to anyone who might threaten her.

Opal is watching her. Stubborn and sullen and a bit uncertain. "You're not even the same anymore, Annie."

"So what's that supposed to—"

"You don't make collages anymore."

"That has nothing to do with you getting lost."

"I wasn't lost! When—"

"I need to know where you are, Opal! Every moment!"

"When are the lumis coming back, Annie?"

"Promise to let me know where you are, every moment."

"I'm here now."

"That's not what I mean."

"Okay."

"Because I didn't know where you were."

"Okay." Opal reaches up to wrestle her curls into a knot.

"Hold on to your paddle."

"Okay . . ."

"Not okay! I thought you were— Did anyone . . . talk to you?" *Is this too vague?*

"Oh no," Dr. Francine assures Annie. "I advocate gentle questioning."

"No," Opal says. "And I didn't go with a stranger who touched me in places I don't want to be touched. So there."

"At least she remembers that much," Dr. Virginia says.

"At least you remembered that much," Annie says.

"Too confrontational," Dr. Francine warns.

"Didn't you ever go investigating?" Opal is so small in her kayak, surrounded by water.

Out here, we're always surrounded by water. Inlet ocean lake bay river—

A premonition?

Annie shivers. "You could have fallen in and—"

"But I didn't."

"—hit your head and not come up again—"

"But I didn't."

"I don't know how I could go on without you."

"You're going on without Mason." Opal's eyes go hard—the way they do whenever she's both angry and sad, and the angry wins.

Better angry than that unhappiness that hooks me in, makes me give her whatever she asks for. Shielding her from Mason's death.

"If I want to, I can paddle away from you, Annie. Fast—"

"You watch it—"

"I can so. Real fast."

"Don't you ever go off by yourself again!"

"Except I can't just leave you hanging over the railing—"

—me and half a dozen talk radio people—

"—having your hissy."

"Don't you let her talk to you like that."

"Don't you ever go off by yourself again! Promise."

That pointed little chin juts up, so determined, and the stubbornness that connects the two of them—*our mother's daughters*—becomes sticky, fuses, till they can no longer release each other. Everything is the same texture—air skin hair clothes land water—so that they're part of their surroundings, only skin separating their insides from the sodden air.

Mason would never let it come to a standoff with Opal. With me yes. But not with Opal. He banters her out of her funk. Gives her a way out. Tells Opal about a time when he, too, got hell for investigating.

Annie takes her cue from him. Tells Opal, "I got hell once for . . . investigating . . . when I was your age. Mom and Dad and I stayed at a lake in Italy and—"

"They never took me to Italy."

"They would have. If—"

"I didn't have one day with them."

"I know. I'm sorry."

"Look look—" Opal points to a great white heron, gliding low above the ducks toward the boardwalk, then veering toward BigC's black cherry tree, where it settles itself, elegant and pearl-white.

"Annie?"

"Yes?"

"Do you know there're nests under the boardwalk?"

"Made from mud?"

"Mostly from nest stuff . . . like twigs and grass. Plus there's a blue crab down here. What's the name of that lake?"

"Lago di Garda. We swam every day. One morning after breakfast the sun was behind the mist, turning water and lake and sky all the same color . . . the color of mist . . ."

"What's the color of mist like?"

"Sort of white and gray and golden . . . like Mom's ring, except half-transparent so you can see through the colors . . . see shapes."

"Spooky?"

"A bit spooky . . . mostly beautiful. While I was swimming in the mist, I could no longer tell where sky began and where water began, and it was—"

"I want to see Mom's ring."

Annie flips her hand so that Opal can see the stone.

"Better not spit on me, Annie."

"I would never spit on you!"

"You said you have to spit on opals to keep them in good condition."

"That's true for the stone, yet, but—"

"Why didn't they call you Opal? You were first."

"They gave me the name of our grandmother, dad's mom . . . Annabelle."

"I don't know her."

"She . . . died when I was two."

"Everyone is always dead."

Tears shoot to Annie's eyes. "That's how I sometimes feel."

"Once my hands are big, you and I can take turns wearing her ring."

"We will."

"Every day we'll take turns, every day, Annie?"

"How about every month?"

"Okay. Two months for me. One month for you." Opal, shimmering like the stone she was named after.

Annie smiles. "Sounds fair."

"Because you wore it for so long already."

"We'll visit each other whenever we exchange Mom's ring."

"Light's coming through your hair, Annie. All red like your nose."

"Hah. You leave my nose alone."

"What happened when you went investigating?"

"Whenever I got tired, I floated on my back, figuring that if I kept moving, I'd reach the other side of the lake. But it stayed the same distance—"

"Because of the mist."

"Because of the mist, yes, and just when I thought I must be getting closer, I was back where I'd started, and there were my parents—"

"Our parents!"

"—our parents, arms waving, yelling—"

"Having a hissy. Just like you."

"—and four police boats searching for me. Operation Rescue. Can you believe that, Opal? I mean, talk about our parents overreacting. I was so . . . angry. I mean, I knew all along where I was."

"But *they* didn't know."

Annie smiles. *I'll have to tell Mason.*

"You tricked me." Opal spoons water with the blades of her paddle. Flings it toward Annie. "At least *I* wasn't swimming."

"You could have been. If that kayak had tipped—"

"Can I race you to the cottage, Annie? You in the car? Me in the kayak?"

"If you promise to be careful."

But Opal is already paddling, blades flying, shouting, "Bet you I'll get there first."

NIGHT, THAT same night, and when Annie awakens, suddenly and sweating, she's flung across the side where Mason used to sleep. *I am alone.* Without him, the bed feels barren, his absence irretrievable.

"Damn you." Having to discover over and over that he isn't here anymore. She feels a blind rip-roaring anger. *"Damn you for not letting me get back to what's familiar. Just not there anymore, the familiar."*

"We could have gotten through this," Mason says.

"No."

"We could have lived apart for a month and—"

"No."

"Six months."

"No."

"I bet you we would have been together again. Ultimately—"

"No."

"I bet you—"

"I couldn't have stayed with you."

"Not even to keep me alive?"

"It's too much work keeping you alive!"

Damn him. Making her forever the woman whose husband killed himself. Annie sees it in the faces of people who know. The speculation. She doesn't speak with them, but her eyes warn them away. *"Be careful," she imagines telling strangers who encounter her. "You have no idea what I'm capable of. The person you see—hair skin eyes—contains someone entirely different. Medusa. Madonna. Flesh-eating harridan . . ."*

FINALLY, THEN, sleeping. Sleeping and dreaming—

—dreaming and walking with Opal on a path of deep sand. Crowns of pitch pines and oaks and black cherry stick from the sand, their trunks long buried. From this forest of treetops we come into a wide rim of high dunes. And now I know where we are. In the Walking Dunes. Opal runs up the yellow slope of sand, her purple windbreaker flapping. Slides down on her butt, laughing. Then up to the rim again . . . purple on yellow . . . but not down, not down on her butt, no longer here but gone . . . beyond the other side of the rim. I scream her name—Opal Opal—run past beach heather and bearberry—Opal Opal Opal—and suddenly remember Napeague Harbor beyond the tallest dune. I run up the yellow slope of sand, along the rim, searching, searching in all directions, and stop running because it's a dream—

Annie knows it's a dream.

She wants to wake up. Tries to wake—

—but I'm trapped inside the dream, have to keep running, searching. Opal Opal—Something purple in Napeague Harbor, ballooning from the shimmering surface. I run. Toward the purple . . . swaying, ballooning . . . toward Opal—

crying—

Crying?

Opal is crying—not drowned in the harbor but crying.

Annie rushes toward her. "Here . . . sweetie?" she whispers, strokes back the curls that so often hide the small face. As she feels Opal clinging to her—tear-blinded the way she used to as an infant—all time vanishes: Opal is in her arms, now, not wet from drowning; is also the infant scrambling forever against Annie as if trying to return to a safer darkness; and the sorrow between them encompasses all sorrows . . . their parents' deaths funneling into Mason's death forever in the same moment.

It rocks Annie, that sorrow. Rocks Opal in her arms. "Sweetie? I'm here." She molds herself against Opal, holds her for a long time while Opal's tears open up Annie's own sorrow, one more layer . . . so many . . . She can open those layers, step inside the folds, or choose to step back as the layers billow and let in more pain than can possibly fly through one opening. As the pain keeps flying at her, Annie doesn't know if the fabric will hold. But she keeps holding her daughter, holding her, tight, tight, till they both slide from tears into sleep.

HER FIRST thought upon waking—spooned around Opal—is that she'll help her find friends. Because Opal has been resisting getting to know the kids in the neighborhood. She'll say something like, "They're being mean."

Not having friends has turned into not wanting friends.

That Saturday, Annie takes Opal for a walk along the bay, stops to talk with families who have children, but Opal drags behind. Four girls are building a sand turtle. They've conned the youngest girl to lie belly-down on the beach, and though she's complaining, they continue to heap sand on her.

"Hold still, Mandy!"

Opal watches, hands behind her back, as they decorate the turtle with seashells and pebbles.

"Why don't you ask if you can help?" Annie whispers.

"I don't bury people," Opal says.

"I got sand up my nose," Mandy yells. Tiny barrettes glitter in her hair.

"Just hold up your head," one girl says.

Another girl laughs. "Like a turtle neck."

Mandy groans, "I will never forget this!"

Opal turns and heads away from the girls.

Annie stays next to her, walking fast. "They're just playing."

"Burying people is not playing."

All at once Annie wants her pink afghan back, wrap it around Opal, rock and soothe her the way she used to. She sees herself knitting the afghan during those long days after Opal came to her. If only she had kept it. But during those two days of clearing out the pond house, she wanted to empty it, starting with Mason's belongings; then her own; and once she'd tossed her denim jacket—faded, with drawings of leaves in delicate lines—onto the pile for Goodwill, it was as if she'd pulled a plug, letting everything else run down that drain, including clothes and shoes and toys and the afghan, everything from her studio—except her work.

All day long, that gaudy afghan keeps at her, as if she'd tossed away every minute she had with Opal while knitting it.

She calls the Goodwill store, asks if it's still there. "Because I would like to buy it back."

"Sometimes we get handicrafts in," a clerk tells her, "but they sell right away.

"It's actually quite ugly. Uneven, in various pinks."

"Our customers like to buy handmade things. Even if they are ugly."

"It's the only afghan I ever—"

"I do remember one. But it wasn't pink. Is it knit or crocheted?"

"Knit. May I leave you my number?"

"Of course. What kind of pattern?"

"Rectangles. Sewn together."

"Nothing in pink," the clerk says.

It keeps at her, the afghan, while she's with Aunt Stormy, getting the Zeckhauser cottage ready for their granddaughter's bat mitzvah party. The painters are finishing up with the interior, a quiet sage and white, but Annie longs for the shrill pink-pink of the afghan. It keeps at her when she takes Opal swimming. When they eat dinner. Even after she tucks Opal in for the night.

"Did you see my car keys?" she asks Aunt Stormy, who's reading on the velvet couch, stretched out with her legs on the backrest, the way she likes to read.

"I have something better for you."

"Meaning?" All Annie wants is to get into her car and listen to the radio people.

Aunt Stormy points to a paddle she's propped against the French doors.

"So?"

"Go and kayak instead."

"At night?"

"Especially at night."

"I don't think it's safe."

"Safer than your roads at night."

Annie digs through her backpack. "I need to drive for a while."

"I took them."

"Why? You said it was what I needed."

"And you did. But it's been a month now."

"I really need to—"

"Let's talk." Aunt Stormy folds the page and closes the book. "You might like this. An anthology of short stories from Chile. Now . . . would you help me with a couple of things?"

"I— Yes, of course."

Aunt Stormy fills the sink with soapy water. Immerses fistfuls of silverware. "From my client supply. I'll give you the keys afterwards. If you still want them."

Annie snaps up a dish towel. "It must be important to you."

"Opal . . . she needs to be with you more."

"She's asleep."

"You'll have to find a way to make this work."

"I'm trying. You know I'm trying."

"You'll come through this."

"How can you know?"

"Because you're both a lot like your mother. Dauntless . . . Exuberant . . . Some people are dealt misfortunes they cannot survive."

"You mean Mason?"

"I wasn't thinking about Mason."

"Well, he didn't survive the three of us. I—"

Dawn in the pond house. Jake gone. And she in her bathrobe, her back to Mason, sickened by what he has become, what they have become together. Mason showing off even in death, already waiting for her to cut him off the rope, forcing her back to that moment when she could have prevented it.

AUNT STORMY touches Annie's arm.

Staring at the spot on her arm where Aunt Stormy left a wet spot and one fleck of foam. Trying to pick it off, the foam, without breaking it. Drying forks. Drying. Too ashamed to tell about the sauna.

"Annie?"

"I'm not . . . ready to talk about Mason."

"Don't then."

"Except to Opal. . . . I think I have to be willing to talk about Mason. For her?"

Aunt Stormy nods.

—to let him inhabit my memories . . . my panic the first time he threatens to kill himself . . . the second and third. My anger when he keeps threatening, manipulating. Thinking: I wish you'd go ahead, saying it to his stunned face, saying it once, and he goes ahead, proves me wrong, himself right, not a liar after all but someone who announced his intentions. Does he surprise himself when he finally does it? He probably imagines my reaction, does it for my reaction.

Drying forks. Focusing on the leafy pattern of the handles. "We used to have that pattern when I was little."

"Your mother and I got it at the same place."

Annie pictures her mother and Aunt Stormy *in a department store, choosing the same pattern. Sisters-by-choice. Here too. Each buying a set of eight on sale, so that if one has a party, the other will lend her the silverware.*

"We were taking classes at the college and waitressing five evenings a week. Enough for rent and tuition."

Annie has seen photos of the place her mother and Aunt Stormy rented together after their au pair contracts were over, a one-bedroom apartment above an antiques store in Southampton. Twin beds. A round table with four chairs. A blue couch. Lace curtains that Aunt Stormy's mother sewed for them in Germany.

"We didn't need much money for food because we ate at the restaurant and had leftovers to take home. A fancy restaurant, too expensive, called Kaminstube—Fireplace Room—though it didn't have a fireplace. Your mother and I got the jobs because we spoke German—the only thing authentic about that place. The owner was third-generation Greek, who liked that South German *umpahhpahh* music. You know?"

Annie grimaces.

"Exactly. More of that on any given day than we heard all those years growing up by the North Sea. We had to wear *Dirndl.* Made us look like upside-down cups with legs sticking in the air."

Annie laughs. "Serving to *Umpahhpahh* . . ."

"On days the owner rounded down our hours, we took silverware and—"

"Took? You mean you stole—"

"We were honorable about what we took."

"I can't imagine you and my mother stealing."

"We kept a tab of how much he cheated us of. And we only took that value in silverware."

Still, it feels weird to Annie, considering how ethical her mother and Aunt Stormy have always been. Or maybe it does fit in with how Aunt Stormy claims her gifts—admiring something until it becomes hers: those tawny leather gloves Annie had bought for herself in Morocco; that silky black sweater that once belonged to Annie's mother; the blue glass ball that still floats from her candle chandelier above the kitchen table, and has multiplied over the years, nine blue orbs so far—thin blown glass—as though the coerced gift were still spawning others.

"Opal asked about Jake," Aunt Stormy says.

If I were my mother, I would have stolen it back.

"Have you thought about letting Opal spend some time with him?"

"I don't know if . . . it's possible to see Jake again."

Jake has called twice. Aunt Stormy told her. But Annie hasn't called back. Unthinkable, being near him again. She failed him, failed herself when she didn't stop Mason. And yet, Jake is the only one she'll ever be able to talk to about what happened.

"May I please say something?" Aunt Stormy asks.

Annie nods.

"Jake has been in Opal's life from the beginning—"

"I can't."

"—and he's like a second father to her."

"Mason didn't like it at all when I said Opal had two fathers."

"This is no longer about Mason. How about—" Aunt Stormy wipes her palms against the front of her jeans. "—visitation, Annie? Certain times that Opal can count on being with Jake?"

"Odd to even consider visitation."

"More odd, yet, to not consider it. Just think about it."

Annie doesn't know what to say.

"For the time being, I need to hire someone to help with my business. I usually do in the summer. If you want—"

"Yes."

"I can pay twenty dollars an hour—"

"That's more than—"

"—and a flexible schedule, so we can both look after Opal till she starts third grade."

"Thank you."

"Some of the jobs . . . we can take Opal along. Like checking on houses when the owners are away. And if you need more time with her or for your collages, you can coordinate a lot of things from here by phone." She motions to a list of numbers on her refrigerator. "My purple pages." Appliance, Chain Saw, Chimney, Electrician, Excavation, Firewood, Handyman, Landscaping, Locksmith, Maid Service, Oil, Plumber, Roofing, Snow Plowing, Window. Several names in each category. Stars by the ones she prefers, lines through those she wouldn't call again. Like Marcy. Category Firewood.

"Honest Marcy has stood me up twice. Didn't call until weeks later. Lied about a death in her family."

"How do you know it's a lie?"

"She says *honest* every other word."

Annie is ready to defend Marcy, befriend Marcy. "People die."

"But with Marcy it's the same cousin. Stanley. I used to date Stanley before I met Pete. First time Marcy told me, scared the shit out of me. Then I called his wife to offer condolences, and Stanley answered the phone."

"Proof enough." Annie smiles.

"SO WHAT *is* happening with your collages?" Aunt Stormy asks.

"I . . . keep postponing." Annie feels uncomfortable thinking about her work. "I do want to go back to them."

"Good."

"Some days I think Mason has taken my work from me."

"If you let him."

"He killed himself where I work. All right? He was so jealous of my work—"

"—but also supportive," Mason reminds her.

"—and it got worse once I had my studio."

"You closed the door on me, Annie. It was different when you still had everything set up in the living room. We could talk then—"

"There are other places you can work," Aunt Stormy says.

"But he's everywhere. It's not as simple as getting another studio."

"Of course it's not simple."

"Thanks for giving me that much."

"I'm on your side, Annie. It's going to be damn difficult to start again."

"You'll be in museums," Mason says.

"I only want to do the work for myself."

Aunt Stormy motions to a corner of the living room. "How about if we clear that? You'll be between two windows."

"We're already crowding you."

"One: You're not. And two: I wouldn't suggest this if I didn't mean it. I'm not into martyrdom."

Annie has to smile. "Then you won't get sainthood."

"Fuck sainthood."

"O . . . kay."

"Let's set up there right now. Unless you want to go kayaking."

"Not particularly."

Together they stack the crates with Annie's collages along the wall between the windows and cover them with quilts and pillows.

"Now you have an *Eckbank*."

"*Eck*—— what?"

"Corner bench. We had one when I was a girl."

AFTER AUNT Stormy goes to sleep, Annie sits on the *Eckbank*, sits with what she needs to begin her collages, and doesn't do anything. Except sit and stare at what she has around her. When she was a girl, the space between Mason and her was narrow. Girl-boy. Boy-girl. Almost one. And what she has come to believe is that the space between two people needs to widen and narrow and widen again. But with Mason it only narrowed more when they grew up.

"What if you leave too much space?" Mason asks.

"You'll lose each other."

"And if you cross the space between you, Annabelle?"

"You crush each other. Or one of us will retreat forever."

"How then does it apply to three people?" Mason says.

Sitting and staring and not doing anything is what Annie does the next day.

And the day after.

But she sits with it. With the feeling of not being able to do anything. With the frustration and failure that come out of not doing anything.

She stays. Stares at what she has in front of her.

"What if you promised yourself one hour?" Aunt Stormy suggests.

Annie feels like throwing up.

"Maybe not even let yourself work for more than an hour."

"Five minutes feels like too much. I probably should just get a real job."

"You have a real job. You can also work with me."

Annie enjoys the hard physical work with Aunt Stormy, lifting and carrying, picking up stacks of drapes and quilts from clients, houses, washing whatever can be washed and taking the rest to the dry cleaner. With Opal, she clears the path to keep it from growing together.

From her own work, she feels split off. From any desire. Still—she gives it that one hour. Day after day.

Nights when nothing will stop the pain, she makes herself kayak instead of driving. Not a shutting out of the pain but an opening to what is around her. The water holds the light longer than the earth. And the radio people don't mind, are right along with her, making her fret over what happens to them when they're off the air. Like the shrimp woman from Walla Walla, Washington. Linda. *Is Linda still hiding out in her house?* And the second-marriage couple from Hartford. *Are Elise and Ben still fighting and keeping lists so that one of his grown children won't get a more expensive present than one of her grown children?* How about Mel and Hubert? *Has Mel kicked out his bully roommate, or are they on a cruise to—*

Annie stays close to shore. To be safe and to gather critter bits: bones and wings and those jingle shells she used to call mermaid's toenails as a child, slipper shells that she used to call devil's toenails. Stuck inside a devil's toenail is the skeleton of a tiny crab.

Aunt Stormy has set up two card tables for her. "Not as sturdy as what you used to have."

"I don't want what I used to have."

Side by side, the tables brace each other, not as flimsy as on their own. Annie covers them with butcher paper, goes with Aunt Stormy to the basement, and returns with empty jars, scissors, leftover fabrics, old photo negatives, tools.

Pete brings over sandpaper and store receipts, the linings of envelopes and worn chamois cloth. Best of all a shoe box filled with old dental tools and X-rays, hundreds of tiny X-rays.

Opal collects dried grasses for her, pinecones and leaves, crooked twigs and Popsicle sticks, beads and lavender, clothes she has outgrown.

And Annie sits with all she's gathered and all they've brought her though she doesn't know if she'll ever be able to make another collage. Sits with her hands still.

One hour. That's what she promises herself. More if she wants. But not less.

ONE NIGHT she returns from kayaking with egg casing that's shiny and ribbed and rattles like armor . . . like a soul. The canvas on her easel is bare, blank, and as she flings acrylic paints at it to stop it from daunting her, she's thinking of Pete, who goes down to the bay every day and does his sequence of stretching and an hour of water-walking, working every muscle, reclaiming his body. She can see why Aunt Stormy loves this man . . . the way he's finding foothold in the sand to keep himself upright, working at sustaining and advancing whatever strength his body gained in the last hours.

She slathers her paint, searching for a way in, and suddenly she can no longer stop because the canvas is opening itself to her imagination. She knows what that's like, knows what it's like to live for that—exciting and frightening and mysterious and familiar. It's as though the image has been shaping itself inside her, months of untapped back work breaking free, now, into another version of raft, dragging her into territory where she didn't expect to be.

Once again, she's using twine for the raft, though it makes her uneasy. But the image calls for that—even if twine suggests rope.

"Is that where you took the idea for hanging yourself?"

This twine is thinner than in earlier versions, and she lays it in an open weave on top of marbleized paper from Italy, all blues and whites, torn into thin shreds that overlap, rising and pushing like choppy waves, making the raft unstable. And on the raft, a momentary sculpture of limbs, dark silhouettes against the low afternoon sun. In motion.

That's what she works toward.

In motion.

Or just before motion.

Or after.

When the impact of motion still resonates.

It can happen within one image, but usually she needs several; and the transition from one to the next is like what happens offstage—essential for understanding what's happening onstage. It's almost like what she once saw at a photo exhibition of places *after* violent crimes had happened there—no bodies; no blood or guts—ordinary places where people walked or sat or passed; yet, the impact of that violence resonated. Nothing concrete. Nothing you could point to and say: This is what has changed. And yet, extreme change, forever, in the soul of those places, in every particle of air and of matter.

Annie's hands are reaching into the collage, building up. Lavender twigs. Dental X-rays. Leaves. An overlay of sheer fabric, a shade lighter than copper. On the raft, the feet of the yellow figure are fused to the planks. The brown figure is light-limbed, quicksilver. As Annie tears into the layers with the sharp point of a dental instrument, an excavator, Pete called it, the surfaces wrinkle and tear . . . those wonderful lines . . . beautiful dark streaks . . . all those marvelous surprises . . . and she feels herself moving into the image, feels something opening to her. Pain? Joy?

Already, the sculpture of limbs is dissolving while the copper sun continues to shimmer on water. And the red girl is there, more of her now. Still watching. Or being watched. *What did I see?* Annie brings her fingertips against the girl's red shape, closes her eyes. Too smooth. Too still. Everything else feels torn and puckered.

THAT SUMMER Aunt Stormy becomes Annie's eyes, her reason, the wise voice that cuts through Annie's confusion as they work together. Sometimes all that holds Annie upright is the pattern of ordinary days. Making breakfast for Opal. Going to the post office every morning. Feeding the ducks.

Nights she works.

In the mail, a Simon and Garfunkel CD from Mason's parents.

"I promised I'd burn a CD of Mason's favorite music for them," Annie tells Opal. "Next time we visit them, we'll—"

"We don't have any of his music," Opal accuses her. "You threw out everything that belongs to Mason!"

"We can download his favorites together if you want."

"You threw out everything that belongs to me! You threw out our house!"

"Because Mason spoiled the house for us. And everything in it."

When Annie calls to thank Mason's parents, his mother tells her she's worried about one of her regulars.

"Old Mrs. Belding. She signed in for her safe-deposit box. I didn't like her son, Annie."

"Why not?"

"He was so impatient with her. Held on to her elbow the entire time. When I unlocked Mrs. Belding's box, he shook the contents into his briefcase. With the three of us standing right there in the vault, though he could've had privacy in a cubicle. And Mrs. Belding not glancing up. I haven't seen her since. And when I went to the bank manager with my suspicion that Mrs. Belding's son was robbing her, he lectured me again that I was too attached to my customers."

"ALL HER tenants inherit BigC's annual battle with the ducks," Aunt Stormy tells Opal and Annie as they watch BigC scrub duck shit from the boardwalk.

But many of the white spots are embedded as if the boards had been splattered with bleach. Every year BigC has the same battle with the ducks. She buys gadgets to keep them away. Whirligigs and scarecrows. When she invites Opal along to Sag Harbor, Annie lets her go; they return with a cordless drill and various things made of plastic, all ugly: three huge owls, a set of porch dishes to match BigC's umbrellas, and a boy doll that's all in one piece with the clothes painted on.

Hollow like Aunt Stormy's rocks, the owls look fake with their evenly grooved feathers and glass eyes. Opal holds them while BigC bolts them to the railing of the boardwalk, and for almost a week, they scare the ducks away.

Rain then, so much rain that it seems Pete's trumpet vines double on sunny days. They creep up the bamboo canes by his garage, around the legs of his outdoor table, grazing your ankles when you sit down, startling you.

• • •

ONE NIGHT, the water is thick against Annie's paddle, and even before she sees the flicker, she knows the lumis are here. Quickly, she paddles back to the cottage, wakes Opal, and paddles with her into the bay. It feels as if all waters around them and way beyond them are saturated with that white-green flicker, heavy with that light—phosphorescent, fluorescent—and will cradle them if they were to leap in, just as it cradles their kayaks.

Opal laughs aloud. Stirs her paddle. A vortex of shimmer. "Mason says they're waterfalls of light."

"True and poetic."

All at once a black duck with a bit of white on its feathers flees from them, wings whirring close to the water.

"Where did it go?" Opal asks.

"I don't see it anymore."

"Can we kayak all night, Annie?"

"For a while."

Maybe kayaking with Opal will take the place of night driving.

Maybe one dawn, they'll launch the kayaks next to the wharf in Sag Harbor, paddle under the bridge and toward the breakwater.

"Tomorrow I'll catch lumis," Opal says.

"Good. I'll come along."

IN THE afternoon Opal takes Aunt Stormy's pitcher, and Annie follows her to the bay, where they find Pete, up to his knees in the whitecaps.

"Aren't you cold, Pete?" Opal asks.

"Warmer . . . than the air."

Annie is amazed how he finds joy in every movement despite his discomfort.

Opal gathers a lumi from the beach. "Feels like snot—"

"Yuck . . ."

"—with sand stuck to it. Hurry up, Annie. Put some water in the pitcher."

Where Annie scoops water from the bay, four fiddler crabs are dragging something away, fighting. One wins, and scoots off with the booty.

Opal lets the lumis slide into the pitcher. "Look look, Pete." She takes the pitcher from Annie and jiggles it.

He staggers toward her, left leg first, dragging his right leg.

Opal takes a few steps into the water until they're both in to their ankles.

"So . . . delicate," Pete says.

A wave splashes Opal's knees. "Mason used to lift me high above the waves."

"No, no," Annie corrects her, "it was my— I mean our father who did that with me . . . and later, I did it with you."

"Not so." Those stubborn, stubborn eyes.

"I would catch you before you'd reach the waves, and I'd lift you high so you'd fly above them—"

"Not so."

"Yes so."

"Not so."

"You're always twisting things around in your head," Annie says. It worries her. Like Opal's stories of the cottage changing overnight. Does all that just come from her imagination? From being so dramatic? Or is it more? Delusions? No—

"Don't you remember, Opal?" she says urgently. "I used to tell you I was turning into a people-wave to stop the water-wave . . ." *How do I remember, Dad? From stories you told to me? From what I still feel in my body: the flying . . . the lightness . . . the certainty that there is a way across. A way I haven't thought of before—*

"Not so."

"I would hold your hands, and then I would let you fly."

"That's what Mason did with me."

"No, no. Mason was there. But he would watch us. You would laugh and gurgle, and I would lift—"

"Mason let me fly over the waves."

"Does it . . . matter . . . Annie?" Pete asks.

"Yes. Of course. I was there!"

"It's . . . what she . . . remembers—"

"It's what she wants to remember."

"It's a . . . lovely . . . memory . . . for her."

Suddenly Annie feels ashamed. "It's just that she hijacks all the good memories, gives them to Mason . . . leaves me out altogether. But she blames me for the rest."

Pete nods. "Not . . . fair."

Not fucking fair.

Opal is adding a strand of seaweed to the pitcher.

Some fistfuls of sand.

Pebbles and shells.

More lumis.

"What if she never remembers how it really was?" Annie asks Pete.

"Then you . . . can do . . . nothing about . . . it."

TIHII. A word her father once wrote with wine on the tabletop and then said aloud. "TIHII." Like the whinnying of a horse. When Annie asked him what it meant, her father touched each letter. "This . . . Is . . . How . . . It . . . Is. And what it means is that I can do nothing about getting laid off. Not make them keep me or pretend that it doesn't matter. This is how it is." When Annie tried out the sound and whinnied, her father laughed, and the lower half of his face widened, while his thick eyebrows curved down, changing the shape of his face. On the table, the letters were drying out. Annie dipped her index finger into his wineglass and ran it across the letters till they glistened again.

Kneeling in the sand, Opal is sifting through her pebbles. "I only want red ones."

"I'll get . . . you more . . . lumis." Awkwardly, Pete leans forward, teeters as he reaches into the bay.

Annie stops herself from supporting his arm. At worst he'll plop down. A soft fall. Aunt Stormy usually busies herself while he regains his balance. Her tact and kindness. Yet being there, close enough, if he were to need her. When Annie first moved in with her, she was appalled that Aunt Stormy didn't help Pete out of her car, that she went ahead into stores or the post office while he was still struggling with her car door. But by the second errand, he usually met up with them. How much of this was unspoken? Did she let him do it alone from the beginning? Or was there a gesture, once, from Pete, or words: *"Let me . . ."*

Pete raises his fist from the water.

"You got one!" Opal laughs.

He lets it slide into the pitcher.

"Good job, Pete."

"That's what . . . I live for . . ."

• • •

THAT EVENING, when the lumis flicker in the pitcher, bodies sheer and airy, Opal asks, "Can I keep them?"

"Not good . . . for them," Pete says.

"Why?"

"They'll get . . . smaller . . . until they . . . vanish."

She leans close to him. "But how?"

"One time I . . . kept them . . . too long and . . . couldn't find them . . . anymore."

"Maybe they jumped out?"

"I think—" Pete shakes his head slow-speed. "—their bodies . . . became . . . one with . . . the water."

She grabs the pitcher. "I want to set them free now."

"Tomorrow morning is soon enough," Annie tells her.

"Now—" She begins to cry, wildly.

"But it's dark."

Aunt Stormy lays one hand between Annie's shoulder blades, rubs gently.

But that's where Mason used to kiss me— Annie twists away.

"We'll take flashlights," Aunt Stormy says. "How about that?"

Annie kneels next to Opal. "It'll be an adventure."

"Catering to her moods again," Dr. Virginia chastises Annie.

Opal sniffles, both arms around the pitcher.

"You two go ahead," Aunt Stormy says.

Outside, everything is louder than during daylight: the creaks of the boardwalk; the rustle of the phragmites; the swish of their bare feet on sand. The bay is flat, without color, but as they walk in, their legs stir up brief green flickers, here and there, all around them. Annie feels lumis against her left ankle, thick, then gone.

"They've been waiting for our lumis," Opal decides.

"What is it about you and those lumis?" Annie means for it to sound playful, but it comes out as impatient.

In the dark, the edges of her daughter's teeth glisten, whiter than her skin, one horizontal line that—for an instant, only—separates into two lines. So small she looks, so heartbreakingly brave, imagining perhaps some magical connection between the lumis and Pete and the bay . . . the lumis vanishing if she were to keep them too long from the bay . . . Pete reclaiming his body by walking in the bay . . . perhaps even—

Annie is sweating.

—perhaps even that she can bring Mason back like that too. If she takes no more lumis. If she gets Pete stronger. If—

"Too shallow here," Opal says.

"Let me know when we're in far enough."

Together, they go deeper.

"Here now." Opal submerges the pitcher and holds it down until the water has flushed out every one of her lumis.

WHILE ANNIE sits in the sand with the cell phone, scheduling window washers for two of the houses, furnace maintenance for three others, Opal is water-walking with Pete. He with small steps, she dancing and jumping around him. Encouraging him even when he stumbles. When he falls. More bruises.

"You can do it, Pete."

"Each day . . . I can . . . do one more . . . thing than the . . . day before."

He gets tired easily. Everything takes such a huge effort. Yet, he keeps trying.

While Opal frets over him. Nudges him to do more.

"You're my . . . coach—" He sways, lets himself down till he sits in shallow water. He's crying. "It has . . . nothing to do . . . with you . . . Opal . . . so hard . . . getting . . . how I used to . . . be."

"You can do it, Pete."

"It'll get . . . better. It always . . . gets better."

That evening, she stays next to him in Aunt Stormy's living room while he reads *The New York Times*, flipping the pages slowly; and she stays even when he tells her to run along, that it will take him all night reading the paper.

"You'll have to take a break for your exercises," she insists.

"Soon . . ."

"I'll make a chart."

"Okay."

"Like in school. You make a check mark next to the exercises you've done. It'll be your job, Pete."

"My job . . . now is finding . . . lost . . . things."

"You think our little girl is looking for sort of a father figure?" Aunt Stormy whispers.

"She's stalking him. I think she somehow believes she'll get Mason back that way."

"I don't get it."

"It's all mixed up with the lumis and getting Pete well . . . meaning if she can bring him back from almost dying—"

"Is that what she says?"

"No, just what I'm muddling through." *If I were her real mother, I would know.* "And I may be totally wrong. She'll be devastated once she figures out Mason is never coming back."

Aunt Stormy motions to her French doors. "Right now, imagine that's all Opal can see through every pane of glass, Mason's loss. But slowly—"

"That's what it was like for me at first."

"—over time, each of these glass panes will be replaced by a good memory for her: Pete getting stronger . . . laughing with you . . . burning the Hungry Ghost . . . new friends . . . her first kiss even. But there will always be that small windowpane with Mason's death. Except it will be one small part of the total, finding its place in proportion to everything else in Opal's life. And in yours."

Annie nods.

"You're starting to see all the other windowpanes. It took me a while too, when Pete became ill. I was so terrified, and losing him was all I—"

"Pete?" Opal shakes his arm.

"Yes . . . ?"

"Do you lose a lot of things, Pete?"

"Yes, but . . . I only find . . . things . . . I've stopped looking . . . for."

"Do you find things you weren't looking for?"

"That's . . . the good . . . surprise. . . ."

"Or things you forgot were missing?"

"How did it happen?" Annie whispers to Aunt Stormy.

"I thought it was a headache—his face and neck hurt. But then he started vomiting. Wanted water. But I didn't let him. I knelt by him, turned his head so he could vomit. Just when I called 911, Pete stopped breathing and—" She shakes her head.

Annie takes Aunt Stormy's hands into hers. Kisses her forehead.

"—so I started resuscitation. Till the ambulance got here. He has damage to the brain tissue on his left side. You can see how he has trouble moving the right half of his body."

"Yes."

"A lot of people let one ailing part make them totally immobile. But Pete keeps moving the rest of him—as difficult as moving is. And his physical therapist is amazing. She wants him to make an effort to do stuff with his right hand. He really believes that he will restore what doesn't work yet."

"Such a way of living altogether."

"But that's what Pete is about. You know I was crazy about him before—"

"Yeah . . ." Annie smiles. "That came through. Even when I was a kid. My mother—"

"But now I'm absolutely awed by him."

"—would talk about the two of you. A great love, she called it."

Aunt Stormy closes her eyes. "What else did she say?"

"She told me about your full moon dates. How you celebrate."

"We still do that . . . even with Pete ill. He's not ready for the kayaks yet, but we drive to the lighthouse—"

"With champagne and cake."

"Yes, and each time we come back with adventure stories. Even when there are no adventures, we find stories in . . . little things, in the way the moon slants across the water . . . the arc of a bird's flight."

IN THE FALL, the upstairs bedroom is closing in on them with various fabrics that clients have returned. Curtains and tablecloths and bedsheets float from the ceiling. Opal likes chasing Annie through those layers and layers, flimsy-warm, some solid, some gauzy, till Annie lets herself be caught.

"Wait till next summer," Aunt Stormy tells them. "Then the walls and shelves will be bare again."

Next summer . . . Annie can't imagine being anywhere else but here with Opal. Three afternoons a week she takes Pete to speech therapy. Afterward, they pick Opal up from school. Opal loves it when Pete is in the car, is more talkative with him than with Annie. At the end of his driveway, she gets out and picks Montauk daisies. Lets Pete, then Annie, sniff her hands. Not flowery. But of earth. A bit like camomile, but stronger. A scent that stands for the beginning of fall, of days shorter, of the certainty or promise of decay. *TIHII.*

Mason

"—we felt so close to each other. Look at me, Annie."

You didn't. Wouldn't.

"Think about Opal. Think about what's good with us."

But you were shaking your head.

"Please—look at me. Do you think this jealousy is easy for me?"

You laughed. You did.

"You don't get it," I said. Just as you didn't get it how it hurt me when you and Jake held hands at his eighth birthday party, something you and I hadn't done yet. That's why I took your present for him, a sketchbook, scratched through the first page with a sharp crayon scribble.

"Oh, I get it all right," you said.

"We will always be married."

"No, Mason."

"If you believe in unconditional love—"

"Love has nothing to do with—"

"What about Opal?"

"She is my sister."

"Opal is our daughter."

"Legally, she is my sister."

"You have thought this out. Opal is yours? The house is yours? I have no rights? Nothing?"

"Do you have any understanding of what happened in the sauna?"

"I love Opal."

"I know that. And I'll make sure you'll be in her life."

"Think about her."

"I do."

"I don't want to live then."

"Don't say that, Mason."

"You don't want the marriage—I don't want my life."

"That again? You can't hold me hostage with—"

"It's your choice."

"Oh no. My choice is leaving."

"And what do you want from me? To tell you: It's all right, Annie? Go? Go and have your life away from me? Well, it's not that fucking easy."

"I'm not doing this to hurt you."

"Just think how much more damage you'd do if you set out to hurt me."

"Blackmailing me with suicide won't keep me in—"

"I am not blackmailing you or wanting some game. I am stating a fact."

"Go ahead then." Your face got so pale that the freckles were like pencil dots.

My belly was ice.

"You know I didn't mean that, Mason." You turned up the collar of your robe as if to hide yourself from me altogether. "But would you really want me to stay because you're threatening me with suicide?"

"I want you any way I can get you."

"Well, you blew that."

"I'm sorry. All right? Christ, you don't believe me, do you?"

"I don't know what to believe from you."

"You were part of it too in the sauna."

"That's why I want out."

"It was just words till you touched Jake. You liked—"

"Yes, and that's the worst thing I have done," you said. "The second worst thing is—"

SEVEN

Stormy

{ *Tribe of the Barefoot Women* }

November, and I'm walking in the flat wash of the bay, jeans rolled to my knees. Outside I'm fifty-five, but inside I'm my true age—twelve. The age I yearned for when I was a child in Germany. The age that has settled itself within me. Waves nudge my calves, chase me toward the foam and pebbles, that ever-shifting border between wet sand and dry sand, till—once again—I run into the bay. Only a few people are on the beach, people with shoes and socks and scarves and gloves. When they see me, they pull their coats tighter.

My feet are warming the sea. When I walk here alone, I often imagine women who have walked here before me and whose bare feet have warmed the bay so that, even in November or January, fish that would have left for milder waters are still here, attracting birds that, in other parts of the region, have migrated.

I think of them as the tribe of barefoot women. The tribe started with the whalers' wives and sisters once they came into their middle years and met on this strip of sand, never a planned meeting, always by chance. They'd recognize one another because their feet would be bare as they'd stride along the ocean in winter. While some women dread the sudden heat in their bodies, the barefoot women return that heat to the sea and absorb from the sea great sources of health that make them more limber with each day they age, more vigorous. It's the kind of health for which they'd have to visit one of the old spas in Europe, like Karlovy Vary in Bohemia, where kings and poets once drank from the hot sulfur springs or bathed in the healing waters.

Annie waves to me from a distance, comes running toward me, hair flying, one red wimple. From this far away, she could be Lotte. Even when Annie was a toddler, Lotte and I could see the boys' competition for her—Mason mercurial, Jake steadfast—and how Annie dazzled them both.

Hell—I miss Lotte. Even more so when I'm with her daughters and feel I'm getting to know her at ages long before I met her. I see her in earlier incarnations, at the age of Opal. It was different when Annie was a child, because then Lotte was still alive, changing with each day.

I WAIT for Annie. Against my face: mist, dense and slick. Around my calves: the froth of the bay.

She glances at my feet, shakes her head, but then takes off her shoes.

"You're not old enough for this, Annie."

She gives me that look from the side.

"I'm serious."

"I don't mind cold water." But the instant a thin wave licks her feet, she yelps. Still, she walks alongside me into the wind, resolutely, her long legs taking larger strides than mine.

"I didn't even ask you," she suddenly says. "Would you rather walk alone?"

"Oh no. I've had my walk alone."

"Mason hangs in me, with me . . ."

I don't want to scare her away with questions. Though I have so many. Questions and the memory of one day when I loved Mason. One day in September when he and Annie were sixteen and the ocean was at its best and all the lifeguards were gone for the season and a young woman walked into the water.

Legs like tree stumps. Her huge swimsuit a meadow above: red and blue flowers on green stretch. From the back, she was a solid rectangle, the only light coming through between her calves and heels, a small upside-down V-shape of light. She whooped with delight as the first wave hit her, glided in like a sea creature returning to her habitat, weightless as her body crested the waves. "Beautiful," Mason said. As she swam out, body rising and falling with the waves, she was agile and brave, a young woman the size of three. But when she swam back in and tried to get out, the surf tossed her onto the sand, massive breasts half-spilling from that meadow stretch of suit. Not strong enough to hoist that weight of herself, she was sucked out into the ocean and scrambled by the next wave. On all fours, she crawled toward shore as if she'd suddenly turned into an ancient woman. Such terror on her face. That's when Mason leapt up and ran toward her, reached her just as another wave pulled her away. He stayed with her, brought her in. Holding on to both of her hands, he helped her to upright herself. And when he walked her to her blanket, talking with her, I felt safe in the world. "You're one of the good ones, Mason," I told him.

"I WANT TO be . . . rid of Mason," Annie says.

I nod. Let her come to me.

"The roads are too icy for walking," she says. "The only safe place to walk is the beach, where the tides have taken out the ice."

"True."

The sky holds a thousand shades of gray. The sand is as cold as the air, but the water is milder. People we encounter are bundled fingertip to toe and stay above the high-tide line. They have no idea how balmy the bay is in November. But small children can feel the breath of the waves on their faces, want to run in and play.

"I want him in a place where—where he'll have to answer the question he used to push at me." She glances toward the shoes she's left above the high-tide line.

"You can still get your shoes."

"I don't need them."

I take her hand into mine. "Your fingers are cold."

"The worst thing I've done is not keeping him alive."

"Oh, Annie. No. None of us could have kept him alive."

"You don't—"

"Only he could do that."

"You don't understand."

The three of them like a basket of puppies. One playful jumble. Not knowing when to climb out on their own. Staying in far too long.

"I should have stopped him," she says.

"Maybe you're not that powerful."

She looks at me, stunned.

"I certainly am not powerful enough to make someone choose death or life. Mason made that choice. For himself. He was the only one who *could* make that choice, Annie. No matter what happened before. No matter if you had the biggest fight ever."

"How do I get out of this then?" she asks. "Of feeling like this?"

"You're doing it."

"No, I'm not."

"Walking . . . taking care of Opal . . . working . . . talking . . ."

"But it doesn't stop. I can't stop it."

"It'll never stop altogether."

"He's still at me."

"It'll be less with each day."

"Doesn't feel like it."

"Not yet."

She picks up a clump of seaweed and slipper snails whose shells—hues of gray and pink—form a quarter circle where they're joined, stacked.

"I haven't known anyone who can pull them apart," I tell her.

Carefully, she tugs. "I don't really want to pull them apart."

"They all start out as males, and they can turn female, but can't turn back. If there aren't enough females, some males in the middle will change gender."

"Amazing. How do they get nourishment?"

"They shift apart a bit—"

"Not now."

"No, when they're less . . . observed, I guess. Then they let in some nourishment and close again."

I LIKE being old enough to walk with the tribe of the barefoot women. At fifty-five, the tides of fire no longer embarrass me as they did when I was thirteen and my body outpaced its memories of itself—playful stubborn shy bookish innocent—and confused me. Not unlike today's heat that leaves my skin red-hot. Except then the sensation was so different, contrary and puzzling, something to fight or give myself to, completely.

I believed I was the only girl with this mortifying heat that could seize me any moment. Like when I looked at some boy. Was the heat evidence that I was attracted? Even if I didn't feel attracted? Only red-hot-clumsy. Was that how attraction felt? Against all reason, all will? Did I have to distrust my body because it might betray me?

AHEAD OF US, stuck into the sand, are sculptures of dry phragmites and narrow bits of shell, delicate and sure to wash out.

"I wish I could take one for my garden."

"They belong here," Annie says firmly.

I let go of her hand. Crouch in front of the sculptures, each different in how the phragmites and the shells are joined. Next to them is a crushed beer can.

"They belong here," she repeats. "For whatever purpose the person who created them intended."

"I'm not taking anything from anyone."

"What if they are a signal—"

"The next high tide will get them anyhow."

"—or a message to someone?"

"Then the recipient of that message better hurry." *I should have let her take her own walk.* Raising the empty beer can as if in a toast, I ask Annie, "Any objection to me taking that for recycling?"

"It probably belongs to someone who passed by later, not to the person who made this."

Seagulls blend into the grays of the sky, are outlined by lighter shades of gray as they move from one into the other.

AS THE heavy brown sand sucks itself around my feet and collects their shapes, I continue along the sea, forever twelve—twelve at any age I have lived since; any age I will reach. Collecting. Retaining. Becoming.

Wanting what's authentic, exquisite. The taste of salt on my lips. The shimmer of light as it soaks through the haze. The grains of sand I will rub from between my toes before I sit on my bed and tell Pete about my walk. He used to run on this beach. But the stroke has shrunk him, made him frail, and he's fighting to reclaim his body with such grit that I love him even more.

I've told him I want to marry him.

"Why . . . now?"

I couldn't tell him: *"Because you need me more."* I said, "Do it for me. Make me an honest woman."

"You . . . are an . . . extremely . . . honest woman."

"All right then. I'm at the right age to be married."

He smiled. "Why?"

"I'd worry less. About you. If we were married."

"But . . . it's so . . . good with us . . . because we . . . don't have . . . marriage."

Annie has told me he inspires her work. She's awed by the way he gets up, slowly, emerging into his body, trembling, his fingers touching the floor, walking themselves toward his feet, his weight on one finger, then another, trembling, each movement taken apart into a thousand components as his body invents the sequence of movements the way an infant does. Invents. And repeats. And remembers. Easier the next time because memory kindles invention. Not declining as he might have. A choice. And his joy then when he shows us he's doing one more thing than the day before.

"Listen," Annie says.

And I listen. To this wave, now, flooding the bank of pebbles. As it recedes, a murmur rises from those pebbles.

"Hear that?" Annie smiles.

"Oh yes."

We listen. Wait. Because the murmur does not happen with each wave. Only when the next wave won't rush in to merge with the receding wave. For this murmur to occur, there has to be that lull between moments, that lull of being one with all that surrounds us, before the pebbles once more stir against one another.

WHILE ANNIE takes Pete for his blood test, Opal and I fry up the fluke I had in the freezer from when Pete and I went fishing the week before his stroke.

Opal dips the fillets in flour. "What does fluke taste like?"

"Almost like flounder, tender and flaky. Your mother used to say they tasted buttery . . . that butter was part of their natural flavor. I'd fry them up for us after she gutted them. The man who rented us the boat showed us how to. We remembered him year to year, but I don't think he remembered us. You should have seen Lotte row. Like an arrow . . ."

Eager for another picture of her mother, Opal leans forward. I think she gets her pictures from different stories, so that Lotte's image is added to and revised, coming together to look like some cross between Annie and me, perhaps, changing whenever Opal envisions her.

I can see Lotte too, in the boat, and I'm there, with her. "No clunking from side to side, the way I rowed. That's why she'd do the rowing. Once we rented the *Big Bertha*—"

"Who's that?"

"It's the name of a boat with an outboard motor. Luckily, it had oars too, because the motor wouldn't start when we were ready to turn back, and Lotte rowed us."

"I need more flour."

"After that, we didn't bother with motors. We loved to fish. When we were still au pairs—"

"What kind of pears?"

"*Au pairs.* It's like nannies. That's how Lotte and I met."

"Not in Germany?"

"We didn't know each other in Germany. Not until we came to America and worked as nannies in the same neighborhood. In Southampton. During the off-season, we used to go to Montauk and rent the cheapest little cottage we could find. We'd buy squid for bait and keep it in the refrigerator until Lotte sliced them up."

Opal grimaces.

"Me too." I laugh. "They were slimy all right, and I'd go outside while she'd cut them up and the black oozed out."

"Like ink?"

"Like ink mixed with gray water. We'd go to a marina on East Lake Drive where we could rent fishing poles and boats by the half day. We had to stay in the harbor, and Lotte would row us about a thousand feet offshore and toss the anchor over the side. We'd fish for fluke."

"What do fluke look like before they're—" She raises a flour-dusted fillet. "—like this?"

"Flat and almost round. Brownish-gray, with eyes on top."

"On top?"

"On top. Their underside is white and soft because they lie in the sand. They're bottom fish. Your mother . . . she'd get so excited when she caught one." *I see us in the boat, wearing shorts and sweatshirts. Lotte dips her fingers into the slime, hooks two pieces of squid. One for my fishing pole, one for hers. Then she bends across the side of the boat and rinses her hands in the salt water.*

"Sometimes we pulled up other fish," I tell Opal. "Lion fish—I don't know if it was their regular name—only that they were ugly. We threw them back in."

I don't tell her how sorry I felt for the fish because the hooks would be through the sides of their mouths. Or how Lotte would pull out the hooks and toss the fish on the bottom of the boat, where they flopped around. I'd keep my feet away from them. Tried not to see their lips all cut open. One fish had swallowed the hook down into its stomach somewhere, and when Lotte tugged at it, the insides of the fish came out of its mouth, still attached to the hook.

But I can tell Opal this: "Your mother would do the messy work, not just the bait but also getting fish off the hooks and cleaning them. I was squeamish. I thought your mother was tough, but when I told her, she got mad at me and said I didn't know how hard it was for her.

"I fried up fluke the day your parents fell in love," I tell Opal. "That's how your mother got your father—with my cooking. Lotte invited Phillip for dinner, and we pretended that she was doing the cooking."

"Why?"

"She wasn't a confident cook. While I enjoyed it. We made Phillip stay in the living room, and then we'd run to and from the kitchen."

Opal laughed.

"I told him I was helping Lotte. When I was done cooking, I went out to a movie, and she carried the food to the table."

I only tell Opal about the dinner part, of course. Not how Phillip and Lotte made love on my couch and left a stain that Lotte couldn't get out. When she confessed how she'd ruined my couch, I was far more interested in what making love was like, because neither one of us had done it till then. Still, I accepted her offer to trade: her table for my couch.

• • •

It's Make Love, not War, Stupid.

We Need a Regime Change.

Listen to the World, George.

All around us, signs bob in the wind. It's freezing, and we're wearing triple layers of clothing. But it's exhilarating to be in New York for the protest, even if the city has barricaded the side streets. To reach the stage on First, where the speeches are held, we have to head north into the sixties and come down First from the north.

Grim-faced police. Everywhere.

Our crowd is moving as slowly as the line for the women's room at a matinee.

"Pete could keep up with this," I tell Annie.

"But the crowds would jostle him."

"You're right. Better for him and Opal to look after each other today."

"The police look terrified." Annie waves to several of them. "Is this where you have the coffee for the protesters?"

She gets them to laugh. To see us as individuals, perhaps—not a crowd of faceless enemies.

Annie and I wear our posters on string around our necks, covering the fronts of our coats. Annie's: **War is Terrorism.** Mine: **Early Dissent is essential for democracy.**

Yesterday, when I made my poster, it took me hours to settle on this slogan, and it still doesn't express what I believe, that if my parents and teachers and their generation had spoken out against Hitler's regime—from the beginning—they would have stemmed the escalation of violence that led to Holocaust.

Way too long. Too formal. Like something that needs footnotes. Better to have just a few words in big letters that people can see all at once.

I wish I could talk with Lotte about how riskly dissent has become. Ever since 9/11, patriotism has been edging toward nationalism. Two of my friends from the vigil are being audited. Some protestors are detained at airports long enough to miss their flights. There are days I feel afraid of speaking out. *That's why I must speak out, Lotte.*

I wish I could tell her about the flags that came up almost as quickly as the Trade Center came down; about the grieving that brought all of us, much of the world even, closer in the days following 9/11, until Bush twisted our grieving to go after oil.

Most of all I wish I could talk to Lotte about her daughters, who've been coming at me with their mother-longing. After Lotte's death, Annie was the one with the questions, wanting to have me fill in what she didn't know about her mother. And now the little one. I'm not enough for them. Can't be enough for them. Because I'm not Lotte.

Some days I search their faces for Lotte. Radiant and gutsy and lovely. Feel Lotte's skin against my fingers when I lift Annie's hair from her eyes, or when do I a tick search on Opal after she plays outside. Her sudden switches from bliss to rage worry Annie, but I've seen Lotte like that, have seen that mercurial side of hers. Like at that concert, held at a Masonic lodge. We were curious, left our seats to go exploring, whispering and laughing. In a dim upstairs hallway, a guard stepped into our way. Before he could say anything, Lotte demanded, "Where is the women's washroom? We're missing the concert looking for a washroom." *Lotte. Showing off*. Like Opal. Who can't balance her rage and bliss the way Lotte could.

Annie used to be gutsy like Lotte, but she no longer trusts herself to be gutsy. I see the change in how she acts with Opal, out of fear that she'll lose her too.

"How many, do you think, on this block?" Annie asks.

"Fifty thousand, easily . . ."

"No. Closer to a hundred thousand."

"And all these other blocks filled with people."

"Look at that—" She motions to a banner ahead of us. **Somewhere in Texas a Village is Missing its Idiot.**

"Mason would have come up with something like that. In comparison ours are wimpy." *Damn.* I've been so careful not to mention him unless Annie does.

She tries to smile but looks stricken. As if remembering his death all over.

"I'm sorry, Annie."

"You're right. In comparison, ours are wimpy."

"Nothing wimpy about peace."

She's looking around as if expecting someone. Or avoiding someone? Maybe for one of the people who came in on the peace train with us, more than thirty people from the peace vigil, starting early in Southampton, adding protesters at stations along the way. When we arrived at Penn Station, our group had over two hundred, and we tried to stay together as we headed east, all along merging with additional groups that thickened into one tide of protest on Sixth Avenue, where we marched north, then east once again, in this city that wouldn't grant us the permit for a march.

By now, we've become separated from everyone we started out with, except Bill from Amnesty International, whose poster, **Shame on You, George,** we recognize far ahead of us. The energy of the protesters is incredible. Envelops us so we don't need to be with people we already know. There are no strangers here.

Annie turns up her collar. "Bet you twenty dollars that Mason would have put something outrageous on his sign."

I play along. "Thirty dollars."

"Better be careful if you start betting against me. It could get expensive. Mason lost thousands to me."

"That's not all he lost." *Damn.* "What a stupid thing to say. It's not even what I believe. Did your mother ever tell you that I can be quite tactless?"

"Yes," Annie says and covers her mouth.

"Extremely tactless?"

"Brusque. That's the word she used for you."

"I thought eventually I'd learn to not be . . . brusque, but so far it hasn't happened."

"But she liked that about you."

"Really now?" I smile. "Brusque, huh?"

"Look at that." Annie points out a sign: **Let's Bomb Texas—They Have Oil Too.**

"So far my favorite slogan was on the T-shirt of that large-breasted woman: **Weapons of Mass Seduction.**"

"I liked that one too."

"What else did Lotte say about me?"

"That you're direct . . . rigorously truthful."

"Also called tactless. I don't mean to be."

"I want to get used to hearing or saying . . . Mason's name without crashing." There's something else beneath her words, wanting to push itself out.

I tell her, "Nothing you have thought or done will ever shock me."

She blinks, raises one hand to her throat, and for an instant it seems that she's weighing telling against not telling, and that telling is winning out. But all at once, protesters are pushing toward us, against the surge of our crowd. Coming back already?

"What happened?" Voices. From different directions.

"They've blocked Second."

One voice. High. "Whose streets?"

"Our streets," others chant.

"Whose streets?"

"Our streets!"

Standing on her toes, Annie is searching the crowd.

"Waiting for someone, Annie?"

"Not really . . . except for Jake . . . Maybe."

I'm intrigued, of course.

Behind her, three people are dressed in duct tape, with duct tape across their mouths. **Say No to Duct Tape.**

"WHOSE STREETS?"

"Our streets!"

"What happened?" I ask a young man as he presses toward us.

"It's closed. Up ahead. Those fuckers— Oops, I'm sorry, madam."

"Well, I'm fucking shocked that you'd use that kind of fucking language."

He laughs aloud. Raises his poster. **Bush is a Fucking Idiot.**

"Don't go back," a woman shouts.

"I'm not even sure Jake is here," Annie says. "And if so, that he'll find us."

Quite a buffer. A hundred thousand people to keep Jake apart from her.

But all I say is, "Where did you tell him to meet you?"

"We left it open."

Suddenly, I'm separated from her.

The mass of bodies closes around me.

King George Rules Through Fear.

I Don't Want Him Speaking on My Behalf.

"Annie!"

"Whose streets?"

A roar: "Our streets!"

"Don't go back now!"

"We'll get through!"

A hand grabs mine. Annie. "Hold on."

I hold on.

"Whose streets?"

"Our streets!" Louder yet, breaking through the chant.

All these different groups, bonding, the young and old, the radicals and the religious . . .

"Let's go back and head north on Third," Annie suggests. "And then see if we can make it over to First."

But I pull her forward. "Whose streets?" I shout.

"Our streets!" A scream now.

"Whose streets?"

"Our streets!" Annie and I join in the roar as we approach the barricade.

A woman gets past the string of uniforms by showing an ID. Then two men. A young couple.

"They must live in that neighborhood," Annie says.

I swing my protest sign to my back. "Do what I'm doing. I'll explain later." Slowly, I walk toward a young policeman with a great black mustache.

Annie snags my elbow. "Don't—"

I tuck her hand under my elbow so that it supports me. "Sir?"

His fingers stray to his mustache. "You cannot get through here." Long eyelids. Bony temples. I imagine him good with sex, a modest man who astounds himself and others.

"My mother— I have to get to my mother."

"I can't let you through, madam, unless you have identification that you live here."

What is it with this madam shit?

"My mother is in a wheelchair." This from me? I've always been superstitious about lying and still believe that you make true what you lied about. "My mother lives over there . . ."

"What's your mother's address?"

I scan the street signs behind him. Near water, I have an intuitive compass, but in the city, I set off in the wrong direction. "Corner of Second and Fifty-seventh, Officer. We have to get to her."

He studies me. His features are so mobile, a mirror to his thinking, and his fingers are on his mustache again. Those beautiful long eyelids. A swell of lust comes at me, so fierce, I want to get him into a doorway. But I remind myself to look distraught and so wobbly that he'll have to envision my mother as a very old woman in a very old wheelchair. Given how I need Annie's arm to stand at all, any mother of mine would have to be close to a century old.

When he waves us forward through a gap in the barricade, Annie hesitates, but then she runs after me. "You'll get us arrested," she hisses.

"I would do anything to see my mother in a wheelchair."

"You told me your mother died when you were in your twenties."

"So I'm resurrecting her."

"Jesus Christ."

"A wheelchair is better than the grave, Annabelle."

WE STRIDE across Second Avenue and avoid a pile of horse droppings with a poster stuck into the middle: **Bushit.** All at once I feel watched. I turn. Search. No.

"Where are you taking me now?" Annie says.

"I still want to get us to the stage area."

BigC is meeting us by the stage, where she's supposed to connect with six women from Ohio who'll sleep at her apartment overnight. At the last vigil in Sag Harbor, she invited Annie and me to stay with her after the protest. When we told her we'd need to get back to Opal and Pete, BigC e-mailed a peace group that's coordinating sleeping places for out-of-town protesters. I wonder how she'll find them.

"We'll never get through," Annie says.

"Don't worry. My mother will get us through."

"You told me she never left Germany."

"I feel really close to her today." I slow my steps, make them unsteady as we approach another barricade.

"Please, don't."

"Your mother wouldn't have hesitated for one moment. Did you know that she never paid for a speeding ticket in her life? One time, in Southampton, we got stopped, and she told the officer she was so glad he'd come along. Asked him, 'How do I get to the other end of town and to the highway? I've tried five times now, and I'm totally lost because this road always spits me out here.' He gave her directions, delighted to be helpful. When Lotte and I did our cross-country drive—"

"Ladies—" An officer holds up her hand. Large nose, expressive eyes. "You have to go back, ladies."

"I understand, Officer. But my mother lives two blocks down from here. She's in a wheelchair and—"

"I cannot let you through."

"—and the nurse is leaving at one-thirty"—I rev up my accent. Usually it's faint, but I can do just-off-the-boat—"and we have to get there before she—"

"Go, go." The officer waves me through. "Not you," she tells Annie.

"Oh!" I make my voice quivery. "But that's my daughter. Annie? Annie, dear, I need you to lift your grandmother from—"

"Go." The officer opens the gap for Annie. Doubt in her eyes. Doubt and the fear of a lawsuit.

When we're far enough away, Annie says, "What about your cross-country drive?"

"Lotte was speeding, and a cop car followed us. When she stopped and the cop came to our car, she said she was only speeding because she'd started menstruating—"

"Oh no—"

"—and didn't have any sanitary pads and was trying to get to a drugstore so she could keep from soaking through the seat and—"

Annie is laughing. "Poor man."

"I still remember him backing away from our car."

"He probably posted it on the bulletin board at the station under 'Excuses we haven't heard yet.' " Annie links her arm through mine. "Mason would have enjoyed getting past the police."

AHEAD OF US, a man and a woman walk with their feet turned outward, so that the feet in the middle—her left, his right—seem about to trip each other, or trip anyone who might try to pass them. But we manage to get ahead of them and turn to read their signs.

Make Out—Not War.

Hail to the Chief. Except the **H** of **Hail** is crossed out and changed to *J*. And the **C** in **Chief** to **T,** so that the sign reads: **Jail to the Thief.**

"Great," I tell them.

"All these months with you—" Annie falters.

"Yes?"

"—have been incredibly . . . peaceful after all that with Mason. I like how our day-to-day life is."

"It's good for Pete and me too, having you and Opal with us."

"Even here at the protest, I feel peaceful. In some bizarre way."

The next barricade is defended by an officer who has the expression of someone who's not brainy but very quick.

I squeeze Annie's arm. Tilt into her. Point past the barricade. But the officer is already shaking her head.

Gently, I ask in my just-off-the-boat accent, "Would you please hear my reason before you shake your head?"

The officer shrugs.

"My *Mutter* . . . mother is in a wheelchair. My *Mutter* needs around-the-clock care. Her morning nurse left. Half an hour ago. If we don't get to my *Mutter* very soon—" That quivering voice . . . I got it right. Also the closing of my throat.

"Mother, please." Annie braces my arm. "Officer—" She takes a long breath. "Her mother, my grandmother, is very old, ninety-seven, and she has severe health problems. She doesn't speak English . . . so even in terms of using the telephone . . . she's helpless. We were supposed to be there an hour ago, but it's been impossible to get through, as you know."

"What's your grandmother's address?"

"Sutton Place," I blurt.

"Sutton Place and Fifty-third," Annie modifies.

"I'm so proud of you," I tell her when we're past the barricade. "The toughest one so far."

"I'm getting into this."

"I like you spunky."

Annie flips my protest sign to the front. Adjusts hers. "She'll come after us and arrest us if she sees that we're part of the protest."

"I don't see any contradiction. We were part of the protest for a while, and now we have to take care of my mother. That officer doesn't want to be responsible for the death of an old woman in a wheelchair."

"You're the one who told me if you use illness or a broken-down car or whatever as an excuse, it'll happen."

"And I believe that."

"Then what's . . . this?"

"Wouldn't it be wonderful if my lie brought my mother back from the dead?" I'm struck by sudden, incredible happiness.

"I can just see you and an older version of you . . . in the apartment that will always be a few blocks from here."

ON THE peace train back to Southampton, I have a sudden longing to hear Pete's voice. It's almost physical, that longing. I picture him walking up the steps to my cottage, slow slow, but no longer with a cane, his body as erect as he can make it, knocking at my door. But though the door opens, I can't see his face. I can't even remember it.

When we reach North Sea, the lights are on, and he's sitting at the table, reading the *Times*. Opal is sleeping on the pile of carpets, one fist around her plastic boy doll.

I step behind him. Hold him hard. "I missed you."

He tilts up his face. His dear, familiar face. Kisses me.

"How was Opal?" Annie asks.

"Sophisticated . . . and . . . delightful . . ."

"Thank you so much for looking after her."

"Is that . . . what I was . . . doing? We . . . both thought . . . Opal . . . was looking . . . after me . . ."

When Pete stands up, one pant leg is higher than the other, and in that heartbreaking moment his bare, veined ankle reminds me once again how frail he is. And yet, what we are to each other—lovers, best friends—is sweet and intriguing. Soon, we'll lie together for another night, skin warmed by each other, and perhaps he'll tell me again that I've become too tender with him. *So many ways of making love.*

I link my fingers through Pete's. Ask Annie: "You want to let Opal sleep where she is?"

"If I carry her upstairs now, I'll only wake her. I don't want her to be scared . . . waking up in a different place than she's used to."

Pete presses his thumb against my palm. "We'll hear . . . Opal from our . . . bedroom."

Mason

"—that I would have liked it even more if you hadn't been there."

I felt like crying—stupid—and I did what I usually do, forced it away. I said, "It showed."

"I bet."

"You always liked him best. Even when we were kids. I'm sorry. I didn't mean to say that."

"We're both saying things we don't—"

"It's just that I had to know what it would be like for you and him . . . and I thought that once I knew, we'd get beyond this and—"

You shook your head.

"I want you to look at me again the way you did when we ran into the waves with all our clothes on. Remember how alarmed Opal was? Told us she didn't want us to be nutty. But then she ran in and splashed us. Oh, Annie, we both did the worst we're capable of. Knowing that will make us better together."

"No."

"I mean it, Annie. I'm going to . . . end it."

"How then will you do it? How?"

"I know exactly how. And once you know, it'll be done."

"I don't want to listen to this."

"Are you trying to rush me, Annie?"

"This is crazy stuff."

"Are you trying to have me do it tonight? Because once I do, you and Jake will never be able to be together."

"Crazy stuff."

"I have never felt this sane."

"That says a lot about your sanity."

"So clever. So very, very clever you are."

"Mason— You need to see someone, a shrink . . . a doctor—"

"Hey, don't you worry."

"You can't threaten something like that and then tell me not to worry."

"You'd really do that for me, Annabelle? Worry?"

"This is one of your uglier games . . . and I'm not playing."

"Oh, but you are. And I'll tell you what scares—"

EIGHT

Opal

{ *Rescue* }

In the morning, snow flurries. More and bigger till it's a blizzard by noon.

Aunt Stormy slips her bare feet into her fuzzy boots and goes for the Sunday *Times*. But her red truck gets stuck in the driveway.

Annie and I help her dig it out.

"Are your legs hurting too?" Aunt Stormy asks Annie.

"You bet. I feel I walked all day yesterday in someone else's hip sockets."

"Must be my hip sockets."

I explain to them, "People cannot walk in other people's hip sockets."

"Well, I think Annie wore mine out at the protest."

I roll my eyes.

WHEN AUNT Stormy returns with the paper, Annie and I build a fire. Pete is fidgety. Walking around. Bumping into things.

"Sit with me," Aunt Stormy tells him as she tugs blankets and rugs in front of our fire.

Pete heads toward the French doors. His elbow hits Annie's easel.

Quickly, I move it aside so he won't knock it over. "What are you doing, Pete?"

"Nothing." He looks so sad.

I try to cheer him up. "Hey, Pete, look at the ducks out there on the ice."

He brings his face against a little windowpane, four rows above where I'm looking out.

"What if they get their butt feathers stuck on the ice, Pete?"

He smiles. "Jesus ducks . . . walking . . . on frozen . . . water."

"Holy ducks." Annie says it like she would say *Holy shit.*

"Why am I not surprised?" Aunt Stormy sounds mad. "Once again, a miscount. The *Times* reports only one hundred thousand protesters."

"There were a million of us," Annie says.

"At least a million."

Annie pokes at the logs, makes the fire big. "Now it feels like New Hampshire, Opal."

"No."

"Not even with the snow blowing?"

"It is *not* like New Hampshire."

"But you like being snowed in."

"Not so." I cross my arms. Put my chin down so Annie can't see my face.

"Wait till . . . spring . . . Opal."

"Why, Pete?"

"Then . . . we'll have . . . dozens . . . of baby ducks."

"I don't know if I'll still be here."

"The ducks . . . will be here."

"Okay."

"You . . . can visit . . ."

My toes start hurting. "Mason isn't here to see the baby ducks—"

Mason. When he gets mad at Annie, he doesn't talk with her. Never ever. Only with me. Talks with me more than ever and in front of Annie. So Annie can hear and know what she's missing. *So there.*

Like when I was five or maybe already six and Mason told me, "Your sister locked me out of my car today."

"I let you into our car," Annie said quickly. "The end."

"He isn't talking to you, Annie," I said.

"That never stops *her*," Mason said.

"Are you having a fight?" I asked them.

"Of course we're having a fight." Mason, all mad. "Wouldn't you if someone locked you out of your car and left you standing by the side of the road and laughed at you through the window?"

"I did not leave you standing by the side of the road," Annie told Mason.

"Then what do you call it? I was standing out there, by the side of the road. You were sitting inside my car."

"Our car. And what I mean is that I did not move our car."

"Your sister locked me out, Opal," he told me.

"It was supposed to be funny," Annie told him.

"Do you see me laughing, Opal?"

"But you— You decided to go nuts and picked up a rock and—"

"Do *you* think it is funny to lock someone out, Opal?"

"Do not pull her in like that," Annie said. "Please. If you want to fight, do it directly with me. Not in this . . . roundabout way."

ROUNDABOUT *round . . . roundabout round . . .*

My toes are hurting worse.

I tell Pete, "Jake isn't here to see the baby ducks."

Pete turns his head slow-speed to me.

"Everyone's not here. Or dead! Except for Annie."

"You have two in me." She kneels next to me. "Remember? We talked about that? How I'm your mother and sister?"

"And when you die, both of you are gone."

"I'm here."

"One person dying can make two disappear. So that would be the worst of all. And then I don't want to be alive at—"

Annie goes ballistic. "You're not going to pull that on me."

"But—"

"You hear that?" Annie looks big and angry. Scared too. "You're not going to pull that on me."

Aunt Stormy says, "I don't think that's what Opal means."

"My daughter tells me she doesn't want to be alive. That's pretty destructive."

I snatch the boy doll.

Run upstairs.

Throw myself on the floor.

Punch the floor till my toes don't hurt.

Then I kick the floor so they can hear me and be sorry.

But no one comes running.

I HOLD the boy doll by his shoes. "Poor baby."

I bang his head against the floor. His shoes don't come off. Nothing comes off. Except two specks of black paint from his hair.

"Poor baby."

His shiny-stiff head sounds like someone knocking on the floor.

I turn myself into a snake and slither to the top of the steps.

"You want me to go to her, Annie?" Aunt Stormy's voice.

"She needs to kick and pound to get it out of her body."

I do some more knocking and kicking. *So there.*

"It's not that Opal wants to hurt herself," Aunt Stormy says. "Rather that after knowing a world without her birth parents and now without Mason, she can imagine herself not being in that world."

"I can't do this again. Those threats . . . those tantrums . . . Not after Mason."

"You're so good with her." Aunt Stormy again.

"I'm a mess with her."

"You're a wonderful mother to her."

Annie bawls.

"I thought you knew that."

Annie. Snot bubbles and all, I bet. Saying, "Mason . . . he was much better with her."

"Up and down," Aunt Stormy says. "Like a man on a ladder—"

Man on a ladder? Mason? Up and down. With me? Mason—

"You listen to me, Annie. From the day you got her, you were the steady one."

"Theatrical . . . what Opal . . . learned . . . from Mason . . ."

Bawling, Annie is. Bawling snot.

"Pete noticed how theatrical Opal was when she was just a toddler. And how Mason cheered her on. Both of them—they love upheaval. Look at how he—"

"None of . . . that . . . now."

"All I'm saying, Pete, is that's where Mason and Opal are alike. They take that upheaval inside themselves, leave the rest of us to clean up. It's safe for her to attack you, Annie. Because she knows you won't go away." A long, long breath from Aunt Stormy. "That's certainly more than I intended to say."

"Opal . . . is listening."

Whispering.

Steps.

More than one person.

I SLITHER back to the boy doll. "Shut up."

But the steps don't come up the stairs.

"I'll rescue you," I promise.

I get the orange rope from inside my snow boot. That's where I hide it for playing rescue. It's from the little kayak, all soft from being wet so often.

The rope is thicker than the head of the boy doll. That's why I have to tie it around his painted-on belt. With two knots. The other end of the rope I hold. Tight. Then I toss him high across the railing.

But I don't let him crash dead. I yank the orange rope back before he crashes on the stairs.

"Stupid baby."

I rock the boy doll.

"Shut up!"

Rock him side to side.

"I'll rescue you."

Toss him across the rod and rescue him. Cradle him in my arms, the tossing and the rescuing and the rocking all-in-one.

So I do it again.

Then I hide the rope for when I'll play rescue again.

"DOING BETTER this morning?" Annie, sitting on the edge of my bed.

I pull the quilt to my eyes. I can't remember how I got into bed. But I'm in my pajamas.

"No school today. You have a snow day." Annie's voice is perky. But her face is worried. "Let's go search for seals. It'll be an adventure. We'll go cross-country skiing on the beach below the Montauk Lighthouse."

"You are being perky, Annie."

She laughs.

So I make her stop laughing. "I can't do this day."

But she doesn't blink. "You'll be glad afterwards."

"I don't care about afterwards."

"I do. But we have to hurry. We got ten inches of snow."

"What if there are no prince bits, Annie?"

"Maybe the princes were lucky."

"Because they got away in time?"

"Sometimes they do. About getting away . . . that snow won't last on the beach because the tide will wash it away."

On the drive to Montauk, squirrels keep running across the road. I count nineteen. Five of them dead.

"This is so weird." Annie swerves to avoid a squirrel.

"Suicide squirrels."

She bites on her lip.

So there.

At the lighthouse, she helps me strap on my skis. Snow races across the sand, low and fast, when we ski along the beach. Annie first because she makes good tracks.

"Like white foxes," she says.

"Like small, fast animals."

"True."

"Like weasels."

"Yes."

"Or smoke. Or like the white bellies of bottom fish."

"Weasels or smoke or bottom fish."

"Bottom fish are funny-looking," I tell her. "Their bellies touch the sand. They scurry along the bottom."

"Aren't you glad we're doing this?" She gets so happy that she slips.

When she tries to get up, she laughs.

I know she wants me to laugh with her. But I don't want to. "What if the seals aren't there, Annie?"

"They're always there in the winter. And at low tide, they climb from the water and lie on the big rocks. Long and fat and shiny. Like huge wet pebbles."

"Maybe not this winter."

"Are you going to leave me sitting in the snow?" She holds out her hand.

I don't take it.

"Opal! Come on—"

"That photo isn't even true."

"What photo?"

"The naked bride photo."

"She's not naked."

"With *me* naked. It's fake."

"It's posed."

"Fake." I glare at her. Pull her inside the hurting so she'll do it for me.

"Don't be so dramatic, Opal."

"The only reason you got me is because my real parents died."

"We both miss them."

"Well—you suck as a mother!"

"And you suck as a daughter!"

We stare at each other.

I'm so scared I can't swallow.

Annie really said that?

"If our parents were alive," she says, "I would still be your sister. They were my parents too and I miss them every single day."

"I don't believe you."

"I don't give a flying—tomato."

"I know what you were going to say. Flying fuck."

"I still don't give a flying tomato."

"Brussels sprout?"

Her eyes are hollow like she's not in there anymore.

"Annie? Annie!"

Waves jab at the snow. An edge of white for a few seconds. Then sand, brown and wet.

"How about a flying Brussels sprout, Annie?"

"So I don't give a flying Brussels sprout."

"Get up!" I hold out one hand to her. "Now! Or you'll freeze your big butt."

Annie takes my hand. Scrambles up. And back into her eyes.

I slap snow from her fleece pants.

"You can ask me about our parents . . . anything you want to ask, Opal."

"I know stuff about them you don't know."

"I'm so . . . very glad for you." Annie slips her hands through the straps on the ski poles.

"From Aunt Stormy."

"I'm so glad for you both."

"Did you know that my father walked faster than anyone else?"

"Good. So let's keep moving."

We stay on the snow. On our right the water and sand. On our left sand and another edge of snow, frazzled from when the tide was high.

"My father walked twenty miles every day, Annie."

"That's a lot. Keep moving."

"My mother had a dog in Germany when she was little."

"Her family had a cocker spaniel. Brigitte. A brown and white cocker spaniel."

"You know my mother's dog?"

"From stories. But when I was little, I used to pretend Brigitte was my dog."

Annie pretends too?

Wind blows through me, but it doesn't get me cold.

"I guess you inherited me, Annie."

"We inherited each other."

"Pretty soon you'll only be my sister."

"All right with me . . . once you're eighteen."

"And then I won't need you as a mother anymore."

"I can't do this without you, Opal." Her eyes push at me.

"Do what?"

"Be a family."

It's taking forever, getting to the big rocks where the seals are supposed to be.

"You can call me your child," I tell her.

"Hallelujah and then some."

"Because I *am* a child."

"Should I be dancing?"

"And since you are taking care of me, you can say *my*. Like in *my child*."

"I'll do that."

This is real. As real as sliding one ski ahead of the other. As real as snow all around us like white foxes. Or weasels. Or the white bellies of bottom fish. As real as, suddenly, Annie singing. Singing without words, her back to me. Like wind singing. As real as those seals—

"Look look, Annie!"

"They're huge," Annie cries out.

"Like ponies."

"Yes, like ponies."

The seals' heads are like dogs' heads. Almost. But their bodies are bigger. Much bigger. And limp like sacks of potatoes. But not lumpy. Smooth like big, big slugs. They slouch across each other, those seals. Melt into one another on those rocks, crusty with shells and salt.

"Three of them there"—Annie points to the gray water—"swimming."

"Where?"

"Those big balls moving—"

"Where, Annie?"

"They're much faster in water than on land. Over there now—where the water is swirling. Each head like the top of a bowling ball."

And now I see them. "But they're darker than the water."

"Yes."

"And when they're on the rocks, they're lighter than the water."

"Because their fur is drying."

"Can you eat seal, Annie?"

"Eskimos eat seal."

"Good."

One seal pulls itself from the waves onto the largest of the rocks.

But another seal blocks its way. Roars and lifts its head so that its back curves like a banana.

When it chases the new seal off the rock, the entire clump of seals ripples.

AUNT STORMY and Pete drive to a moving sale in Noyack to look for a sewing machine and more dishes for her business. But they bring back a dog. He's for free to a good home. And he already has a name.

"Luigi . . ." Pete's voice is baby-talk. "Come and . . . meet Opal."

Luigi's eyes are almost all white. That's how he rolls them when he crawls backward. Away from us. He's only up to my knees. But the white shows the red around his eyes, makes him look nutty.

"Luigi?" I kneel down to make myself little.

His nails scratch the floor as he stuffs his butt into the corner.

If he could get away through the wall, he'd do that.

I hold out my hand. "Luigi?"

"Don't be scared, Luigi." Annie squats next to me. "Why are they giving him away?"

"They've bought an apartment in the city." Aunt Stormy spoons dog food into a dish. "We said we'll try him out. Take him home for a week so you and Opal can be part of the decision."

"I don't want to try him out. I want to rescue him," I tell her.

"We'll see. I've been thinking about getting another dog . . . after Agnes, for a while now. And I like mutts so much better than those overbred dogs."

"Mutts have . . . better . . . dispositions."

Luigi is breathing fast. In and out and in and out. The fur on his skinny sides going in and out. Like he's been running a marathon.

Aunt Stormy sets his dish down by the sink.

We all step away to let him go there and eat.

He whimpers. His fangy little teeth show. But he doesn't move. Just watches us with his white eyes.

We step away even more. Pete doesn't need to touch the wall anymore. Just walks close enough to the wall to catch himself if he has to.

Luigi comes out of the corner. A few steps.

"He's sniffing the air," I whisper.

"He's obviously hungry," Annie says.

"Luigi . . . ?" With one foot, Aunt Stormy moves the bowl toward the dog. "This is so good. Come and eat. Luigi?"

"Move it . . . closer . . . Stormy."

She does.

Luigi scurries back. Shaking and panting, he stretches his nose and neck toward the bowl. But his tail stays pressed in the corner.

"He's hungry," Annie says, "but afraid to eat."

"Let's leave him . . . alone. Out . . . we'll go out."

"Let's go into my bedroom," Aunt Stormy says.

After we close the door, there's jingling from the kitchen.

"I bet it's the name tag on his collar hitting the bowl," Annie says.

• • •

When the jingling stops, we return. Luigi's bowl is in the living room. Empty. He must have licked it all the way there.

But he's cowering in that same corner.

"Good dog," I tell him. "Good licker."

"Maybe that can be his corner for the time being," Aunt Stormy says.

The next morning we buy Luigi a bag of dog food with the picture of a puppy on it.

When I set his food dish and his water in the corner, he runs off and hides behind the velvet couch.

Twice, he comes close to the dishes, only to back off.

Suddenly I know why. "I bet those moving sale people kicked Luigi. When he was eating."

"You may be right," Aunt Stormy says.

"Because the not-eating happens when his back is turned to us. Or to the room."

"So if we put his food and water out from the wall, he can get behind them," Annie says, "and keep his back to the wall."

I take his dishes, move them away from the corner. Once again, we go into Aunt Stormy's bedroom.

The jiggling again, then.

And he is eating when we come out. Eating cautiously, eyes rolled up.

That's how he eats every day. With a clear view of everyone.

When I take him outside, he stays so close that his nose bumps against my legs.

We buy him a doggie bed. Round and stuffed with cedar chips. When he puts one paw on it, it rustles. He yelps. Runs away. Returns and circles it.

"Afraid of anything unfamiliar," Annie says. "Poor thing."

After three days Luigi starts sleeping on the doggie bed.

Aunt Stormy's favorite vet is on Shelter Island.

She takes me along on the ferry. It's tilting and cutting through the ice. Crunching.

When the vet lifts Luigi onto the silver table, he tries to scramble away, toenails clicking.

But the vet holds on to him. "Good trick, little fellow," he tells Luigi.

"He doesn't even let us brush his hindquarters," Aunt Stormy says. "Try not to touch him from above." The vet's hands are quick and gentle. Even when he gives Luigi a shot.

"Luigi is our dog now," I tell him.

"He's lucky. Now remember, when you approach Luigi, only touch his head from beneath."

"Why?"

"It'll help him get more confident. He's had a rough time so far in his little life. And he considers you the alpha dog. Get on the floor with him. Nose to nose. So he'll feel at the same level."

I bend my knees till my nose is across from Luigi's.

"Good. Like that," the vet says.

I snake my hand along the cold table. Up Luigi's legs. Cuddle the front of his neck.

"Yes, like that," the vet says. "You're good with him."

When we walk to the truck, catbriers hang like veils from high branches, glittering with frozen rain. A necklace of pearls. I didn't know they could be beautiful.

"Now we don't have catbriers anymore," I tell Aunt Stormy.

"I try to get them all," she says.

Wind grabs me. Makes me dizzy. I laugh.

When we take the ferry back, it's almost dark. Spooky. The crunching through the ice is louder.

"I bet Mason would kayak in the ice," I say.

"It's far too dangerous."

"He could wear one of your wet suits."

I have a photo of Mason and Aunt Stormy in wet suits. They posed on the boardwalk. Afterward, Aunt Stormy said she hated the feel of the thick rubber. "Toe to hair panty hose, armor style." But Mason said, "I like the way they feel snug-like."

In the dark, whiteness of broken ice.

Whiteness of stars.

I bet it's like that where Eskimos live.

Mason

"—me more than dying."

"That you're not winning?"

"That we're no longer looking out for each other to win."

"You're betting against yourself, Mason."

I turned away from you, Annie.

"Where are you going?" you asked.

"To see Opal."

"It's too early."

"May I please sit in her room, please, before you tell me when and where I can see my daughter from now on?"

"Just don't wake her."

But when I went into Opal's room, she was sitting up in her bed, frowning at me.

"Hey . . . Stardust."

"Why are you fighting with Annie?"

"Can't hide anything from you?"

She shook her head, pulled me into a hug of her sleep smell. "Are you going to make up with her, Mason?"

"It's what I want most in the world."

"More than anything ever?"

"Yes." As I held her, I wanted this moment—before she'd get up and go to school—to be more special for her than any moment we'd had together so far. But already I was imagining her five, six years from now, a teenager who'd rather be with her friends than with me. Who'd be embarrassed by everything I did or said. But I would smile. Pretend it didn't matter. Or that I hadn't noticed.

Yet, I already feel cheated out of being with Opal. Do you ever do that, Annie, imagine her years from now and miss her so terribly already?

"Are you crying?" Opal asked.

I turned my face from her. "No," I lied and suddenly remembered that day she'd fought to get away from me, Annie, from my touch, and though I'd known it was because of Aunt Stormy's lotion, I'd felt bereft.

"Stinky," Opal had cried. And she'd been right because that lotion stank of coconut and pineapple.

"Like tutti-frutti," I said, trying to convince her, "but you're so fair, you really need sunscreen." Holding Opal—she was so little, Annie—I slicked lotion on her face and neck and arms and—

"Stinky! Stinky! Stinky!" She kicked me, got away.

But I caught her. "Oh . . . hold still, Mophead. Please?"

Howling, she threw her body back. In her eyes the ferociousness of animals who chew off their limbs if trapped. *Or yours.*

"No, Mason—"

"Put your fingers down, Opal. I'm almost done."

I wish I hadn't been so impatient with her, Annie. She was clawing at her face, screaming and kicking, rage climbing from the earth through her feet, rising inside her body, filling her belly before she crammed it down into earth again—

So much wilder than you, Annie. More like your mother's wildness.

—and already Opal was running wobbling weaving along the edge of sea with me chasing but not catching her, letting her stay ahead of me, the same distance, till she ran off her rage and plopped on the sand. I carried her back to you, Annie. He was there too, Jake, whispering to you—

"You *are* crying, Mason." Opal stood up on her mattress.

"Don't fall off. I'll tell a Melissandra story if you sit down."

"Melissandra is a tucking story. I don't want to sleep anymore."

"Don't tell me you've never heard the morning version!"

"I have never heard the morning version." She sounded delighted.

I waited.

"All right." She sat down.

I touched my nose against hers. "First, Melissandra tucks you in."

"That *is* the evening version."

"Almost."

"So where is she?"

"Let me see if she's around." I flattened myself against the floor, checked under Opal's bed. "Here she is . . . hiding under your bed as usual." I popped my head up next to Opal's, said in the high Melissandra-voice, "So, kid . . . what's your name?"

"Opal. What's yours?"

"Melissandra," I said, hissing the double *s,* rolling the *r.*

"How old are you, Melissandra?"

"Eight years and one week and three days."

Opal's lips were moving. Counting. "That's how old I am. Except I'm one day older than you."

"Shucks."

"You go to school, Melissandra?"

"Kindergarten."

"You're much too old for kindergarten."

I shook my head. "I like kindergarten. It's my third year in kindergarten. I'll stay there forever."

"You can't."

"Yes, I can. Because I'm going to be a kindergarten teacher when I grow up."

"How about your night job?"

"I still got that."

"How many lollipops did you eat last night, Melissandra?"

"Fifty-seven."

She laughed. "You'll throw up."

"No way. Lollipops are good for me."

"No, they're not. You'll get cavities."

"I love cavities. They're my hiding places for chocolate."

She laughed aloud.

"I have one hundred and eleven cavities," I said.

"I have two fillings."

"Let me see."

She opened her mouth, wide. Yawned.

"Only two?" I clicked my tongue. "It's because you brush your teeth too often. That's simply not right."

She giggled.

"I never ever brush my teeth." I gathered the quilt around her shoulders. "You still have an hour of sleep before you get up."

"Tell me more about Melissandra."

"Melissandra has to leave . . ."

Opal pulled at my hand. "Promise she'll come back?"

I kissed her cheek, and as I stood up, I was seized by a vertigo of loss and devotion, and I—

NINE

Jake

{ *Group Home* }

Don't rush it, Jake warns himself when he gets to the vigil in Sag Harbor. On the wharf, he stays two rows behind Annie, where she won't see him right away. The urgency to tell her how he saw Mason die has built with each day, has become stronger than any hunger he has felt, any desire or fear.

A breeze in the air. Candle wax and salt. He hasn't stood this close to Annie since that strange, sad day of watching *The Graduate* with Mason's parents.

People tip the wicks of their candles toward one another, pass the flame, talking about an American student who was killed in Palestine today.

"An Israeli military bulldozer ran across her—"

"Covered her with earth—"

"Breaking and suffocating her."

"This is supposed to be a silent vigil."

"On the radio they said Rachel Corrie fell."

More protesters than at the last vigil, when Annie didn't see him and Jake didn't have the courage to talk to her. But today he will.

"The house belonged to a Palestinian doctor."

"I read on the Internet she lay down to prevent the demolition."

"No, she stood in the way."

Jake heard about her on the radio when he was driving here. He thinks of her as a girl because she's a daughter, dead now— *A girl. A daughter.* Thinks of Opal's impulse toward all or nothing—what martyrs are made of.

"—and it backed up over her, the bulldozer, after crushing her."

"How old was she?"

"Nineteen."

"Twenty-three. She's from Washington State," Jake says, loud enough for Annie to recognize his voice.

She spins toward him. Eyes furious and glad and scared.

"Please?" he says.

Aunt Stormy gives him a candle, already lit. "Jake," she says. And kisses his cheek.

He wraps his arms around Aunt Stormy, careful to keep the candle away from her long brown hair. Holds on to her the way he wishes he could hold on to Annie. "I heard on the radio that Bush said tomorrow is the last chance for peace. That's been with me. That and the girl, Rachel Corrie."

Aunt Stormy lets go of him. "Until tonight I believed we could stop him and his insane war."

"Such a different mood," Jake says, "from the protest in Manhattan, when peace still felt possible."

"So you were there?" Annie asks. Was she disappointed she didn't meet up with him? Relieved?

"I couldn't find you." It's a lie. But only half a lie. Because when he saw her in New York, he was suddenly sweating in the ice-cold air, certain that this was the last time he'd get to talk to Annie, certain that he'd blow it. Unless—

Unless he found words that would open into another last time.

And another last time after that.

He'd already lost Mason, and he needed to save that last time with Annie, postpone it till he was more prepared. And so he shadowed Annie and Aunt Stormy. Moving closer. Getting calmer. *Because it doesn't have to be today.* Shadowed them till a cop let them through a barricade. Last Jake saw of them were their protest signs, flopping on their backs.

• • •

WHEN THE procession of protesters walks up Main Street, candles bobbing in a queue of lights, he keeps next to Aunt Stormy. It's one of the first mild days after a rough winter. He's left his coat in the car, wears his corduroy blazer open.

"Where are you staying, Jake?" Aunt Stormy asks.

"I'll find something."

"Would you like—"

Annie elbows her. "Some of the hotels have winter rates."

"Good idea," Jake says. "I was hoping to see Opal too."

"She has a new friend," Annie says. "A girl her age who lives five minutes down the beach from us. Mandy."

"It's taken a while," Aunt Stormy says. "Oh no—" She taps the shoulder of a bald man walking ahead of her. "Excuse me? Do you know that you have the logo for Mercedes-Benz on your protest sign?"

"It's a peace symbol."

"The vertical line in the peace symbol runs from top to bottom. In the logo for Mercedes-Benz it stops halfway down."

"I'm so embarrassed. I guess it shows I'm new at this."

"We're all glad you're here."

"You must think I'm a complete idiot."

"No, no," she assures him. "I just thought you'd want to know for your next vigil."

"Mercedes-Benz." He laughs. "I ride my bicycle whenever I can." He continues walking with Aunt Stormy. "Would it be appropriate to hand out some flyers with a quote I got off the Internet?"

"What kind of quote?"

"Something Göring said at Nuremberg. Here." He takes a rubber band off a rolled sheaf of pages.

Aunt Stormy reads aloud: " 'Naturally the common people don't want war . . . But, after all, it is the leaders of the country who determine the policy, and it is always a simple matter to drag the people along.' "

"That's so true," Annie says.

"Keep reading," the man with the Mercedes-Benz logo says.

" 'All you have to do,' " Aunt Stormy reads, " 'is tell them they are being attacked and denounce the pacifists for lack of patriotism and exposing the country to danger. It works the same in every country.' " She folds the quote. Shivers. "Exactly what they're doing here," she says. "Thank you for bringing it along."

"Can we talk, Jake?" Annie asks. "Please?"

He's startled. "Sure. Yes. Sure."

"You want to go for a drive tomorrow? Maybe a walk?"

"Sure."

"And—Jake?"

"Yes?"

"Don't get all dressed up."

JAKE IS still wondering what Annie meant by that when she's in his car. While he got dressed, he changed his clothes from plaid pants to jeans to plaid pants. Returned once more after starting his car and got back into his jeans. But kept on the white oxford shirt. And parted his hair.

His body feels comfortable near her body, instinctively wants to be near her, but he drives without talking, waits for Annie to start so he won't say anything to scare her away.

She looks straight ahead.

Jake is not about to talk about Mason. Still, without Mason, there is silence between him and Annie, the absence of Mason. *On the raft, I wanted him dead, and he saw that in my face just before I pushed him underwater. And did it for me, the killing of himself—not then, but in Annie's studio. When he must have seen it again in my face, the wanting him dead, while I stood outside his window, watching him get ready to die, maybe betting on me running in to rescue him—*

If he tells Annie—tells her in a way that'll make her understand—what happened when Mason killed himself, it will clear away this misery between them, bring them back to how it was before that night in the sauna, or even to before that, when they were children and he loved her fearlessness and believed he would become fearless too if she loved *him* best.

But what if he told her and she thought that he killed Mason? That he went inside her studio and killed him? Because that's what Jake wanted to do in the sauna. Wanted to kill Mason. Stop him. But didn't. Kill or stop him. Didn't. Just as he didn't go inside the studio. He's very good at *not* doing something. *Coward.*

Annie will believe him.

She knows more than anyone else how Mason can get you to do things you don't want to do.

He should tell her right now. "That morning, after you took Opal to school—"

"Opal talks about you."

"How . . . how is she?"

"Everything is so . . . very hard for her, Jake. Not her schoolwork. But just getting through the day. Her tantrums. And that . . . relentless unhappiness of hers. I'm knocking myself out to undo it. But she won't let me."

"It must hurt, seeing her like that."

Annie nods.

"Does she bully you with it?"

"How?"

"To get what she wants. Like Mason."

"I don't think it's like that. But I do offer too much. To undo her unhappiness. It's so much in my face . . . and it accumulates if I can't undo it. It feels I'm always . . . dancing around it, protecting her from herself . . . while she's flinging shit at me."

"Let me be there for her?"

"Yesterday her foot went through the bathroom floor. It's sort of punky in front of the sink. She's been testing it, hopping up and down, seeing if it'll give, but when it did, she felt betrayed. Got pissed at me."

He thinks of asking her again to let him help.

But he doesn't want to push.

A sign: RESIDENTS ONLY.

Jake slows his car. "Remember those drives my family took on Sunday afternoons?"

"Yes?"

He takes a turn into the street. "My parents would pick the most expensive neighborhoods they could find. Private or No Trespassing. From the backseat, I'd hear them guess the prices of houses that were ten times the size of ours. Comment on their styles. My mother"—Jake smiles—"she'd be planning additions—we'd be driving slowly, like this, very slowly—while my father would be building gazebos and trellises. When I was little, it felt we were always one Sunday away from moving into one of those places, but gradually I became afraid that we were just moments away from being arrested for trespassing. I'd imagine the three of us in jail."

At the end of the RESIDENTS ONLY street, big copper statues of greyhounds flank the entrance to a driveway. Skinny loins. Rear ends sloping as if they were about to urinate.

When Jake makes a U-turn, a man in a blue jogging suit strides past the greyhounds, one hand raised to stop Jake's car.

"You're in big, big trouble now," Annie says.

"Aunt Stormy will bail us out."

"Hah." An almost-smile.

The man comes up to Jake's window, tilts his head to check inside. "May I help you?"

"He does not sound like he wants to help you," Annie whispers.

"May I help you?" His hair is swept from his forehead like gray wings. Or rather like the thighs of mice.

Thighs of mice. Jake reminds himself to tell Annie. Imagines her laughing.

She undoes her seat belt and leans across him. "Yes, thank you. You may help us."

"This is a private road."

"I sure hope so." Her arm lies against Jake's chest. "A private road is one of our prerequisites."

Jake breathes slowly. To keep her from noticing that she's touching him. To keep her from remembering and moving her arm away. But it's more than that. Breathing—

"Now tell me . . ." Annie's neck is lengthening, the span of her shoulders opening. "Which of these . . . estates is in foreclosure?"

Breathing. Slowly. And then Jake knows. *To keep myself from pushing Annie away.* His body hates her touch. Hates how horrible it felt to fuck her in front of Mason. He lowers the back of his seat. Leans away from her.

"You must be mistaken," the man says.

"Your place, by any chance?" Annie asks.

"We have no foreclosures on this street."

"Well, one of us certainly is mistaken," she says. "Understandable, of course."

"Why?"

"The bank has not made it official."

"I am certain—" But the man's voice does not sound as certain as before. "—that we have no foreclosures on this street."

"I'm loving this," Annie whispers into Jake's ear.

He turns from her breath . . . warm and rife with the smells of all she's stuffed into her mouth.

"I feel like a trespasser," she whispers.

"You are," Jake says. "We are."

"Forget we mentioned anything," Annie consoles the man.

"Absolutely," Jake says. "We only know because my brother-in-law is a vice president at the bank that holds the mortgage."

Annie's eyes flicker.

"So what am I supposed to make of this?" the man asks.

"You'll find out soon which one of your neighbors it is." *Showing off for Annie. Mason-behavior. Pushiness. Lying. Amazing myself—*

Don't think about Mason.

"All we're doing today," Annie explains, "is checking your neighborhood to see if it's . . . well, suitable."

"Suitable," Jake echoes and feels the conspiracy, the fun. It's how it used to be when they bonded against Mason, bouncing off each other . . . imagining.

"Suitable?" Sweat above the man's lips.

Jake waves his hand to dismiss any concern.

"Suitable for what?"

"It may not suit our . . . mission anyhow," Annie says.

"Even though the zoning does allow for . . ." Jake waits.

"Allow for what?" the man demands to know.

"Well," Annie says, "it's not really official yet."

Jake can tell she's loving this. He turns off the engine. His sleeve on the ledge of the window, he raises his face to the man. "May I ask you something?"

"Yes?"

"Is it always this quiet here?"

"Of course." The man looks dazed.

"Because that's our foremost prerequisite. The quiet."

"The quiet," Annie agrees. "In an area of such . . . exclusiveness, we assume neighbors do not interfere with each's other's . . . privacy."

"What are you saying?"

"Lovely people." Annie's smile is angelic.

"Now you listen—"

"Not to worry," Jake assures him. "These are lovely young people in the process of being reeducated."

"We do not use the term *reform school*," Annie explains. "It's rather a—" She sinks in her seat. Waits for Jake.

Who is thinking, quickly. "A residential learning center." *Carrying this even further than Mason could have. With more imagination. Except that Mason's voice is louder. Was louder. Or is this my real voice? There all along?*

The admiration in Annie's eyes is intoxicating.

"Private, of course," Jake tells the man, but he's glancing at Annie. "Since they're all from exclusive families. You know the type."

"These young people fit right in to your neighborhood," Annie says. "We expect the success rate to be encouraging because their . . . offenses are relatively mild."

"Offenses?"

"Crimes . . . if you must say."

"Even though," Jake reprimands her, "we don't like to say."

"I'm so sorry. I hope it won't go on my evaluation."

"Once more, and I'll have you in front of the board."

"I know. And I appreciate this."

Jake sighs. "They're juveniles, which of course makes all the difference."

Annie nods. "Lovely young people . . . fortunately still juveniles. Experimental, at this stage—"

"But very promising," Jake interrupts.

"—to have young people like these govern themselves without . . . adult interference."

"Guidance," Jake says. "Please! Guidance!"

"Sorry. Guidance."

"These young people are eager to become part of a community once again," Jake assures the man, "and your neighborhood . . . such tranquillity, ideal."

"You must be . . . mistaken."

Annie smiles at him, gently. "As I said, one of us most certainly is mistaken."

"Still, we have facts you don't have access to." Jake starts the engine. "At least not for a few weeks. Good day now."

• • •

By the time they've made a left from his street, they're howling with laughter.

"Certainly."

"Most certainly."

"Exclusiveness."

"Words I hate: exclusive, superior, elite . . ."

"Lovely young people."

"Still juveniles."

Mason would have loved this. And then Jake wrecks it and says it aloud, "Mason would have loved this."

Now his name is there between them.

They sit stunned.

Until Annie says, "Not nearly enough on the line for Mason."

"Your seat belt."

"We have a history of stuff we did on the line."

And each time Mason has to up it. Make it more exciting.

"Some of it was just kids' stuff." Jake reaches across Annie to buckle her in.

"The sauna thing was not kids' stuff."

"Usually I managed to keep it from getting that far."

"Not that night."

"No. And not in Morocco, when you risked our lives, staring at that man's crotch."

"His eyes . . . on me, like hands, Jake."

"It was dangerous and childish, turning to us and laughing about him."

"I wanted him to feel what it's like to be stared at like that."

Nights in Morocco, Jake slept with Annie's clothes, just one item, on his pillow, breathing her. One morning when she returned to her room, she saw him with her blouse on his pillow. "My hair was wet," he said quickly, "and I didn't want to get the pillow stuffing all wet." He was amazed she believed him. Still, he kept explaining. "So I kept your blouse between my hair and the pillow. To keep it from getting wet . . ."

• • •

"OUR LAST night in Tangier I could hear you through the wall," Jake tells Annie.

"I didn't think of you until afterwards."

He looks at her, puzzled.

"It had to do with the people in the room on the other side. They woke us up around three in the morning, kept us awake, loud and long. In the morning at six, Mason and I moaned and bounced around. To get even. We didn't even think you could hear us."

"Maybe you didn't. I'm sure Mason did. And that he—" Jake shakes his head.

"Say it."

"I'm not sure I should say this."

"You can say anything to me."

"When?"

"What do you mean?"

"Except for today, you haven't let me talk to you." He shakes his head. "How can I—"

"Don't say it then."

"Mason wanted me to hear."

"That's sick."

"Mild, compared to . . . what we know he was capable of."

She draws her knees to her chest.

He wonders if she's imagining him in Morocco on the other side of that wall . . . imagining what he must have felt . . . imagining him breathing her scent on his pillow . . .

She shivers. "Every day . . . I find him all over again . . ."

It's always about Mason. Jake keeps driving. "He threatened to kill himself that summer at camp."

"Why?"

"If I didn't lie for him. It happened the day you visited us."

"You were on the raft. I found you there. I—"

"How long . . . before we saw you?"

"What was the lie he wanted from you, Jake?"

"Mason was stealing bakery rolls. Every morning, at breakfast, we made our own lunch. Everything out on the long tables: eggs and rolls and cold cuts and cheese. Lots of store-bought bread but only one bakery roll for each boy. To eat for breakfast—still warm—or save for lunch on a tray with his name printed on a tag."

Annie is waiting, and as Jake tells her, he is right back there *at camp with the smell of camphor and pine needles and mold and yeasty bakery rolls.*

"Mason loved those rolls. We all did. He'd eat his at breakfast and fix himself a sandwich for lunch from store bread. But then he'd sneak to the lunch tray before anyone else, steal another boy's roll, and stick that boy's name tag into his sandwich."

"Switching tags." She nods. "Sounds like Mason."

"Some boys caught him one noon. They were watching to see who was stealing their rolls. He got away, hid out in my cabin. That's where I found him. He was crying, saying, 'It was mine. I'm not a thief.' "

"What did you do?"

"He wanted to run away and for me to come along. But I wanted to stay. He said he'd stay too. But that I had help him and tell everyone I fixed my roll for him in the morning and stuck his name tag into it."

"Did you?"

"I was the one friend he had there."

"And he gambled losing you."

"He promised no more stealing, no more switching of tags."

"But he still did it, right?"

"Sometimes he'd steal two rolls and toss the name tags on the floor . . . as if testing how much I would lie for him."

"Testing . . . You know, every day I cut him down again, Jake. It doesn't matter that I live in a different place now, that I've left my worktable behind. I have to cut him down again, already knowing that any moment I'll find him again . . ."

"Hey— I'm so terribly sorry." He touches her wrist, prepared to have her flinch, but she doesn't. He's the one who flinches, suddenly queasy. He yanks his hand away. "I couldn't bear it if I'd already lost you both."

"I'm so . . . fucking tired of cutting him down."

Jake's heart is hitting his collarbone. "Are we accomplices then?"

"What if I had been enough for him?"

"Nobody was enough for him. Nobody could have been."

"The more separate I felt from him, the more he held on." Annie brings her forehead to her knees. "You think that's what he wanted all along—to kill himself . . . make his death ours?"

"Then he's the only one who got what he wanted." It sounds so clear to Jake. If only he could believe it. Believe that Mason did not count on him to stop his suicide. Believe that Mason did not wait to step off Annie's work-table till he was sure Jake would come running. *Making his death mine.*

"He liked to get away with things," Annie says, "that other people get caught for."

He can come into my house any time because his parents pay for him. Can trash my room. Or ignore me. Some mornings I have stomachaches knowing he'll be there soon.

"But much of it was . . . wonderful when we were kids. Right, Jake?" Annie raises her face. "The three of us . . . not letting go of each other?"

The three of us.

A knot.

A tangle.

Bunching out to one side, then another.

Wanting Annie to like me best. Wanting Mason to like me best. Yet knowing I'm second choice for both. Still—impossible to refuse their love, though it makes me feel worse.

"Right, Jake?"

No. That's what he wants to tell her. He says, "Yes." *Easier. With Annie and with Mason. Hard to say no when they want me to say yes. Still—it wasn't all no. It was yes too.*

"As a boy," Jake starts, "I used to think he'd die if you and I ended up together."

"You were strong enough to stand losing me to him."

"What?"

"Because you still had the two of us."

He shakes his head. "I had to keep you safe so that—"

"Babysitting us?"

"You think that's what I wanted?"

"Babysitting the way your mother did?"

"Come on, Annie. It wasn't like that."

"We could count on each other . . . you and I."

"Yes?"

"Always, as a child . . . pretending I liked Mason better . . . I had to so he wouldn't hurt you or break things that were yours. Hiding that I liked you . . . And I'm still doing that. Even though he's no longer alive." Annie shakes her head. "To kill himself after he set us up like that—"

"So we'd feel too guilty to ever be together. Did you ever feel that our friendship had to be secret?"

"Like having two parts to our friendship, yes . . . the open part in front of Mason, and then the secret part."

"He was at his best when he was with both of us, when he was the center."

"Things always exciting . . . that intensity of his."

"But when he switched it off, we tumbled."

"Oh no—" Annie looks stunned.

"What is it?"

"We're still talking about each other through him."

Jake stares at her. *It's true.*

"There's more of Mason in our conversation than of you and me." She covers her face. "I don't want him to. It's what we did when he was alive. Talk about him."

"If we didn't start, he did. His favorite subject."

"Ours too. Admit it, Jake."

"Admit? All right, this is what I'll admit: I'm afraid that, without Mason, you won't find me very exciting. You liked it when you had both of us around, adoring you."

"It made me feel special in school, having two boys like me but— You and I were the ones swirling around Mason like a couple of loopy bugs around light . . . and we're still doing it, Jake. Even without him. Letting him—" She laughs without joy.

"And here we are again," he says, "speculating what Mason might have done or thought or wanted of us. What Mason wanted—" He stops himself.

"See what I mean?"

What Jake meant to say is that Mason wanted him and Annie to be fully charged. But it feels dangerous to say this. Disloyal.

"I don't want to feed on him, Jake."

"Maybe he is feeding on us."

"Some nights I wake up, revolted at his violence . . . to himself. To me. Mostly to Opal. Other times I feel almost . . . relieved—it's not the right word, but I can't think of a better one—relieved that he is no longer . . . here. Promise you'll never tell anyone?"

He nods. "That day we sold lemonade—I think even then the blueprint for our friendship was there. Who we were . . . and were to become."

She is listening closely.

How much more can I say without pushing her away? "Do you ever think he created situations where he could feel justified being jealous?"

"All the time. That was his high, being jealous."

"Winning you every day?" Jake asks.

"Or you."

Jake wonders how much she encouraged Mason's jealousy.

"Actually, he was not as amorous as it may have seemed. There was a lot of show, touching me . . . when you were around."

The bone? The warm-up? Jake feels a silent scream inside, holds it in. *Getting me to fuck you for him.*

"What, Jake?"

HE PARKS at the end of Ocean Road, stares at the waves, furious.

"What is it?" she asks, not touching him though her voice is touching him.

Getting me to fuck you for him. He feels queasy.

"Jake?"

"Getting me to fuck you for him," he says, jolted at having said it.

She crosses her arms, fingertips on her shoulders, bends forward, lips moving.

"I can't hear you, Annie."

Lips moving. Rocking herself.

"I was the stand-in," Jake says.

"Have you ever thought— No."

"What, Annie?"

"That it was the closest Mason could let himself come to fucking you?"

"I've made every effort not to think that. Or that maybe he wanted both of us."

"Fucking both of us by making us act it out for him?"

"We did."

"Only to shut him up, Jake."

"Or to please him?"

She's rocking. Rocking herself. Lips moving. And finally Jake can make out what she's whispering: "Mason did not survive the three of us."

"If you ever want to talk, Annie, about that night and Mason's death—"

"Aunt Stormy says quite a few people have drowned here." She motions to the water.

"Because there's something I have to tell you."

"It's a beach without lifeguards. That's why."

"Annie?"

"People who can't get beach passes swim here. Like the undocumented workers. One more document not available for them."

"LOOK LOOK, Jake. A mud snail." Opal holds out the shell, sets it into his palm.

"Pretty cool." So far, he has given her five hugs.

"Mason says if you dribble water on your skin, it'll move around." She scoops water into his palm.

After a moment he feels it, a slight pulling of membrane against his skin. Creepy. Like velvet sliding across his hand. He wants to shake it off. But for Opal, he holds still.

"Better put it in the water, Jake."

"Good idea." He pulls it from his palm, sets it into the bay.

The water is still cold, the sand too, but he and Opal are building a sand castle with garden shovels. Already it's waist high, with a driftwood pole and curls of dried brown seaweed.

Annie watches. Doesn't help. Just watches them.

For what? To try out my father potential? It's obvious how much Opal has missed me.

"We need shells for decoration," Opal decides and runs off.

He follows her. Carries the shells she picks up.

"Jake, look—" She stops.

Huge letters carved into the sand. GIVE WAR A CHANCE.

"That's sick," Jake says.

Opal tramples across WAR. Tramples the three letters till the sand is flat. With the tip of her right sneaker, she prints PEACE into the space.

"That's ingenious," Jake tells her.

"Can you eat that seaweed?" she asks him when they press the shells into the walls of her castle.

"I'm not sure."

"They sell seaweed salad at the fish market."

"That's probably imported," Annie says. "This here may be polluted."

"Ouch—" Opal cries out.

"What is it?" Annie asks.

"A shell. It's too sharp."

"Can I take a look?" Jake asks. "Dr. Pagucci on splinter patrol."

"It's not a splinter."

"Then we'll have to improvise. You used to get more splinters than any of my other patients."

"You don't have any other patients."

"Dr. Pagucci limits his practice to family. Because everyone else would have fired him by now."

"I'm not your family. You are so stupid."

Sand in the pinpricks of his wing-tip shoes.

"You are stupid because you don't come see me."

"I'm sorry."

"If you don't have anything else to eat, then can you eat seaweed?"

Jake can tell she wants this answer to be yes. Is she planning survival out here in case she doesn't have anyone left? "Do you still have my phone number memorized, Opal?"

"Yes."

"It's good to remember the phone numbers of everyone who loves you."

Everyone who loves you. Mason—

Mason chasing Opal along the beach, getting farther away till their figures merge, one shape for an instant and then Opal rising as Mason swings her onto his shoulders. Then one shape again, one figure set atop the other, as he gallops toward Jake and Annie, closer, Opal laughing and shrieking, her fingers holding on to his forehead. "Mophead," he calls her.

"Oh no," Opal cries out as licks of tide start coming in. She clicks her tongue, stomps her feet, arms snaking the air above the castle as if she were a shaman.

Jake feels such affection for her as she dances around her castle.

"You're my Mophead," he says.

"Don't call me that!"

"What can I call you?"

"Fuck off, Jake." Such fury. Then a look of horror as if she were waiting for him to die.

"What did you say?" Annie asks.

"Jake is still alive. So it wasn't that."

"I want you to apologize to Jake."

The blue-green of the water gets closer, turns into foam that slicks the sand around her castle.

With his feet, Jake drags sand into a moat. "You think we'll save our castle?"

"It is not a castle." Opal takes her shovel and whacks the surrounding sand toward her castle, raising the wall. "You should know."

"I should?" Jake pulls ditches into the sand to divert the water.

"Because you helped build it, Jake."

"I thought it was a castle."

"Stupid . . . ," she mutters. "And now you think it's a castle."

"If it's not a castle, what is it?"

"A dragon house."

"Of course. A dragon house."

"No, it isn't. It's a dragon school. That's what it is." She pushes her flat hand toward the ocean as if to stop traffic.

Already the tide is at the lower walls of her dragon school, flattening all details.

"Over here, Jake. More sand. No. Not there—"

Why doesn't she destroy her dragon school before the waves overtake it? *It hurts less if you break it yourself instead of waiting for someone else to break it.*

But Opal is still working to save the last turret of sand, digging another moat even as her dragon school falls to the waves.

Mason

—stumbled. Steadied myself with one hand on my daughter's mattress. She was getting smaller and smaller—

"Don't go, Mason."

I blinked, and she was back, her real size. "Sleep

tight, Stardust—" Once more, my lips briefly against her forehead.

Like ice, my belly.

The sky even darker now, Annie, than when you and Opal got into the car.

Drive carefully. It looks like a hurricane about to start, though it doesn't feel like a hurricane. The sun like an old bruise. The way I'd imagine it after a fallout. No moisture in the air—just this harsh dryness.

Cold . . . so cold—

In your studio, I pull your cashmere shawl from the back of your work chair. You'll never get rid of that barn smell in here, animals long gone, even though you scrubbed the walls, the floor, the rafters. I take a piece of rope from your supplies, wrap your shawl around myself and am suddenly in my parents' house, cold like the vault at the bank, and the cacophony of piano as another child struggles through a lesson . . . ,

There is nothing of yours, Annie, I want to destroy—except myself.

I know what you'd say: "Don't be so dramatic, Mason." Or rather: "Don't be so goddamn dramatic, Mason."

But think about it, Annie. Now that I no longer have you, I can abandon myself to death—

"The idea of death," you called it when I talked about it.

The difference? What does it matter? If the idea of it is leading me to death? Remember *Spoorloos*, Annie? That Dutch film about a woman who's kidnapped at a gas station? Saskia. Whose lover, Rex, wants to know so desperately what has happened to her that he makes a pact with her killer to let him experience the same death. So that he will know.

I know.

I know what it's like when you need to know so desperately that it kills you, Annie.

I know what's it's like for Rex when he wakes up and finds himself buried alive.

Tell me what is worse, then? Reality, Annie? Or what you imagine reality to be?

Your shawl around me, I curl into myself on the floorboards, knees drawn against my chest. As a baby, I sucked on my toes when I curled up like this. My mother told me. It amazed her. Delighted her.

I tell you this, Annie: Of all that used to matter there's just one thing that's still important to me. The belief in being able to win you back, no matter what I do. I can stand anything if I have that, the magic of winning. Except winning in the sauna was not winning. The cost outweighed the booty, and I'm furious with myself. Furious with you for deserting me. And winning, of course.

Are you waiting to see how far I'll trust you? To measure how much you can trust me before you come back? Don't wait too long. I know about tests, about pushing beyond the—

My eyes and throat itch.

Your shawl . . . suffocating, the weight of it. But when I throw it off, cold air rushes at my skin. I'm shaking . . . coiled into myself on your floor. Shaking. But I won't stop to put on more clothes. If I let myself stop for anything, I might not go through with it. Oh, Annie—

TEN

Annie

{ *The Peace Nest* }

Outside: thundering. And on the television similar sounds as Iraq is battered by bombs. The flicker of intense light. Onscreen and outside our window. All heavens striking back at us for starting this war today.

"Such a lie that we're liberating the Iraqi people." Aunt Stormy is furious. "Expecting them to run toward our soldiers, welcoming them."

I agree with her. "And the arrogance, calling it terrorism when the Iraqis defend themselves."

"Of course they'll defend their homes. Just as we would defend our little piece of earth. That's what we're attached to. Not a ruler."

Suddenly a commercial, the Viagra guy, wiggling his crotch while running out a front door to the music of "We are the champions . . ."

"That man is so ugly," I say, "makes me want to swear off sex."

"You?" Aunt Stormy mutes the TV. "What sex?"

"I can't believe you'd say that."

"You and Jake are—"

"There's nothing happening."

"So true. A nun-in-training and a monk-in-training. You certainly wander about like a nun. All bundled up."

"Any other observations?"

"Oh . . . just that your parents hoped it would be Jake for you."

"They never said."

"Of course not. What could we have said?"

"You too?"

"I was hoping for Jake but betting—as you would say—on Mason, especially after Morocco, when all he talked about were those wedding plans . . . like he was afraid if he let up for five minutes, you'd run off with Jake. What we thought—" She shakes her head. "I don't know if you want to hear this."

"Tell me."

"We thought you picked Mason because that was the only way to keep the three of you together. Jake was always going to be there. But Mason would have gone off sulking for good if you'd picked Jake."

My head is spinning. "In the end though . . . that's the choice Mason forced on me . . . on us, and then he killed himself."

"The ultimate sulking for good."

"I love you for not asking details. Someday I will, but . . ."

"When and if . . ." She points to her heart. "You know I'm here."

She keeps the mute on when it's back to bombs striking buildings, a landscape of sand, eerie in its noiseless devastation.

The only sounds from the kitchen . . . Opal rattling the box of dog biscuits, training Luigi. To sit. To stay. To not beg at the table. "Only the trainer should feed the dog," she insists when we offer to carry the huge bag of dog food. "Otherwise it's confusing for him."

Last week, when Luigi got into some dead fish by the inlet and rolled himself, Opal tried to hide the stink by spraying him with Aunt Stormy's perfume. Even after I bathed Luigi, he still smelled of lily of the valley, sweet and cloying.

"The far right has been planning this since the early nineties," Aunt Stormy says. "Many groups working toward this. And it's growing."

"But it's not hopeless," I say, "and exactly for the reason you mention. Think about it. Because we can plan too."

"But think of all the damage in the meantime."

"Think of that peace service in Bridgehampton . . . about lasting for one day longer." Yesterday evening, I felt comforted when one of the speakers at the First Church of Peace talked about how African Americans had always lived with not being heard . . . how they'd managed to survive by coming together and lasting for one day longer, one year, ten years.

"We can't afford even one hour." Aunt Stormy begins to cry.

"I've never seen you so discouraged."

"I am so . . . very cold."

I wrap my afghan around her. Knead her shoulders through the pink yarn. Yesterday, when I opened one of the boxes Ellen and Fred had packed, I found the afghan wrapped around several collages. And here I believed I'd given it to Goodwill. Although I wouldn't choose those shades of pink now, I'm so glad I have it again because it's part of Opal's first few months with us.

In the kitchen the phone rings. Opal runs for it. "Hello?" Such eagerness in her voice. Then disappointment. "Oh . . . For you, Aunt Stormy."

I bet she hoped it would be Jake.

"Or is it that you hoped it would be Jake?" Mason asks.

"Drop it!"

"Be careful, Annie. Don't encourage something you can't take forward."

AUNT STORMY takes the call in the kitchen. When she returns, she's grinning. "Our least favorite client."

"Life-in-the-Colonies."

"Remember how I've been talking about getting rid of him?"

"Oh yes."

"He wouldn't even say hello. Started right off with 'Guess what now.' So I told him. 'We have started a war.' He said that wasn't it, that his new cleaning service already quit on him."

"I wonder why . . ."

"Then he told me, 'You must find me someone reliable, Stormy. And if they can't come right away, you wouldn't mind doing the cleaning this one time, right?' I started to say that, yes, I would mind. But he cut me off the instant he heard yes. 'You're the best, Stormy,' he told me, and when I said, 'Yes, I *would* mind,' he said in his uppity tone, 'Well . . . I stand corrected.' Guess what I told him, Annie."

"To sit down?"

She laughs. "Yes, in the same tone, 'Well . . . sit down already.' "

"It's good to see you laugh," I tell her, "even if it's over Life-in-the-Colonies."

Wind traps itself in our chimney, a wail that oddly sounds like bombing.

"Let's build an osprey nest," Aunt Stormy says.

"In the storm?"

"Once the storm stops. I need to . . . do something to counteract that violence. I know it won't make any difference to the people of Iraq, but I feel so powerless that I need to make something peaceful. Today."

WE ASSEMBLE a wooden frame, staple wire mesh to the edges to make a platform for the nest, gather twigs and sticks and grasses to weave into that mesh.

"I want the nest to be a circle," Opal says.

Aunt Stormy and Pete pull grapevines from the back of her shed. He's getting back to the body I remember, to that flexibility, can touch the ground again and help Aunt Stormy in the garden. His focus has been on healing—stretching and therapy and walking—inspiring me.

After he and Aunt Stormy twist the grapevines into a wreath, they hook the wiry tendrils into the mesh. Together with Opal, I weave long phragmites through the squares of mesh until, gradually, the nest starts to look like a peace symbol.

"It won't be . . . high enough," Pete says.

"We can try." With red string, Opal ties some of her favorite shells to the vines.

We all attach things that mean peace to us: Pete's roses, almost wilted, splashes of deep pink among the grasses; Aunt Stormy's amethyst and a long clear crystal; a shell I found at Sagg Main the day before, shades of brown and beige.

"Your shell," Pete says to me. "Like different . . . colors of . . . skin."

"I've had this amethyst for a long time," Aunt Stormy says. "Waiting to use it."

"The amethyst waited for this too," Opal says.

All around us the scent of earth warmed by longer periods of sun. Working together out here stills our hearts, gives us reprieve from our sadness and fear.

I kiss the top of my daughter's sweaty curls. "It's a magnificent nest."

"Who knows if we'll ever get ospreys," Aunt Stormy says, "but if we do, we can watch them build it up."

"They like their . . . nests higher than the . . . surrounding treetops."

"Could we make it higher?" I ask.

Aunt Stormy shakes her head. "The studs of the boardwalk are not long enough to support anything taller than this."

She's using the cordless drill she admired away from BigC last month when one of her fake rocks blew into the inlet. After she chased it in her kayak, she borrowed BigC's drill, drilled holes into all her rocks, and leashed them to trees. "This drill of yours," she told BigC, "is so much easier than dragging an extension cord around . . ." She went on and on till BigC insisted she keep it.

I get felt-tip pens from the cottage, cut long strips of paper. "Let's write words that have to do with peace. And then braid them into the nest."

"I don't like your felt-tip pens." Opal stomps one foot on the boardwalk.

"So much . . . for peace," Pete says.

"They are all soft and squishy like some other kid has been leaning on them."

"You . . . are the only kid . . . here."

"Look look, Pete, a candle ghost."

"It's a great . . . white heron," he says.

"Candle ghost!"

"A good name for . . . it."

"Let's leave the rest of the twigs on the ground," Aunt Stormy says, "so the ospreys will find them for building up their nest."

We bolt our platform to the end of a long pole, raise it, and connect the bottom of the pole to the railing where the boardwalk starts. Aunt Stormy has already drilled holes, and while we hold the post in that wobbly position, she tightens screws and braces. Above us, bits of sky and the pink of Pete's roses show through the mesh.

"Look look," Opal cries. "Our osprey."

"It doesn't happen this quickly." Aunt Stormy tilts her face to the sky. "It *is* an osprey."

And there it is, circling above.

"It's checking out the nest," Opal insists.

"During their first year, ospreys don't return north," Aunt Stormy says.

"But after that, they come back to where they were hatched. To hunt and to fish."

"Here it has been looking for a place to live," Opal says, "and here we are building it."

"Well . . . the young ones do need lodging," Aunt Stormy says. "Because the parents live more than twenty years."

"Here, chickie chickie . . ." Opal sings to the osprey.

Pete motions to the platform. "I just hope . . . they deem this worthy . . . lodging."

"For us, it'll be a reminder of peace," I tell Opal.

"A reminder of all the work we did," she corrects me.

—WALKING, OPAL *and I are walking through sand basins . . . up a wide rim of high dunes. The same beginning . . . she runs up the yellow dunes, slides down on her butt, playing and back up again, purple-on-yellow, and then suddenly is no longer there. I can't find her, scream her name—Opal Opal Opal—how could I forget how close Napeague Harbor is?—Opal—running up the dunes and all over the crest of the dunes searching in all directions. Making myself stop because it's a dream—*

—I know it is a dream, and I will myself to wake up. But I'm frozen—

—inside the dream. Climbing up the rim of the dream to get out because I'm afraid of what's next, because each dream opens up more, and I already know that, any moment now, I'll see something purple in the bay at the bottom of the dune—there it is, now—swaying as though it's been there for too long. And know in my heart that my daughter has drowned. Because I looked away. How can Opal have run so far? And now I'm running, running—

—while trying to wake up from this dream—

—running deeper into *the dream and toward the purple beneath the surface. Ballooning—*

—I've known this, have been here in other dreams, have failed to heed the forewarning—

—running, skidding, sliding . . . terrified to know for sure. Even more terrified to climb out of the dream and never know for sure—

—and so I stay. Decide to stay in the dream—

—running skidding sliding toward my daughter, who's floating facedown, who has been facedown in the water far too long to survive. But maybe not.

Maybe this time I— Crouching. I'm crouching—there, now—grip the back of my daughter's windbreaker, yanking—yanking hard—

Shaken, I sit up in bed. Reassure myself that my daughter is breathing. *Alive.* Asleep. *Dry.* The bright green digits of the clock are at 4:18, and in the almost-dark of the room, I suddenly feel content. Opal is safe. And it is my doing. It makes me feel grown up, somehow, for a short time at least grown up. As I feel my heart quieting, I'm grateful it's Mason who's dead—not Opal. I wouldn't trade. Would offer him to the gods, the fates, to keep her safe. *Collateral. Insurance.*

I run down the steps to the kitchen, snatch Opal's windbreaker from the blue pegs where it hangs with other jackets, and stuff it behind the crates that make up the corner bench. *There.* She is safe now, my daughter.

And I will continue to keep her safe. Upstairs, her left cheek has slid against the bedsheet, tugging her mouth sideways, sleep-puffy. There is the certainty that she will sleep another two or three hours. The certainty of the next day. And it is all right that nothing else can be as certain as this moment. I slip back into bed, curl myself into what's left of the heat from my body, see Opal running along across the boardwalk, laughing, and as I'm drifting toward sleep, I promise myself to watch for her moments of joy, settle her within the memory of those moments, so that I can evoke her like that whenever I need to. And remind her of that joy.

In the morning I wake up with that familiar panic: *I am alone.*

But then I think immediately: *We're safe now.*

I wrap my arms around myself, hold on to myself, to that moment of peace, and wonder if, gradually, these moments will last longer . . . like recuperating from an injury, say, and being able to walk for five minutes without pain, ten minutes . . . gradually no longer bracing yourself against the pain . . . no longer living with the anticipation that—any moment now—you'll hurt again. Until pain is no longer the first thing to fill you upon waking.

OPAL STANDS below the peace nest, squinting at the sky, waiting for her osprey to return.

"You scared it away," she tells BigC, who stands on her boardwalk, waving both arms as if to take off in flight, her method of shooing away the ducks.

"I only scare ducks away."

"I feed them," Aunt Stormy whispers to me, "and BigC continues her duck prevention schemes."

Her latest project: a scarecrow that's already splattered with duck droppings.

"May I invite Opal to the kite store in Sag Harbor?" BigC asks me.

"Say yes, Annie? Yes?"

"Yes," I say.

They return with chocolate chip cookies and two fluorescent pinwheels that make noise when the wind turns them.

No more ducks.

For a few days.

Every day, Opal checks the nest several times.

Still no ospreys. But the first duck returns. And soon others.

Two great white herons check out our peace nest. When they fly off, they leave huge white splotches on BigC's boardwalk.

"When they first came to the inlet," BigC tells me, "I was hoping they would stay."

"Maybe they will."

"Not on my boardwalk, Annie."

DR. VIRGINIA is talking at me before I can start the car, hawking her newsletter, restating her 800 number three times. *"Or you may subscribe online at www.deardoctorvirginia.com."*

"Enough of you," I tell her.

"I feel used by my sister," Sybil from Mattituck tells Dr. Virginia. "She invites me to her apartment whenever she wants something from me, but then once she gets what she wants, she ignores me and doesn't return my calls."

"Your sister is setting boundaries with you, Sybil."

"Yes, but I think it's ungrateful to do that after I—"

"Looking at a relationship with a sibling in terms of gratitude is excessively needy."

"But I thought it would be different this time. I mean, I gave her my—"

"Here you go again. Trying to force others into gratitude. No wonder your sister doesn't want to talk to you."

Orange striped drums—markers for construction during the day—are stored along the shoulder of the road. No streetlights. Everything dark.

"I'm wondering if I made the right decision, Dr. Virginia. You see, before the operation, my sister was calling me twice a day. And at the hospital we were so close that I thought from now on we'll get along so much—"

"What operation? And please, be specific."

"I donated one kidney to my sister. Oh—you want me to be specific. My left kidney."

I love it whenever Dr. Virginia is too flabbergasted to snap at her callers.

"And it's my older sister," Sybil adds.

"Would you trade one of your kidneys to get me back?" Mason asks.

"Don't—"

"You'd do that for me, Annabelle, wouldn't you?"

I feel it again, that sense of something having gone too far and of having missed the moment when that happened. The moment when you can still turn back. Like when I locked Mason out of our car. We'd been joking, and we were both laughing when we switched driving and he got out and walked around the back while I slid across the seat to the steering wheel. I felt playful when I locked the passenger door. But Mason didn't laugh. Just yanked at the handle and yelled for me to open the door. I was still waiting for him to laugh with me. Then, quickly, everything changed. He picked up a rock, a flat rock the size of his hand. "I'll break the windshield if you don't let me in." I was afraid to unlock the door. But I did. Because I was even more afraid not to. "You should know by now that I'm vindictive," he said when I let him in.

"I didn't believe you," I tell Mason.

I switch to Dr. Francine. A commercial for a divorce lawyer: "You can call me at 800-DIV-ORCE. Divorcequick will grant you a legal divorce—"

"How is that for timing?" Mason laughs.

"—or annulment within twelve hours, and without travel, even if you can't find your spouse."

"I know where to find him," I tell the radio voice.

"You mean dig me up," Mason asks.

Headlights behind me. Sudden and fast. Much too close.

"Asshole!"

"That's where assholes belong," Mason agrees. "On your tail."

"That's for sure."

I pull over. Let the car pass. A Hummer. Like a tank. Just then I notice a sign: EMERGENCY STOPPING ONLY.

"You think that constituted an emergency?" I ask Mason.

"I hate Hummers."

"So does Pete."

"They use up more of everything," Mason says. "Space and gas. Plus they're damn ugly. And because of their weight, Hummers qualify as farm equipment . . . meaning tax breaks."

Suddenly I miss him. *"Do you ever think Opal's hurting started before she was born?"*

"During the accident or before?"

"During . . . I think."

"Maybe if you can't be safe in the womb . . . when can you be safe then?"

"She used to show her joy," I tell Mason. "Now she only shows her sadness."

"Maybe she just won't let you see her joy."

"To punish me?" I see Opal dancing around the tulip tree. Such joy.

"Lola would be better off with me, Dr. Francine." A man's sad, belligerent voice.

"But she belongs to your neighbor."

"I've been taking care of her for two weeks."

"Oh, Bob . . ." Dr. Francine sighs. "I understand how you've come to love—"

"Without me, Lola would have starved."

"I believe your neighbor was acting responsibly," Dr. Francine tells Bob, "by asking you to feed his cat while he was in Costa Rica, and—"

"The only mistake that neighbor made was letting this nutcase near his cat," I tell Mason.

"But if I hadn't fed Lola, she'd be dead now," Bob tells Dr. Francine.

"—you were acting responsibly by taking care of the cat."

"I'm not giving Lola back." A sharp click as Bob hangs up.

"Preparing himself for the life of a fugitive," Mason says.

Dr. Francine sighs.

"There goes her sigh button again," Mason says.

"I'm worried about Lola."

"You think Lola is really a cat?"

"Only you would ask that."

"Why?"

"Your bizarre imagination."

"Which you used to love before you—"

A road sign encourages drivers to call for car pool information. I imagine a car pool of widows heading with me into the night, comparing stories of their husbands' deaths.

"Remember when Opal pulled blossoms from our tulip tree?" I ask Mason.

"I loved how she was dancing around the tree."

"I loved watching her too . . . but I would have liked to enjoy the tree. You let her wreck it."

"She did not wreck it, Annie."

"I don't like to be the one who always says no."

"Then don't."

"The way I survived was by becoming a beast, Dr. Francine." A gravelly voice. "Three years and five weeks in a Vietnamese prison camp."

"But at least now you're free," Dr. Francine says.

"No, I'm not."

"But, Marty—"

"To stay alive, I had to give up ethics and hope . . . human values . . . because all that would have meant death. I clawed to stay alive. From day to day. All belly and cunning."

"When I walked with Opal around that tree later . . . told her how much more we'd all enjoy it if we could still see those blossoms, I felt . . . prissy."

Mason laughs. "You can be prissy."

"Watch it." I feel oddly calmed, buoyed by Mason's generosity toward Opal. I can be like that with Opal too.

"That must have been devastating," Dr. Francine says.

"I still do it. Live like a beast." Is that pride?

"We all carry sorrow," Dr. Francine says. "And we have to find a way to live with that sorrow."

"Ask Opal to tell you her Melissandra stories," Mason says.

EARLY EVENING, and I'm sitting by the window, looking toward our nest, waiting for something that will live here. A shifting of focus, instead of waiting for the next horror of war. But Aunt Stormy turns on the news, and once again I'm furious.

American soldiers heavily armed—

kicking down doors—
bursting into houses—
shoving people—
overturning furniture—
scattering papers—

Aunt Stormy takes a jagged breath when a soldier writes a series of numbers on the skin of an Iraqi man.

"I never expected that . . . violence from Americans."

"Oh, I knew it could happen anywhere," Aunt Stormy says. "I used to think if we understood how it started in Germany, we could prevent it from happening in the future. But there's been a different kind of understanding coming at me . . . from the opposite direction, present toward past. Because of what's happening to Americans, day by day, being manipulated into fear and superiority—

A newscaster is pushing a microphone at a group of protestors: a transvestite with a twin towers hair-do, Texas cheerleaders waving a caricature of Bush. No longer funny. In Iraq people are dying.

"I'm not talking about the Holocaust, Annie, but 1933 when Hitler seized power. And I'm not comparing him to Bush—that's too easy. But what we have is that same breakdown of ethics. The limitation of civil rights. The dehumanization of a . . . perceived enemy, of evil as identified by the far right. Here, the Patriot Act. In Germany, the Enabling Act. Creepy, how similar they are."

She motions to the television screen. "Justifying torture . . . imprisonment. And we're implicated—you and I."

"Annie!" Opal comes running down the stairs from our bedroom.

"Every human being is capable of that," Aunt Stormy says.

"Can I play outside?" Opal hops from one foot to the other. Twirls.

"Go ahead. Run and dance. But only where I can see you from the window."

She heads for the door. "Where is my windbreaker?"

"I . . . don't know." I hate lying to her. Still, if you remove one part of a dream, you undo the dream, break its sequence.

"It was hanging from the second peg."

I feel superstitious. Unreasonable.

"I want my purple windbreaker!"

"Oh . . . that windbreaker. You've outgrown that."

"Not so."

"It looked . . . funny in back. It puckered. Where you couldn't see it."

"Liar liar pants on fire . . ."

"Drop it, Mason."

"It really didn't look good on you anymore," I tell Opal. "We'll get you another one, okay?"

"Not okay."

"You can pick a new color. You must be getting sick of purple."

"You don't even know that purple is my mother's favorite color. You don't know anything. You stupid—"

Aunt Stormy catches her in a hug. "How about saving this for our Hungry Ghost? Here's a piece of paper. Now you can write it down and save it in the ghost box for a most excellent fire."

Distracting her . . . it's what my mother used to do with me when I was little. *Finding our mothers in different ways . . .*

Opal shields her left hand around what she's writing. "And I don't have to tell you or Annie what I write?"

"Oh no."

"Unless you want to," I say, wishing I hadn't.

"I don't want to!"

"Stop sniping at me!"

Aunt Stormy gets the ghost box we've decorated with crepe paper and leftover fabrics from her business. Bright colors, red and purple and gold.

Opal makes mean little eyes at me. "Promise you won't read it?"

"I promise."

"We all promise," Aunt Stormy says.

"What if it happens then? What if I write down that Annie is stupid and the ghost takes her away?"

"All our Hungry Ghost does is burn away what's in the box. He won't hurt people or take them away."

Opal folds her paper, slips it into the box. "This is for our Hungry Ghost."

Mother-by-choice, then?

I kiss Aunt Stormy's face.

"Hey . . . ," she says, surprised, and kisses me back.

Not just choosing sisters as she and my mother did, *sisters-by-choice*, but also choosing mothers, daughters?

The air around me feels spacious and light and complete, mine to breathe, to keep, and all at once I know I'm ready to work.

• • •

I WAIT till Opal is asleep before I retrieve her windbreaker from behind the *Eckbank.* Purple and hooded, it's lined with thin white cotton, almost new still. I could return it to my daughter—

But I need it as the background for my collage. I crumple and rip the purple fabric, glue it to a canvas and overlay it with beach glass, driftwood, a circle of dried catbriers . . . no longer dodging my panic and sorrow and rage but letting them become the background against which I'm reconstructing our lives the way Pete is reconstructing his body . . . layers and circles . . . paint and glass and seedpods that want to spill beyond the canvas . . . transforming superstition into a loss that did *not* happen: Opal drowning.

Water, then. The raft—

Again? I raise dental X-rays to the lamp. The hint of bones . . . shadows of flesh . . . light coming through from above. If only I'd had them for the windows of my Train Series. For the raft then, now. Linked, the X-rays make up planks. Like vertebrae.

What if Opal recognizes the fabric before it has become something else? But then what I begin with always changes—it's part of what pulls me in, that risk of entering without knowing where I'll emerge. Still, I work quickly in case she wakes up, keep a towel nearby to hide the canvas from her.

What'll happen if I become as much part of that image as Jake and Mason? That long-ago fear rises up to meet me again, leads me toward seeing more.

They're underwater too long.

One head rises.

The other is underwater too long. Mason—

But it's true for the collage . . . the blue hinting at shadows beneath . . . hinting at bodies . . . and there's a richness in that. I have to resist forcing them up to the surface, the boys. *It's just a trick of—*

No. Not a trick.

I saw this.

This is what I saw.

And I have to let the boys stay where they are. Mason underwater. Have to let it be disturbing—not only to me in the making but to anyone who'll see this.

I'm working. Working. And now the other head rises . . . Mason . . . both visible now . . . yes, shoulders and arms . . . Jake and Mason, hooting—laughing? no, not laughing—hoisting themselves onto the raft, torsos glistening, drawing together in the center of the raft, a knot of arms and legs—

Do they imagine me there between them, warm boards against our feet, the heat of our bodies, there?

Or is it only for themselves, the heat of their bodies?

Once I see, it's there, between them. Has been between them since that day on the raft. I wait to feel surprise. Nothing.

Only on the raft?

Only that day?

What about Morocco?

THE SUMMER after the three of us graduated from high school and went to Tangier, we had cropped hair that bleached under the sun while our skin stayed orange-brown from the instant tanning cream Mason had bought. We never got a normal tan—just that orange-brown and white stripes bordering our new haircuts.

Our combined parents had made hotel reservations for us, a room with two beds for Mason and Jake, a single for me, where I kept my clothes, as if that would appease Mason's parents if they were to call and check on us. In reality, Jake stayed in the single, while I slept with Mason. Our first night, we talked till late, made plans where we wanted to go in the morning. Then Jake slipped away to the narrow room with the narrow bed.

But the next day I felt assaulted by men's stares wherever I went—stares and mumbled words close to my face and the smacking of lips—stifling in a way no one could have told me it would be. I'd traveled with my parents, had loved being in Italy and in Mexico—but Morocco confined me, pissed me off.

Jake stayed next to me. "I'm here, Annie."

But Mason didn't get it when I freaked out.

That afternoon, I urged Mason and Jake to explore the neighborhood without me. "Just go," I said. "I'll read. I'll take a bath."

While I waited for the tub to fill, I sat on the bed and looked through our guidebook, read the same passage twice, too upset to take it in. All I wanted was to get out of Tangier. I read a different chapter. Stood up to get my journal from my backpack. Wet, the bottoms of my feet. Wet. Water, rising through the rugs. *Damn. Damn.*

I shut off the tub faucet, grabbed our towels to soak up the water, but they got brown from dirt that oozed from the rugs. I smuggled them into the laundry room across the hall, absconded with fresh towels. But after four sets, the rug was still damp, and we had to sleep in the narrow room, where the rugs were dry.

"I'll have to sleep in the middle," Mason announced.

"Why is that?" Jake asked.

"Because I don't want you to sleep next to my future wife."

"Your—what?" Jake asked, stunned.

"If she's in the middle, you're next to her," Mason said, "and if you're in the middle, she's still next to you. You know how I am when I get jealous."

"When was all that decided?" Jake asked him, but he was staring at me.

"Sometime in first grade," I said. "I haven't thought about it in a while."

Spooning. Mason spooning me tight on the narrow bed. His thigh thrown across me. "How about next summer for our wedding?"

"Would you two like some privacy?" Jake's voice, so hurt.

"Let's just sleep," I said, "all right?"

But when I woke with sun in my eyes, the space between Mason and me was cool. I turned over. Mason's hand lay on Jake's hip—*that's where it must have fallen while they slept, unaware*—and Mason's body was curled around Jake's back. My stomach felt weird. I eased out of bed. Filled a glass with water. *How embarrassed those two will be to see themselves like that.* I laughed. Drank more water. Got my camera. Snapped a photo. Thinking I'd paste it into their next birthday cards and really embarrass them. I was ready to tease them when they woke up. But then I didn't. Maybe because Jake was crabby when he opened his eyes. He'd always been like that when startled from sleep.

I wanted to get away from the two of them.

Away from the disorienting maze of Tangier.

Asilah was different, white and open, high on the cliffs. We walked through the Medina without being hustled, entered the shop of an old black weaver and watched him weave while we tried on the soft jackets he'd made. He had such dignity and kindness, was a Muslim, talked to us about the extreme poverty in his country, about men having to be out there hustling for their families.

His daughter, a young, heavy woman, made tea for us, and I could smell the strong mint as the old man spoke about people learning to live with others and to live with themselves. I bought a jacket, and we drank the mint tea—its taste as pleasing as its smell. The daughter served, was reluctant to sit with us though I asked her to, but when she let herself down next to me, she smiled and touched my wrist.

The old man untied a string of wooden bracelets, inlaid with tiny stones, and asked me to choose one as a gift. Most were too small to fit over my hand. But he selected the one for me that fit. I wore the bracelet when we explored the ramparts high above the sea, and when Mason grabbed me—playful at first but then not—he tried to pull it off my wrist; and I bit him, wrestled him by the sheer drop of the cliffs, and all along Jake screaming for us to stop it. But his eyes were glinting.

And I went to him.

"STILL ANGRY at me?" I sit down on the back steps next to Opal.

She flexes Pete's pocket mirror in one hand while Luigi hunts the reflection of the light. Muscles taut, he waits, then pounces upon the flicker in the grass.

"He's so much healthier," I tell Opal. "You take good care of him."

But she doesn't look at me.

"Just the fact that he's getting into mischief," I say, "is a sign he's getting more confident."

She flashes her mirror for Luigi.

He's been ransacking the neighborhood, carrying his booty home—a doll once, a feather duster, a tennis ball, a pair of sunglasses, a sweater—and tucking it behind his cedar bed as if burying bones.

"Do you feel like telling me a Melissandra story?"

"Maybe Melissandra offed herself too."

"I don't think so. I have a feeling she's still around."

Opal takes off her shoes. Cups her toes with her hands.

"You want me to rub them for you?"

"No."

"Are they hurting?"

Opal shrugs.

"How about if you and I make up a story about Melissandra?"

"She's not yours!"

"I hate it when you throw me away like this."

"I'm not throwing anything."

"I thought it was getting . . . easier between us. And I hate it that this stuff is happening again."

"What stuff?"

"You working so hard to throw me away. Will you listen real closely to what I'm going to say?" I wait for her to nod, and when she doesn't, I say very slowly, pausing between each word: "I. Am. Not. Going. To. Leave. You."

"What does that have to do with the price of wheat in Bulgaria?"

I have to laugh. "Where did you get that?"

"Pete."

"Very good. Is that the beginning of a smile?"

"No."

"How about a story about our dad?"

Now she's listening.

"TIHII."

"What are you, Annie? A horse?"

"That's what he used to say. TIHII. It means: this is how it is."

"This is how what is?"

"Stuff we can't do anything about. Like you being stuck with me and no longer having Mason."

Opal tilts her mirror, and Luigi chases the light.

"Our dad told me TIHII made him peaceful inside."

"Why?"

"Because peace takes up so much space, there isn't room for anger and sadness and—"

"I don't like this story. I want the one of how I began."

"You began inside our mom . . . inside the same space where I got started too." I wait for Opal to tell her part of the story as usual.

But she's lifting the dog into her arms. His legs and belly and red-tipped penis stick up as she rocks him.

"You—" I continue, "—began nineteen years before me."

"No, I didn't."

"Yes, you did."

"No, I didn't."

"Yes, you—"

"You can't even get that right, Annie."

"Stop sniping at me, will you?"

"I began nineteen years *after* you! Not *before* you!"

"I said *after*!"

"You said *before*!"

Siblings, for sure. We could be sniping at each other all day.

"Must you be so exasperating?"

"Exasp— What?"

"Irritating. Maddening."

"Yes, I must!" She pushes out her lower lip.

"Anyhow, I was already nineteen—"

"You have to start from the beginning, Annie."

"You—" *Help me out here, Mason—* "You began nineteen years *after* me. Got that?"

Opal nods. "And now I'm nine. Nine plus nineteen is twenty-eight. That's what you are."

"You began inside the same space where I got started too. Got that?"

"But not inside you."

"Not inside me."

"I never lived inside you. Because I don't belong there." Separating herself from me. Still seeking our mother.

As I am. "You lived inside our mother, and she let me touch her belly so that I could feel you move."

"You forgot the blue light, Annie."

"Our mom imagined her baby levitating in blue light."

"You could feel my foot."

"Like a step—"

"A *quick* step," Opal corrects me.

I loop one arm around her. "You want every single word in the sequence you remember, right?" My voice has softened.

She nods. "You could feel a quick step from the outside when my mom let you touch her belly."

"A quick step." I feel the story swelling between us.

"And I punched you with my tiny fist."

"You punched me with your tiny fist. And I already loved you."

"And then I got born and she died. The end." Opal shrugs off my arm. Leaps up and lets Luigi slide to the ground.

He squeals. Hides behind my legs.

"I'm sorry," Opal whispers to him. She kneels in the grass, holds out her hands to him. When he finally comes to her, she lifts him into her arms.

"He's all right," I say. "Would you like a new story about our mother?"

She nods. Kisses the dog's moist nose. "I'm sorry, Luigi-dog."

"Our mother believed we can know about people by looking at their mouths . . . know what's been happening inside them to shape lips into joy or discouragement or anger. Her favorite ones were mouths that rested, that didn't need to smile or talk or move or pretend. She said she'd never seen a peaceful mouth and restless eyes in the same face."

"Sometime you have restless eyes, Annie."

"We need more dog food," I tell her. "Want to go to the hardware store with me?"

"I don't care."

"Well, I do."

"Okay."

In the store, she studies the seed packages, keeps her back to me.

"Why don't you help me pick out some seeds? Which ones look good to you? Carrots? How about if we grow sunflowers . . . or pumpkins or . . . cucumbers?" *Ridiculous, how I'm trying to bring her to me.* Still, I dangle seed packages in front of her, tempt her with photos. "Zinnias? Corn? Rattlesnakes? Chocolate Santas?"

She's working hard not to smile.

"We have to support our troops." A woman's voice. By the shelf with insecticides.

The man who is with her says, "Now that it's happened, we need to make the best of it."

"You make the best of it when you're in the midst of a flood." Heart pounding, I talk quickly before they can tell me to go to hell. "Or an earthquake. Sticking together. Making the best of what has already happened. But to make the best of a corrupt choice simply because it happened?"

"I did not invite you into our conversation," the woman says.

"I'm sorry. But too many people still can't believe that their government could be doing anything wrong."

"I wish you had stopped with *sorry*." She turns away. Dalmatian pattern boots with loud heels.

"Enough, young lady," the man tells me and follows her from the store.

"Mason says you can tell the tourists by their shoes," Opal whispers.

"Good observation." I pick up a can of wildflower seeds. Jiggle it. *Like rain on a roof.* "You want to plant wildflowers?"

Opal gives me her ancient glance, cronish and wise.

"Don't say it," I warn her, hoping to provoke her into rebelling.

And she does. Loudly. "If they're real wildflowers, they don't come in cans."

But any smile from me would turn her quiet again. *I hate playing these games with her. So complicated. Still . . .* I click my tongue. "Such a little cynic."

She straightens herself. "Not little."

"Still—a cynic."

And she smiles. Finally, finally smiles.

How I knock myself out for that smile.

Mason

—you could stop anything, Annie.

An avalanche eating up a mountain.

A tidal wave.

The rope clears the rafter. First toss. I thought that part would be harder. Maybe I was born to be good at this—what do you think, Annie?

When I slip the rope over my head, I'm suddenly not so tired anymore. It lies around my neck—enough rope for eight necks, imagine.

I climb on your worktable. A bit of your work—me—another one of your masterpieces. You don't like that word, Annie. How about one of your creations, your inventions—

Why don't you fucking choose?

All right, another one of your undertakings—

Undertake.

Undertaker.

Under—

Too irreverent. Even for us.

Your tabletop wobbles, that church door—weird to be thinking of it coming from a church—and I make sure to be right above the center, above your filing cabinets. Because it has to be tight, the rope, before I tip the door, step off—

You could still stop me now.

You know what scares me, Annie? That if you knew, you wouldn't stop me—

But that's not true. It's me. Who can't stop. Because of what I've done to our love.

A flicker of light in the dark morning. Headlights? Are you back home, Annie? I wait for the car door to slam. Wait for your steps. For the resuming of all that ever mattered to me—you and me and Opal.

Something moving outside? But only silence. Still, I keep waiting, body tight and clammy. Because now I know what it's like to be without you.

No longer able to call you to me, Annie . . . to laugh and scheme and be outrageous together.

Is that you?

Oh Annie—

Does silence then move with a sound of its own? A trick concocted from wanting. From too much wanting.

The sky . . . fuzzy and ashen and the smell of

yeast. Chewing and swallowing the thief. Swallowing the it's wrong. Till three boys trap me in the hallway where I'm chewing and swallowing. Every morning, eating mine for breakfast already wishing I could have it for lunch, swearing to myself I'll save it, be a good person—

Then the boys. "Thief."

Still chewing and ashamed and afraid and wanting more.

Calling me thief. Punching me.

"No. It's mine." Running from them. Hiding out in Jake's bunk. Wanting to hide forever and crying, ashamed to tell him. Still, telling him. Promising: "I'll do you, Jake, if you tell them it was yours." Pity in Jake's eyes—

Pity? And the shame inside me thicker for the eating and the lying and making Jake lie for me and—

"Jake—" Backward breath eating my voice eating the rope firestorms pelting the window Jake by the window melting all glass all caulking all—

"Jake?"

Here?

—firestorms melting the three of us no longer three no longer even one melting—

Annie?

Ask me, Annie, what's the worst thing—

That I don't know the way back.

Because even if you absolve me, how can I, Annie?

Air smelling of yeast and faraway smoke, and I'm drifting—

—dreaming that I'm sleeping—

—drifting becoming a pattern of light on fire—

—shifting and being fire—

—rocking against a square of window filled by smoke that covers the sun—

—and all those Canadians still waiting for rain—

—funny thinking of all those Canadians waiting—

—and I can't quit shaking—

—can't quit rocking against the window till it shatters—

—till I become fire—

—all those Canadians waiting for fire—

—till I become shards of milky glass—

—that pierce my skin hot—

—hot pressing hot against my chest—

—against my lips—

—oh Annie—

—my throat—

—breathing against it hard

—breathing and floating—

—film of light burning my eyelids—

—drops of sweet red fire—

—lifting my bones to the surface—

ELEVEN

Annie / Jake / Opal / Stormy

{ *Hungry Ghost* }

{ Annie }

"The police are trying to find out who dug through the sandbank between the pond and ocean," Annie tells Jake as they lift the kayaks from Aunt Stormy's truck.

"So that's why it's so mucky," Jake says.

The launching area off Georgica Pond has receded, and the ground is swampy. When they drag the kayaks through the shallow water, dark mud sucks at their ankles, releases them, and closes around them again.

"Disgusting sounds," Jake says.

"Usually, the town opens that gap every spring so that fish can spawn in the pond," Annie says. "Then it gets closed and, in the fall, opened once again to let the fish into the ocean. Except this year, the rains flooded lots of basements, and when the town refused to let the residents drain the pond into the ocean, someone did it secretly."

"Maybe it took just one shovel, middle of the night, to make enough of a break for the force of water to push more sand aside and— Damn. I'm stuck."

"Try this." Annie eases herself into her kayak.

"Then we'll never get out."

"Trust me," she says in a deep-deep voice.

He laughs. "I trust you all right." But when he sits in his kayak, he can't move forward or back. "I am so stuck."

"Time for some butt-surfing." Annie demonstrates by wiggling her kayak forward, sliding her hips and torso in the direction of the open water.

Jake attempts to bounce forward. "Wait for me." Mud flies from his paddles.

"Like this." Annie plants one paddle blade into the muck ahead of her, wiggles and pulls herself forward.

"I hope they catch the ones who did it. It messes up that fragile balance of freshwater and salt water."

When they come past the first bend of the creek that leads into the belly of the pond, they feel the swell of the ocean.

Just then a swan—wings spread, beak raised—slides toward them as if running on water. They paddle, hard, veer to the right to get off its path.

"It looks pissed," Annie says.

"I bet it's protecting a nest."

"They can be aggressive. Break bones. Turn over boats."

"I wonder if we should go back."

Far ahead of them is the distant border of sand where the pond merges with the ocean. "As long as we respect the nesting area, we're all right."

Jake motions to something white in the reeds, more than a hundred feet away. "Must be the female."

Half-rising from the water, the male charges toward them, puffed up like a carousel swan.

"Get away, you—" Jake raises his paddle like a flyswatter.

But the swan is taller than the kayaks, and he keeps advancing, hissing, neck extended as if to strike.

"Get away, you son of a bitch," Annie yells, paddle swinging. "I'm sorry—"

Her blade strikes the chest of the swan.

She feels sick. "I'm sorry. Get away—"

The swan swerves to the left, keeps himself between the kayaks and the female in the reeds.

"Let's give him a lot of space," Jake says.

Gripping their paddles, ready to use them against the swan, they get past him, paddling as fast as they can past the huge houses that are set back from the pond. A deer grazes on a slope of lawn.

"Never just one deer," Mason says.

And there are three more, feasting on shrubs that border the long veranda. No fear at all. Here, deer are considered a pest, but in New Hampshire, Mason used to feed them, buy salt blocks for them to lick, and watch them with Opal from the window.

"You know how Aunt Stormy tells the difference between a year-round house and a vacation house?" Annie asks Jake.

"Tell me."

"Year-round people don't need that many rooms."

He laughs.

"Aunt Stormy says some of these go for over fifty million."

"Crazy."

When they reach the sandbank, he strands his kayak. "Remember, we still have to make it back past that swan again."

"Are you scared?"

"Yes." He pulls her kayak ashore. "You?"

"Me too." She turns her kayak over, spreads a tablecloth across it. "But I don't want to think about the swan now."

He opens their picnic basket. Pours red wine into metal camping cups. "What is it like for you, living in North Sea?"

"It's an . . . easy fit. Familiar. And lovely."

"Will you stay?"

"My mother once said this place wraps itself around your heart." She passes the focaccia bread to him.

He slices fresh mozzarella cheese and tomatoes.

Mist swirls from the ocean, sheer spirals of moisture that race across the blue of sky, the green of shoreline.

"Will you stay?" Jake asks again.

"For the time being . . ."

"How long is for the time being?"

Annie smiles. "That's exactly what Opal asked Aunt Stormy after we moved in last year. And she told Opal, 'For as long as you want.' "

"And you?"

"I'm on the list for substitute teaching. I could do that and my own work. Aunt Stormy has fewer clients in the winter."

A thickening of the mist . . . darkening.

Houses and trees become shadow cutouts, are blotted up.

The color of air and water and sky all one, cocooning them on this shelf of sand.

Only Jake here, close by.

She aches to touch his lips, his dear, dear face. *No—* What if any passion between them can only move through Mason, a conduit, a current?

"We still have to make it back again," she reminds herself.

"We could stay here," he whispers. "Just the two of us."

"On the way back . . . if we keep way to the left and together, far away from the female . . . we'll be safe."

"Let's wait out the fog." Jake's face, paler than the mist.

Everything gray on gray . . . shimmering . . . and the ocean louder now that she can't see it . . . that rolling disorientation.

With one thumb, she brushes the corner of his mouth, across his lower lip.

"Annie—?"

"You had some sand there." She pulls her hand back. "Because anything else would be . . . awkward," she says quickly to prove to him that it really was just sand even if it's a lie. "Because it wouldn't work." She feels relieved. Something has been solved.

He hesitates. When he says, "Yes," her heart constricts.

"It'll be better for Opal . . . not to, being together as friends . . . only."

Jake looks miserable. "Do people still use that word?"

"What word?"

"Platonic."

"Ah, that word," Annie jokes. But it feels fake.

"So . . . do you think we're handling this well?"

"Sort of. Yes. I think."

"Because this is what we both want now?"

"Right. To leave . . . sex out of it."

"A pact . . . And then we can have our friendship again?"

"Not if we blame each other."

"Oh, Annie, I don't blame you."

"Not if only one of us carries the . . . guilt. But if we were to carry it between us, as we carry Opal . . . like that, yes, in a weave of . . . of kindness, together, then we can't fall through."

"Just as the pain will be ours too. Within that weave."

"Yes."

"We can do that," he says, but his eyes are sad.

"We're lucky we can," she says. *But then why does it feel like the end between us?*

"There's something I need to tell you," Jake says.

She nods. "I'm listening."

"Not now. But when I come back in August for the Hungry Ghost. Pete says I can stay with him."

She squints at him. "You sound . . . grim."

"More scared than grim, Annie."

{ Stormy }

"Please, tell Mr. Bush that his acting job aboard the *Abraham Lincoln* was ridiculous," Stormy tells the operator on the other end of the White House line. "To posture there in a flight suit and declare 'Mission accomplished' demonstrates to the world how arrogant and ignorant he is."

Every day, the White House answering machine greets Stormy with the same lie, that her message is very important to the president, and every day she's stunned by the beauty of her surroundings, juxtaposed with the madness of war. Both real.

"Please, tell Mr. Bush that he has pushed this country into an immoral war, and that people can see through his lies and justifications." As always she gives her name.

In Nazi Germany, I could have been shot for this.

She continues to speak out though she's no longer sure that her voice—or an accumulation of voices like hers—can make a difference. That belief has become disillusion. Disillusion even in the *act* of believing that made her question her parents for not speaking out after she'd lived in America for a year.

One night, when she wakes up, sickened by the violence toward the people of Iraq, Pete is already awake.

"Do you ever feel implicated as an American?" she asks him.

"Of course." He reaches for her.

"So do I. Just as I've felt implicated all my life as a German."

"Most Americans won't. They . . . grew up trusting their government."

"Europeans are more skeptical."

Stormy keeps calling the White House even if the only person who'll hear her words is some minimum-wage phone operator.

"I'm calling regarding the staged rescue of Jessica Lynch from an Iraqi hospital. Please, tell Mr. Bush that he's using her for his propaganda. Victim and heroine in one."

The end of May, when Bush goes to Auschwitz and compares himself with the liberators of the concentration camps, Stormy cries. When she's calm enough to phone the White House, she says, "One of Mr. Bush's greatest transgressions so far, a disrespect for the victims of the Holocaust, using Auschwitz for another one of his photo ops." She checks the Internet for the press coverage. No shock. No rage.

"Is it too dangerous a subject for the press?" she asks Pete. "Doesn't anyone dare fault Bush for posing at Auschwitz?"

"Or that insipid Laura," Pete stays, "for standing on . . . the train track to Auschwitz with a red rose." He draws her close to him. "It's a terrible time. I find some strange . . . comfort in little rituals. I put a candle in . . . my window. I go to a vigil."

"Is it foolish to expect results from the protests? Is it, Pete?"

"No. Of course not." He kisses her on the lips, the chin. Over the months, his face has been reemerging, the muscles defined once again. His former self arising as he works around what ailed him. Adapting. And as a result, strengthening himself.

The microwave is humming today's tea . . . camomile and peppermint. Sweet. Soothing. *What soothes?* Seeing Annie work again. Reading to Opal. Pete's arms at night, and now.

Nudging herself deeper into his embrace, Stormy locks her arms around him. "Some days I feel I'd fly off without you, and what keeps me on the ground is seeing you heal."

"I like having you on the ground right . . . here," he whispers, "with me."

{ Jake }

When Jake returns in August for the Feast of the Hungry Ghosts, he brings a dragon kite for Opal. For Annie a CD by Annie Gallup. "Another Annie who tells stories," he tells her when they cut bamboo canes behind Pete's garage for the ghost's chest and tepee skirt.

Afterward, they drive to the nursery where Jake wants to buy a rosebush for Pete. Between the bedding plants and flowerpots, two little boys are dragging their comfort blankets, swiping off leaves and blossoms, while their father strolls along, talking on his cell phone and pulling a red plant wagon.

"Yuppie parenting," Annie says.

"And how does one define that?" Jake is sweating.

"Like that." Annie motions toward the boys. "Too precious to be refused anything."

What if—once he tells her how he ran and let her find Mason dead—she won't talk to him again? Still, unless he tells her, they can't move forward. He isn't sure what's beyond that forward. Only that not telling Annie is in the way.

What's important is to stay together today, Jake tells himself. To steer every word into discussing the kind of rose he'll buy to thank Pete for the invitation to stay.

Annie picks up a morning glory vine, the blue of faded denim. She hesitates. Then abruptly sets it back down.

"You don't want it?" Jake asks.

"Not really." She looks upset.

"Because I'd be glad to get it for you."

"It's not about that."

The boys bounce against their father's plant wagon. Turn it over. Run off while he scoops up the plants that are still intact and, with one foot, swipes the others to the side of the path.

"And all that without stopping his phone conversation," Jake says. "What a talent."

"You forgot your plants," Annie yells after the man.

He gives her a bored glance. Turns away.

"Creep," Jake says.

Annie picks up the pot with the morning glory. "I guess I didn't want to get it because I was afraid that shade of blue would remind me of Mason. But how can I deprive myself of a color because he loved it?"

"You are amazing," Jake says. "Do you know that?"

"Maybe it can remind me of what was good with Mason."

"You're more generous than I am."

When they get back to the cottage, BigC is on her boardwalk, unwrapping a huge roll of Bubble Wrap. She waves. "I'm taping it to the wood and leaving air underneath."

"Why is that?" Annie asks.

"So that if ducks step on it, they'll topple over and get spooked and won't come back."

But the instant BigC tapes the Bubble Wrap to the wood, ducks swarm toward her from all directions, drawn by the crinkling of plastic.

"Must evoke memories of Wonder Bread plastic for them," Jake says.

Annie laughs. She seems happier to Jake than in the spring, when he saw her last. No longer so cautious with him.

{ Opal }

"Don't make the ghost too scary," Opal says.

"What would you like to change?" Annie is making the ghost's hands from old bamboo rakes.

Opal steps back to inspect the Hungry Ghost. His chest one huge triangle. It comes up from his waist. Ends with his straight shoulders. His head is set above the shoulders with no neck. Hair made from tinsel. Eyebrows from licorice. A papier-mâché nose. Bulging eyes from the halves of a tennis ball that Luigi has carried home.

"I don't like yellow eyes," Opal says.

"You want to change the color?" Annie asks.

"Purple. All purple with a little white around the purple."

"Climb up." Aunt Stormy boosts Opal onto the kitchen table. "You do the eyes. Afterwards you and I'll tape crepe streamers to the ghost's sleeves."

Annie dips a brush into an old salsa jar where she's mixed glue and water. "Here."

"But it's dripping."

"Brush it quickly across the tennis balls."

"Gross. They're all chewed up, the eyes."

"You'll cover them up. Keep brushing. Good. Like that." Annie tears purple tissue paper into long strips.

Yesterday, Opal and Annie took the jitney into the city and bought lots of spirit money in Chinatown. Tissue paper in purple and red and yellow. Tinsel in silver and in gold. Crepe streamers and sparkling yarn.

"Now the tissue paper."

"On top of the tennis ball eyes?"

"And then brush more glue on them, yes."

"Excellent." Aunt Stormy smells of the perfume Pete gave her for their anniversary. Not a wedding anniversary. But of the day they met.

Opal wrinkles her nose. Maybe if she asks Pete to give Aunt Stormy chocolate instead, he'll do that. And she'll get to eat some.

"You like his eyes better now?" Aunt Stormy asks.

Opal nods. "Just don't give him red fangs."

{ Annie }

They carry the Hungry Ghost across the boardwalk to Little Peconic Bay—Opal supporting the head, Jake the feet, Aunt Stormy, Annie, and Pete in the middle.

"What are you hiding under your shirt, Opal?" Aunt Stormy asks.

"Nothing."

"Looks from here like nothing is making a bulge all around your waist."

"You'll see. Once we burn the ghost."

After they cross the inlet and the sand, they set up the ghost by the bay, where quite a few of their friends have arranged a potluck dinner on tables covered with bright cloths, friends from the neighborhood and the elementary school and Aunt Stormy's business, from Women in Black and Amnesty International. The ghost teeters above them, framed by the colors of sand and bay and sky, its bright banners and crepe streamers rippling, one with the flux of water and birds and wind.

Opal is too excited to eat more than a few bites. Then she runs off, along the edge of waves, away from the other children. Just as the moon comes up, faint and pink, she returns with driftwood and the carcass of a horseshoe crab.

"Look look, that moon is for the children."

"Why is that?" Annie asks her.

"Because it's still light outside. That's when the moon belongs only to children."

"That's beautiful. I didn't know that."

"Yes, you do," Aunt Stormy says. "Your father told you about the children's moon."

"Are you sure? Because I don't remember."

"That's what your father called a moon that's visible during the day, when the children aren't asleep yet."

Opal scatters her driftwood around the figure of the ghost and offers the horseshoe crab to Jake. "No more little boxing gloves underneath, see? No more pincers."

He takes it from her with the shell curved down.

"The tail only seems scary," she assures him.

"I'm glad you told me." With his free hand he tucks her curls behind her ears, lets his thumb linger on her neck.

Aunt Stormy nudges the ghost box underneath the statue with her bare feet and spurts lighter fluid on the garments of the ghost.

More than a year now since Mason's death. And what Annie has written on the page she plans to burn is: *Mason's hold on us.*

"The horseshoe crab only uses the tail when it's upside down," Opal says. "To flip itself back."

"Sadly, not soon enough for this one," says Jake.

But she laughs. "That's because seagulls got to it first and picked it clean."

When Pete tugs matches from the pocket of his fuchsia shirt, Annie reaches for them. What if he doesn't step back quickly enough? But he doesn't yield them to her. His chin has a stubborn set to it, and all at once she can see his former sharpness again, his handsomeness. On his first try, he lights the match and tosses it. A sudden whoosh as flames fill the robe of the Hungry Ghost, the chest, the banners, and soar to the head of the figure, turning it translucent with golden light.

"On the Feast of the Hungry Ghosts," Aunt Stormy begins as she does every August the night before the full moon, "we make offerings to the Hungry Ghosts—"

"—to send them away happy," Opal finishes for her. Suddenly, she yanks an orange rope from beneath her T-shirt and takes four steps toward the fire.

Stricken, Annie wants to run after her, but she makes herself stay, closes her fist around the piece of paper in her pocket, *Mason's hold on us.*

{ Jake }

"Opal!" Jake starts toward the fire. Feels Annie's hand on his arm.

"No." She tells him.

"But—"

"Opal needs to do this."

Hurling the rope into the blaze, Opal stomps her feet and screams, "Take away the stupid rope, you ghost." Then she bolts for Annie. Butts her head into Annie's middle. Topples her on the sand before Jake can catch them both.

Annie is wheezing but holding on. Tight. Holding on to her daughter. "That was very brave."

"Are you two all right?" Jake brings his arms around them. Lets go. But stays crouched next to them.

"We're all right," Opal says and burrows deeper against Annie.

"Take away war!" Aunt Stormy tosses newspaper clippings into the fire.

"All war machinery," shouts a man from Women in Black.

"Ten-bedroom McMansions!" A teacher throws real estate brochures into the flames.

They all feed the flames: driftwood and dried seaweed, broken slats from sand fencing, newspapers and glossy ads and pieces of paper they've written on.

Jake stands up. "The bulldozer that killed Rachel Corrie!"

"Entitlement attitudes!" shouts a neighbor.

"Greed!"

"All the dictators of all the world," says one of the Amnesty members.

"Flashy stores!"

"Twenty-bedroom McMansions!"

Jake lowers himself onto the sand and rubs Opal's arm. Lifting her face from Annie, she gives him an unsteady smile—part unnerved, part victorious—and nestles her spine against Annie so they can both see the burning ghost.

"Language that uses words to obscure the truth!" Valerie, the poet, steps forward. "The Healthy Forests Act. The Patriot Act. No Child Left Behind."

"The Clear Skies Act too!" yells the man whose peace sign used to be the Mercedes-Benz logo. He waves an index card. "I found a Rumsfeld quote on the Internet. Listen to what he says about weapons of mass destruction in Iraq: 'Absence of evidence is not evidence of absence.' "

A groan rises with the flames.

"Take away any chance of Bush . . . being reelected next year!" Pete hollers.

"Absolutely!" BigC raises her tiny frame.

"Of course he won't be reelected."

"Even people who voted for him are disgusted with him," a neighbor says.

"The protests are getting larger," Aunt Stormy says.

In that moment, when the entire ghost becomes flames, they are all superimposed: they can see the figure and one another, all half-transparent, nothing blocking, all seen at once. Lit, the Hungry Ghost grows brighter than the sand, the bay. Brighter than their clothes. And suddenly Jake is heartened by the certainty of the people around him. *Of course they're right. Of course Bush won't get another term.*

Where the triangle of chest used to be, the flames sculpt a face, living features of fire encased within the structure of the Hungry Ghost.

Released.

Annie leans against him, her shoulder against his upper arm.

He holds steady.

Feels her leaning with the added weight of Opal.

His heart is flying.

But he holds steady.

Wants to stay like that with her forever in the suddenly muted color of predusk, the ghost the only brightness in its warm-yellow hue. *What we want the Hungry Ghost to take away . . .*

The flames wane. Taper off. And in that final stage, like everything, they see the statue without what covers the bones. Then: radiance.

{ Annie }

Annie is in that dream state of making where her fingers roam across images, alight, flee. This raft too is built up from strips of dental X-rays, and the hazy planks are far enough apart that bits of photo flicker through, more yet through the sheer fissures between the planks—two men sleeping on a bed in Morocco—while atop the planks two boys wrestle each other.

How they performed for me. Not just on the raft. And how I encouraged them. The girl—no longer suggested by a red elbow or shoulder or profile—has become part of the image, a solid red figure.

Outside, the dog is jumping around Opal and Mandy. Annie still thinks of her as the turtle-girl. Last night, Mandy chased Opal around the dwindling fire until Pete handed out candles to the children. They set them into pockets of sand, and when he lit them, all the children trailed after him, from candle to candle, a long curve of tiny flames.

Now the girls are lugging Aunt Stormy's rocks around, laughing and crawling underneath, popping up and teasing the dog. But Luigi scratches at the rocks, does not back away.

Annie still feels the heat of the ghost's fire on her face. She's excited about the dimensions of the raft, but not about the clean edge of the red girl. Too much all of one thing . . . taking over, separate from the rest. What she needs are bits and pieces. Like old lace?

Jake, by the door. "Am I too early?" Dressed up and pale. Blond hair combed back from his forehead and ears. That unbecoming drab-olive shirt.

"I thought I'd be done before you got here."

"I can wait."

She crushes hydrangea petals across the lower half of the girl.

"Am I distracting you?" He seems jumpy. Easily startled.

"It doesn't have the depth of the green yet." She motions to a wrinkled and jagged band of green, dunks her wide brush into the glue-and-water jar, swings across the petals without flattening their lacelike circles.

"You want me to wait outside?"

"You sound eager to get away."

"No, no . . ."

Annie can still see one edge of red, while the other edge has softened beneath the gauzy petals.

{ Jake }

This is what Jake sees in her collage: various depths of water. Reflections. Blues in the upper half of the collage. The lower half a strong brown with other colors coming through . . . orange and amber. A bog, perhaps.

"Is that a bog, Annie?"

"Could be . . . What matters is what you see in there."

"And the red girl down there, to the right?"

"That's the one area where it goes flat on me."

"Could that be you?"

"To me it is." She picks up scissors, cuts a hand from shiny yellow paper.

Jake peers through the raft where two figures emerge. Two men, spooning. The hand of one man on the hip of the other man— "What is that?"

"From Morocco. The night the tub overflowed."

Mason's salt-sweaty smell comes at Jake in a rush of longing and disgust. To keep from falling, he stands by the wall. "That's not how we slept."

"I didn't make it up."

—Mason's hand on my hip. His face pressed into my neck. Our features blunt. Sleep-flattened. Skin-flattened— "That photo?" he asks.

"While you were sleeping."

"But why?"

"I thought it was funny. Then. I was going to tease you but . . ."

"But you didn't."

"You woke up, and it was different. I don't know. It wasn't funny anymore."

"Why now?"

"To see."

"Is that why you're doing the raft again?"

"You sound like Mason."

"I'm not—"

"He used to get . . . squirmy when I did a raft collage. But now you too?"

Mason's face pressed low into that dip between my shoulders. Sleep-flattened—

Annie dabs glue on back of the shiny yellow hand she's cut out. Builds up the hand of the yellow boy who swims with the brown boy next to the raft.

It agitates Jake, the boy's yellow hand. It was yellow before, but not as big and obvious because it was the same rice paper texture as the figure. But now, raised and shiny, it overlaps the forehead of the brown boy.

{ Annie }

"I was so . . . naïve. Was I, Jake?" Annie's breath is high and fast.

"No." He keeps staring at her collage.

"On the raft too. You and Mason. Not just in bed, there."

"It wasn't like that."

She rinses her brushes. "You loved him, right?"

"I loved you both."

"Really loved *him*."

"I loved you both. And then only you."

"You don't have to pretend . . . about loving me."

"It's not like that. Because I do love you."

"But not love me in that way of wanting me."

"That way too."

"With both of us?"

"Not with Mason. No." He shakes his head.

"Then what is this?" She faces the raft. And is stunned. Because she has done it . . . gone beyond sequence, revealed everything at once: two boys grappling leaping vanishing arising bucking—echoes from layers beneath layers where two men sleep entwined on a bed in Morocco forever and there—the surface smooth again and the boys grappling leaping vanishing arising bucking and the girl getting closer and being inside the image and not just looking on. Echoes. Forever and again all at once. *One of us always watching* . . .

"Annie—"

She laughs. Exhilarated. Terrified. *At last.* "It's possible then."

{ Jake }

Possible?

What's possible then?

Jake wonders if she's thinking of her love for him, the complications of that love.

Her face is flushed.

So much still possible—

Is it even fair to burden her just so that he can quiet his conscience?

What if this—how he saw Mason kill himself—is the one secret he'll need to keep from her?

He can do that.

Carry it alone—no matter how it weighs on him?

Easier than not having Annie and Opal in his life.

Is that cowardly?

Noble?

"I've done it, Jake." She's still looking at her collage.

"Done what?" He steps next to her, and the image of the boys and the raft shifts itself, supersedes the image of Mason killing himself, cancels it, and becomes a far more significant secret. A secret he can trade for the secret he'll carry alone, a secret he can tell Annie without losing her, making her believe this is what he intended to tell her.

"About what I wanted to tell you . . ."

"Of course." She seems startled, brought back from some place he can't go with her.

"That summer at camp when Mason was stealing—"

"You already told me."

"Not everything."

"Let's sit by the window so I can watch Opal and Mandy."

"It's always been there . . . but far away. And telling you feels . . ." He shakes his head. "Nasty. When I found Mason hiding in my cabin, he was in my bunk. Crying and saying, 'I'll do you, Jake.' "

Annie breathes out carefully.

"I ran. From Mason. From the cabin—"

"From your own wanting?"

"I don't know, Annie. Perhaps from my confusion about wanting? I ran to the lake and jumped in and swam to the raft with him following and stepping behind me on the raft and getting hard. Not just Mason. Me too. Hating myself and hating him for standing with me and feeling him and waiting—" Jake says it all in a rush, and already his shame and horror and grief at seeing Mason die in Annie's studio are fusing with what he felt as a boy when he wanted Mason dead. That same shame and horror and grief. Entwined and true.

"But then I saw you, Annie. On the shore. And I pushed Mason away. Fought to keep him from me till we fell into the lake. But we were still holding on to each other. Still holding. So I pushed him away. Down—"

"You held him down?"

"That's what still bothers me most. That I wanted him dead. And now he is." Inching closer to the secret he can't tell her. Confessing without losing her.

She gets up. Touches her collage . . . that shiny hand.

Outside, Luigi is barking at Opal and Mandy, who are scooping cracked corn for the ducks from the metal can and securing the lid with the bungee cord. Luigi follows them, tail wagging.

"Remember us at that age?" Jake asks.

She nods.

"Running around. Playing hide-and-seek."

"You looked so mad when you swam in from the raft. And you ran off."

"I felt . . . nasty." Jake can't look into her eyes.

"Mason was giddy and so happy I was there. But you—"

"Then I got sick."

"—ran off."

"Sick from eating red Jell-O."

"I thought you were mad at me. And I didn't know why."

"I wasn't mad at you, Annie."

{ Annie }

But she's leaning toward her collage, toward what she saw that day, the red girl's entire body now inside this dance of fleeting transformations—real to unreal and real again—and she already knows that what she sees will continue to calibrate, and that this too—Jake telling her—is a moment in her life that will shift and align itself.

She feels wise. Generous. Impatient with anything less intense and true. "It started for me that day," she says. "Falling in love with both of you."

She recalls the pull toward both of them—

Or was it rather toward what she believed she spied that shimmering day between them?

But what she spies now, that moment, is Jake waiting, and she's no longer watching but immersed as she swims toward the raft where there's only Jake—*Jake only*—reaching into the water for her as she hoists herself onto the warm planks.

{ Opal }

Fiddler crabs. Scooting like shadows across the sand. Hundreds of fiddler crabs.

Opal floats. Floats with Jake and Annie and Opal down Alewife Brook. The tide carries them into the harbor. Past the sandbar where a woman and a man wave to them. Square bodies. Square chins. Black hair.

"What are you people on?" The woman laughs.

"Noodles," Opal yells, letting the ends of her long foam noodle bounce from the water.

"One year our parents drifted with the incoming tide all the way to Alewife Pond," Annie tells her, "and when the tide didn't turn, they had to walk back."

"They heard the mussels sing," Opal says.

"How do you know that?" Jake asks.

"They told Aunt Stormy, and she told me. You want to see the mussels, Jake?"

"Sure." He pulls on his goggles.

"They live by the underwater wall. Want to see, Jake?"

He follows her underwater.

Feathery plants sway with the current. Touch Opal's neck. And there it is . . . tiny caves and bridges.

"Magical," Jake says when they come up for air. He heads toward Annie. "Like a miniature of that ancient wall of caves in Morocco."

"Don't get out, Jake," Opal says.

"Just for a while." He lies down next to Annie. Shuts his eyes.

"Look look at me!" Opal jumps up in the water. "Jake?"

"I can hear you splashing."

"But you're not looking at me."

He points to his bald spot. "I'm watching you through my third eye."

"You're lucky you're so fair," Annie tells him. "That way it doesn't show so much."

"Lately, I've been using a little mirror to check the back of my head."

"Now how many men would admit that?"

"Jake!" Opal yells.

He squints at her. Waves to her. "Remember when you said Opal has two fathers?" he asks Annie.

{ Annie }

"Let's do another float with Opal." Annie runs into the brook. Lifts Opal into her arms and swirls her around.

Jake follows her, and they walk against the outgoing tide, along the shallow edge, where the vivid colors of pebbles dim and revive with the motion of water.

"Look!" Opal has found a feather, still attached to a bit of cartilage.

"A critter bit," Annie says.

"You can have it."

"Thank you." Annie tucks it into the hollow core of her noodle before she gets back into the current.

Where they come around the bend of the sandbar again, the man is burying the woman, and suddenly Annie recognizes them—the people who come to the beach to bury each other. They inspired a collage when Opal was a baby. At first Annie didn't know what it was going to become, didn't know those shapes though she had traced them in the sand; but once she identified them, they reminded her of another collage with overlapping circles. *A Thousand Loops.* Motion disguised as inertia. Encapsulated within those rounded shapes.

When they get back to their towels, Opal and Jake fall asleep, but Annie holds the critter bit in her hands, and already her fascination is drawing other impressions to it . . . hills of two bodies against the sky . . . lumis, yes, lumis flickering in the sky . . . light. And though it will become something different, it will always carry the breath and energy of that first inspiration, though it may no longer be recognizable as that. *It's a way of coming into myself.* Maybe she'll see them again next summer, the man and the woman, mounds of sand defining their large bodies.

{ Opal }

Opal tries to curl herself back into sleep. Above her, a flutter sound. She squints. It's the umbrella. Its shade on her face. Her forehead against something soft and warm. Freckles. *A field of freckles.* Annie's arm.

"Jake sleeps like that," Annie tells her. "Sleep was so important to his mom that she never interrupted it—not even when Mason and I wanted to play with him."

"I didn't know that." Jake sits up, yawning

"Because you were asleep," Opal says. "Duh."

"Duh yourself." He wrinkles his nose at her.

Annie strokes Opal's forehead. "All the day-care kids had to walk on their toes when Jake took his naps."

Opal rubs her eyes. Burrows against Annie. *Freckles and sun.*

Annie's hand keeps stroking her. Down her back. Across her shoulders. "A spoiled sleeper, Jake was. Gloomy if his nap was interrupted. That total lack of understanding of why anyone would wake him."

But Jake says, "I don't believe that."

"Why not?"

"Because the day-care kids came first for my mom."

"You can't be serious."

"I picked up all the toys . . . the mess you made."

"Your mom made us whisper when you slept . . . only gave us soft snacks so the crunching wouldn't wake you up. You were the only kid I knew whose mom let him stay home from school because he was tired."

Jake looks embarrassed. Foxy.

"That respect for sleep . . ." Annie smiles. "As if sleep were earned, as if interrupting it would be equal to depriving you of what you deserved. Spoiling you so."

"How about a story?" Opal asks.

"Good," Jake says.

"A Melissandra story."

"That would be . . . yes." Annie bends forward, lips apart.

"So . . . what's your name?" Opal asks her.

"My name?"

"Just say: Annie."

"Annie."

"I'm Melissandra," Opal hisses.

"Is that how you say it?"

Opal nods. "I'm bratty and smart."

"I know a girl like that," Annie says.

"And I work nights. In a lollipop factory. I eat all the lopsided lollipops." All at once Opal knows that Mason will make up other stories for her. And that Melissandra will be forever one day behind her. Even when she's grown up and goes on dates.

"Why only lopsided lollipops?" Jake asks.

"How old does a girl have to be when she can go on a date?"

"Oh . . . about thirty-five," Annie says.

"Don't listen to her, Opal," Jake says. "I think it's more like sixteen."

"Twenty-six," Annie says.

"Sixteen," Opal says.

Annie lifts Opal's curls. "What's that glitter you've got hidden in your hair?"

"Mandy's glow-in-the-dark barrette. It'll glow even more when the light is out."

{ Annie }

When they get home, Opal pulls on socks and starts sock-skating in the kitchen. Her red curls fly around her ears, and she's humming to herself.

Annie steps back. Opal would stop if she knew Annie was watching her. When she was little, she used to show off, clown for Annie. Now she hides from her.

"The only one hiding is you," Mason says.

Annie wonders if she'll miss him when she longs for excitement. But he's gone. And her life will never be quite as tumultuous again.

Opal pirouettes, and Annie steps toward her. Applauds.

"Annie, look look, I'm playing Ice Capades. And I'm dancing. Because remember what happened after I punched you with my tiny fist?"

"Tell me."

Opal raises her pointy chin. "We danced together, I and my mother and you."

"On my wedding day. Yes." Annie takes off her sandals, skates with Opal, but her bare feet get stuck on Aunt Stormy's kitchen floor.

"Not like that, Annie!"

"How then?"

"You need socks." Opal dashes up the stairs. Returns with balled-up socks.

Annie unrolls them. Puts them on.

"Slide . . ." Opal shows her how to slide.

Could I possibly love her more if she were my birth child?

Annie slides. Toward the window. The door. And into a wall. She laughs.

"Here you go again," Opal teases her, "breaking everything."

The rare laughter between them. But for now—as Annie sock-skates with her daughter in the kitchen—that laughter outweighs the despair of war within her. And she knows she'll hold on to moments like this. She'll have to.

After dinner, when Annie carries the trash outside, the air smells of smoke, blanketing all other smells, all nuances, making everything a flat, uniform gray as if the entire north were burning; and all at once the ground slaps against her shins, and she's heaving, the earth dry against her palms, and all she can breathe is the smell Mason must have breathed when his death was about to happen. *One catastrophe summoning another: death not by fire but by rope.*

Hands tugging at her—

Heaving, she is heaving in the haze of smoke, on her hands and shins. The day Mason killed himself, she heard on the radio that several Canadian villages had to be evacuated, and she still remembers thinking how amazing it was that fires five hundred miles away could be so evident where she lived.

Large hands tugging at her.

"Did you fall, Annie?"

Jake on the ground. With her.

Spiky, pale hair as if sketched in.

Night through the ends of his hair.

"Annie? What happened?"

"Maybe I . . . slipped?"

"Did you hurt yourself?"

"No."

Next to her the burst trash bag . . . orange peels and coffee grounds and chicken bones—

His arm now, supporting her as she sits back on her heels.

"Can you smell that smoke, Jake?"

He's sniffing the night. Says, "Yes."

She wipes her palms against her thighs and tries to stand up.

"It's just Pete's fireplace." Jake's skin is darker than his eyebrows and hair. Darker than the whites of his eyes and the white of his teeth. *Jake—*

As she touches the skin around his mouth, her fingertips tingle . . . dissolve. He presses his lips into her palm, and she can feel the flat of his teeth . . . the hint of skeleton . . . of what abides, and beyond that the momentum of his body—

This has nothing to do with Mason—

"Swim with me, Jake?"

"First, we'll have to get you upright." He eases himself against her, and she stands up.

When they reach the boardwalk, they're suddenly ambushed by desire, by an urgency that was theirs when they were twelve and had their first kiss, winter and all those layers of clothing, and still they could feel each other as if skin to skin. As now, only now, clothes shed, the wisdom and habit of skin as though the rapture had waited for them, grown to meet up with them here on this boardwalk, the post with the peace nest against Annie's back.

They don't move beyond this portal till Annie whispers, "So much for chaste love."

Laughing, then—*and Mason far away, far enough*—laughing and running naked into the bay, the light, the vastness, and as they swim out, far beyond the small, choppy waves, risking uncertainty, the sea swells around them, finding and nuzzling them everywhere at once till they become water, membrane, all. And yet, when they surface, the haze of smoke reaches them even here, and it comes to Annie that it isn't amazing at all for fire to span great distances, that sorrow and fire can leap, accost you from hundreds of miles away and target your soul, nest inside your bliss, and that the scent of any fire—even a match struck in a nearby house—can ignite your sorrow.